"...page-turning...Joan Johnston does
contemporary westerns to perfection."
—*Publishers Weekly*

"A top-notch craftsman..."
—*Romantic Times*

♥ ♥ ♥

"Vicki Lewis Thompson is one of those
rare, gifted writers with the ability to
touch her readers' hearts and their funny bones."
—*New York Times* bestselling author Debbie Macomber

"Thompson keeps the reader entertained
with witty dialogue and mesmerizing love scenes
full of tender sensuality."
—*Affaire de Coeur* on *Manhunting in Montana*

JOAN JOHNSTON

is the celebrated author of thirty-eight books and novellas that have appeared on national bestseller lists more than fifty times and have been translated into nineteen languages in twenty-five countries worldwide. Joan writes historical, contemporary mainstream and category romance, and has won numerous awards for her work from Romance Writers of America, Georgia Romance Writers and *Romantic Times Magazine*.

VICKI LEWIS THOMPSON

began her writing career at the age of eleven with a short story in the Auburn, Illinois, weekly, and quickly became a byline junkie. Then she discovered she could write books— and she's written a lot of them! The year 2000 saw her fiftieth book on the shelves. Vicki lives in Tucson, Arizona, and has two grown children and a husband who encourages her to write from the heart.

JOAN
Taming the Lone Wolf
JOHNSTON

Single in the Saddle
VICKI LEWIS THOMPSON

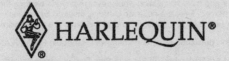

HARLEQUIN®

TORONTO • NEW YORK • LONDON
AMSTERDAM • PARIS • SYDNEY • HAMBURG
STOCKHOLM • ATHENS • TOKYO • MILAN • MADRID
PRAGUE • WARSAW • BUDAPEST • AUCKLAND

ISBN 0-373-83456-X

HARLEQUIN SPECIAL Vol. 4

Copyright © 2001 by Harlequin Books S.A.

The publisher acknowledges the copyright holders
of the individual works as follows:

TAMING THE LONE WOLF
Copyright © 1995 by Joan Mertens Johnston

SINGLE IN THE SADDLE
Copyright © 1998 by Vicki Lewis Thompson

This edition published by arrangement with Harlequin Books S.A.

® and TM are trademarks of the publisher. Trademarks indicated with
® are registered in the United States Patent and Trademark Office, the
Canadian Trade Marks Office and in other countries.

Visit us at www.eHarlequin.com

Printed in U.S.A.

CONTENTS

Taming the Lone Wolf

Joan Johnston

Chapter One

STONY CARLTON took a bite of his hamburger and tried not to listen to the scene unfolding behind the counter of the Buttermilk Café between the waitress and a guy who seemed to be her boss. For a man used to solving other people's problems with his wits— and now and then a gun—it was impossible not to eavesdrop, given the agitation in the woman's voice.

He looked around the empty café. No one else was there to come to her rescue except him—and he wasn't exactly the knight-in-shining-armor type.

"Come on, Bud, I've told you I'm not interested," the woman said.

"Aw, Tess, just one little kiss."

"I said no."

"You oughta have a little more gratitude, seein' as how I let you leave so early in the day."

"You let me leave early because I come in two hours before everyone else," the woman replied with what Stony considered amazing composure.

"Yeah, well, you owe me for givin' you a job when you had no experience."

"I've got experience now, Bud, a whole year of it. I've got work to do, so if you'll just let me by—"

Stony heard muffled sounds suggesting a struggle. He set down his burger, wiped his hands on a paper napkin and threw it down as he left his booth headed for the counter. The man, Bud, had the woman, Tess, backed up against the wall beside the coffeemaker. She was fending off his attempts to kiss her, turning her head away and shoving vainly at his burly shoulders.

"Hey, Bud," Stony said.

Bud turned and glared, clearly irritated at being interrupted. "What?"

"Let the lady go."

"Butt out, mister."

"Afraid I can't do that," Stony said.

"Yeah? So what are you gonna do about it?" Bud snarled.

Stony was over the counter in an instant, as though it wasn't there. He grabbed Bud by the scruff of his food-stained T-shirt and slammed him against the wall, holding him there with his arm rigid, his palm pressed against the center of Bud's chest.

The waitress shot out of the way and stood at the kitchen door, hands clutched together, green eyes wide with fright.

Stony ignored Bud as though he were a bug on the wall and turned his attention to the woman. "You all right, ma'am?"

She nodded her head jerkily.

Stony had been in the Buttermilk Café probably once a month in the past year, yet he hadn't paid any attention to the waitress. Since he had sworn off women a couple of years ago, he had made it a point not to spend his time looking at the pretty ones, so he wouldn't be tempted to go back on his promise to himself.

Tess was definitely pretty.

In fact, she was the kind of woman it was hard to dismiss. Her auburn hair was pinned up off her neck, but it had that mussed-up look, with lazy curls at her temples and ears and throat, as though she had just gotten out of a man's bed. The green eyes that stared warily back at him from a heart-shaped face were curved at the outer edges, like a cat's. Her nose was small and straight, her chin dainty. She had an alabaster complexion, which suggested she didn't get outside much, because the Wyoming sun burned the hide off you summer and winter.

. He had avoided looking at her figure because he found it so alluring. She had a bosom—about big enough to fit his hands—that drew a man's eye, a tiny waist and feminine hips. And she was small enough to incite a man's protective instincts. He was tall, over six feet, and he suspected her head would barely reach his shoulder.

"I'm all right," the woman said. "You can let Bud go."

Stony had completely forgotten about the man against the wall. He turned to Bud and said, "What is it going to take to convince you to leave the lady alone?"

"What I do in my own place of business is none of your concern," Bud retorted.

Stony glanced at the woman. "Do you welcome this gentleman's attentions, ma'am?"

He watched the dark flush start at the V neck of

her peach-colored waitress uniform and skate up her throat to sit like two roses on those alabaster cheeks. Her green-eyed gaze flitted from him to Bud and back to him.

"I...uh...no," she said. "But—"

He cut her off by turning his attention to Bud. "The lady wants you to leave her alone."

"There's nothing you can do to stop me," Bud said smugly.

"I can testify in court when the lady files a harassment suit against you."

"Why, you— She won't have to file no suit, because she's fired!" Bud said heatedly.

"Bud, no!" Tess exclaimed.

Stony glanced at Tess and was surprised to see she was angry—with him!

"Now look what you've done!" Her fisted hands found a perch at her tiny waist. "I was handling things just fine on my own before you showed up."

His eyes narrowed. "The man was pawing you."

Her chin lifted mulishly. "I've been putting Bud off for a year, and—"

"This has been going on for a whole year?" Stony said incredulously. He turned back to Bud, who was still pinned against the wall. "You've been mauling this lady for a year?" He gathered up a bigger handful of Bud's T-shirt.

"Wasn't doin' nothin' she didn't want," Bud said. "Widow-woman needs a man more'n most."

"A widow?" Stony's glance darted to Tess.

"My husband was killed a year ago," Tess said in response to his cocked brow.

He saw from the flash of pain in her eyes that it was still a raw wound. Her boss hadn't done anything to help it heal. Far from it. Stony resisted the urge to slam Bud against the wall again. He forced himself to let go of Bud's T-shirt and take a step back, afraid he would hurt the man if he held on to him much longer.

Stony wasn't sure he had solved anything. Maybe he had made matters worse. He refused to ask Bud to keep the woman on, when it was clear if he did that Bud would continue to press unwanted attentions on his waitress. But Tess apparently wanted—maybe needed?—the job.

"What will you do now?" he asked Tess.

"Get my job back, if I can," she answered with asperity. She walked over and straightened Bud's rumpled T-shirt. "Come on, Bud. What do you say?"

She managed a crooked smile, but Stony saw her chin was trembling.

Bud shot a malicious look at Stony, then said to Tess, "You're fired, honey. You can pick up your check at the end of the week."

"But, Bud—"

Bud jerked his thumb toward the door. "Out." Bud turned to Stony and said, "Now get out from behind my counter."

Stony went back over the counter the way he had come. He glanced at the woman from the corner of his eye as he made his way back to his booth and sat down. He picked up his hamburger and took a bite, but it was cold, and he had trouble swallowing it.

He watched Tess argue in whispers with Bud and

saw Bud vehemently shake his head. He watched her take off her apron and drape it over the counter before she headed for the kitchen. He waited for her to reappear. He wanted a chance to talk to her, to make sure she was going to be all right, to see if there was anything he could do to help. Although, with the kind of help he had offered so far, he wouldn't be surprised if she turned him down.

He waited maybe two minutes. When Tess didn't return, he threw some money on the table to cover his check, grabbed his shearling coat and Stetson off the antler coatrack and hurried outside to the snow-covered sidewalk to see if he could find her.

Stony wasn't thinking about his vow to stay away from pretty women. He wasn't thinking about anything except his need to make sure Tess would be able to make ends meet until she got another job. That should have been his first warning. Not that he would have paid attention to it. Stony was the kind of man who would stand bare-assed in a nest of rattlers just for the fun of it.

He stopped dead once he was outside and looked both ways. The snow was still coming down in large, windblown flakes that made it difficult to see very far. She was nearly to the end of Main Street, which was only one block long in the tiny town of Pinedale, walking with her head bent against the wind and her winter parka pulled tight around her.

"Hey!" he called. "Wait for me!"

She took one look at him and started to run.

TESS WAS TRYING HARD not to cry. For the past year she had been deflecting Bud's attentions with flip humor. Only, last night her three-year-old daughter, Rose, had been sick, and Tess hadn't slept much. When Bud had approached her, nothing witty had come to her tired mind. Then that awful man had interfered and made everything worse!

She had been fired.

The desperate nature of her situation was just now sinking in. She had no savings. She had no job. In a town this small in the middle of the off-season there wasn't much likelihood of finding another. Especially if Bud kept his promise to make sure none of his friends in the restaurant business hired her. She didn't even have the money for a bus ticket to somewhere else.

Damn you, Charlie Lowell! How could you lie to me? How could you be a thief when you knew what would happen to us if you got caught? How could you go and get yourself killed like that? And for rustling cattle! I hate you, Charlie! I hate you for dying and leaving me alone.

She should have taken one of the marriage offers she had gotten over the past year from the cowboys who came into the Buttermilk Café. Or the Pinedale police chief, Harry DuBois, who had proposed to her for the second time only last week. At least then she and Rose would have been sure of having a roof over their heads.

She liked Harry, and he was good-looking in a rugged Harrison Ford sort of way, but she hadn't been able to feel anything—let alone love—for any man since Charlie had died. Besides, she wasn't sure she wanted to be married again, not after what had happened with Charlie. She had been deliriously in love when she had married at sixteen. She was barely twenty, but she felt much older and wiser. She no longer gave her trust so freely or completely.

But if she wasn't going to let a husband support her, she had to do a better job of it herself. She had barely been able to cope with her disillusionment and grief over Charlie's death during the past year. She hadn't done much planning for the future.

It seemed the moment was upon her. She was going to have to make some plans, and fast, or she and Rose were going to find themselves out on the street in the middle of a Wyoming winter.

"Hey! Wait for me!"

Tess glanced over her shoulder and saw it was that man from the café. He was coming after her! She wasn't sure what his intentions were, but she didn't plan to stick around and find out. She took off at a run, headed for Harry's office. He would protect her from the madman following behind.

Maybe she would have made it if the sidewalk hadn't been covered with a fresh dusting of snow that concealed the treacherous ice below. Or if she had been wearing a decent pair of snow boots instead of the cheap, leather-soled shoes she wore for work. Tess hadn't taken three steps when her feet skidded out from under her. She flailed her arms in a vain attempt to catch her balance and reached out with a hand to break her fall on the cement walk. It turned out to be a fatal error.

Tess heard the bone in her wrist crack as soon as

her weight came down on her arm. She cried out in agony as her body settled on the cold, hard ground.

The interfering stranger was beside her a moment later, down on one knee, his dark brown eyes filled with concern.

"Now look what you did!" she accused.

"What I did?"

"If you hadn't been chasing me—"

"I wasn't chasing you. I was coming after you to—"

"This is all your fault!" she cried, hysterical with the realization that with a broken wrist she wouldn't be able to work for weeks. Not to mention the fact that she had no health insurance and no idea how she was going to pay a doctor to fix her up.

The tears she had so ably kept under control through her most recent disaster could no longer be contained. She fought the sob that threatened, but it broke free with a horrible wrenching sound. Then she was crying in earnest.

She felt the stranger pick her up, being very careful of her wrist, which he settled in her lap, and stand, cuddling her against his chest.

"It's all right, Tess. You're going to be fine. I'm going to take care of you."

She should have resisted. She should have told him in no uncertain terms that she could take very good care of herself. Instead she turned her face to his chest and surrendered to his strength, thinking how good it felt to give her burdens over to someone else, even if it was only for a few moments.

"I'm taking you to my Jeep," he explained as he

began walking. "I'll drive you to the hospital, where someone will take care of your arm."

"I don't have money to pay the doctor," she mumbled against his coat.

"Don't worry. I'll take care of it."

They were such wonderful words. She had been in charge of so much lately, and the burdens had been so heavy. She was more than willing to hand everything over to someone else for a while.

"What's going on here?"

It was Harry. Harry must have seen what happened from the picture window in his office.

"She fell and broke her wrist," the man said. "I'm taking her to the hospital."

"Tess?" Harry said. "Do you want Stony to take you to the hospital?"

Stony. So that was his name. And Harry knew him, so maybe he wasn't a madman, after all.

It took too much energy to answer, or even to turn around and look at Harry. She nodded.

"All right, Stony," Harry said. "I'll follow you there."

"I can take care of it," Stony said, his voice rumbly against her ear.

"I said I'd follow you," Harry insisted. "My patrol car is parked down the street."

Stony didn't argue; he merely turned and headed for his Jeep.

Tess was feeling drowsy, which wasn't surprising, considering the amount of sleep she had gotten last night. She had also hit the back of her head against the pavement when she fell, but it was only beginning to hurt because all her attention had been focused on her throbbing wrist.

"Stony?" she murmured.

"What, Tess?"

"My head hurts."

"You must have hit it when you fell. I'll have the doctor check it out."

"Tess?" Harry said.

Answering took too much effort.

"Looks like she fainted," Harry said, hop-skipping on the dangerous surface to keep up with Stony's long stride.

"Knocked out by the fall, I think," Stony replied.

"I only closed my eyes," she mumbled. "I'm still awake."

"I'll be right behind you," Harry said, sprinting—insofar as that was possible considering the icy walks—for the police car parked nearby.

Stony set her in his Jeep and buckled her in. She heard the engine rumble, and things got a little hazy. Behind her closed eyelids she was seeing a picture of the tall, lean, broad-shouldered man who had come to her rescue in the café, his dark brows lowered, his eyes feral and dangerous. And the man who had looked down at her as she lay hurt on the ground, concern etched in his granite features.

His face was weatherworn, with deep brackets around his mouth and a mesh of crow's feet around his eyes that evidenced a life lived out-of-doors. His straight black hair needed a cut. It hung at least an inch onto his collar, and a hank of it was forever falling onto his forehead.

When he looked at her, his dark brown eyes held her in thrall. They were lonely eyes. Or, at least, the eyes of a man used to being alone. They offered sympathy. They asked for nothing in return.

She had seen him in the café before, but not regularly, so he lived around here somewhere, but maybe not right in town. There were lots of cabins along the river in this isolated place where a lone wolf could find solace from the world of men.

She wondered what he did for a living. Judging by his Western shirt, jeans and boots, he could have been another cowboy. But a mere cowboy wouldn't have taken on Bud, who was big enough, and meaty-fisted enough, to be downright intimidating. Stony hadn't blinked an eye at confronting him. So he was probably a man used to being in charge, rather than one who took orders, a man who knew his own strength and used it when necessary.

But he wasn't a cruel man, or he really might have hurt Bud. She had seen how angry he was, but he had kept his rage on a tight leash. He was agile and strong and—

Stony jostled her broken wrist when he picked her up to take her inside the hospital, and the brief agony jolted her awake. But she couldn't seem to get her eyes open. Tears of pain seeped from her closed eyelids.

"Sorry, Tess," Stony said. "Hang on, and the doctor can give you something for the pain."

Tess drifted in and out of consciousness, aware of the murmur of voices, the sting of an injection, the buzz of the X-ray machine, the warm wetness of the cast being applied around her thumb, from the middle of her right hand halfway up her arm.

She heard the word "concussion" and realized that was probably why she felt so woozy. So it wasn't only the lack of sleep that made her feel so impossibly tired. She heard the doctor say she would have to stay overnight so she could be watched. But she couldn't stay, because she had to go pick up Rose from Mrs. Feeny.

"No," she muttered. "Can't stay. Have to go home."

"Be reasonable, Tess," Harry said. "You're in no condition to leave the hospital."

"Have to get Rose."

"Who's Rose?" she heard Stony ask.

"That's her daughter," Harry said.

"She has a daughter?"

The shock in Stony's voice made her smile. She wasn't sure if the expression got to her face.

"An elderly lady keeps the little girl for Tess while she works. Mrs. Feeny, I think," Harry explained.

Mrs. Feeny was very strict about Tess picking up Rose on time. Otherwise the old woman charged her triple. With all the extra she was going to have to dole out for the doctor, she needed every penny she had.

"Have to pick up Rose." She tried to get up, but a palm flattened her.

"I'll do it," Stony said.

"The kid doesn't know who you are," Harry said. "I'll do it."

"I said I'll do it," Stony countered. "After all, this is my fault."

Tess wanted to smile again. Stony sure had changed his tune. Maybe he was feeling guilty. He ought to. This *was* all his fault!

She welcomed Stony's offer to pick up Rose. For some reason, Rose had taken an instant aversion to Harry. Her daughter had a way of making her feelings known. Tess licked her dry lips and said, "Okay, Stony. Pick up Rose."

"Tess, you don't know a thing about the man," Harry said. "He—"

"Don't interfere, Harry," Tess murmured.

"You heard the lady, Sheriff. She can make her own decisions without any help from you."

Tess realized she hadn't told Stony what to do with her daughter. "Take Rose home," she added.

"I'll do that," Stony said. "Don't worry, Tess. She'll be safe with me. I have lots of room at my place."

His place?

She had meant take Rose to her own home. Of course, he didn't have the key, and Mrs. Feeny, who was also Tess's landlady, was hardly likely to let a stranger into an upstairs apartment in her own home. So maybe it was better this way. Only, she had no idea where Stony lived. How would she find him when she wanted to reclaim her daughter?

She managed to force her eyes open a crack and sought out Stony's face. "Take me, too," she said. "Rose needs me."

"For heaven's sake, Tess," Harry said irritably.

"You're in no condition to do anything but lie flat on your back in bed. Stay here in the hospital where you belong."

The situation was desperate. She reached out and grasped Stony's hand. It was big and warm and callused. His strength made her feel safe. "Rose needs me," she repeated. "Take me, too."

"All right," he said. "I'll take you both to my place."

"Promise?"

"I said I would."

He didn't sound too happy about the situation, Tess realized. But she wasn't about to let him out of his promise.

"Thank you." Her eyes sank closed again.

If she could rest for a couple of hours, she would be fine. Stony could pick up Rose and come back for her. She would rescue her daughter from the clutches of the interfering stranger...as soon as she could get her eyes open again.

Chapter Two

"WHERE AM I?"

"You're at my place, a cabin along the river about twenty miles from town. Don't you remember the ride here in my Jeep?"

"I...sort of. It's all kind of fuzzy."

Tess's gaze darted from the male face bathed in shadows beside the bed, to the natural pine log walls, to the wedding ring patterned quilt that covered her, and back to the face made even more attractive by a night's growth of beard. The faint mauve light filling the window across the room suggested it was nearly dawn. The snow had stopped, but it weighted down the branches of the Douglas firs outside the cabin, creating a real-life picture postcard.

She reached for her head with her right hand before a sharp pain and the weight of the cast reminded her that her wrist was broken. She switched to the left and gingerly touched the lump on the back of her head.

"Does it still hurt?" Stony asked.

"My scalp's a little tender, but my head doesn't ache like it did." She realized what was missing and sat up with a jerk that made her dizzy. "Where's Rose?"

"Still asleep."

"Where?" she insisted, reaching out to clutch Stony's forearm. It was as hard as a rock. She realized what she was doing and let him go.

He gestured with his chin. "Right there beside you."

Tess realized why she hadn't seen the child. The bed was huge, and Rose was curled up in a pile of sheets and blankets on the other side. Tess took another look around at the heavy pine chest, the rocker with clothes thrown over the back, the man's wardrobe, and realized she must be in Stony's bedroom.

"I thought you said you had plenty of room," she accused. "Rose and I are in your bed, aren't we?"

"It was the only one in the house big enough for the both of you," he admitted with a crooked smile. "Rose refused to sleep by herself."

Tess turned back to her daughter and leaned over to brush a red curl from her daughter's cheek. "Did she give you a lot of trouble?"

"No more than two or three green-broke broncs."

"Oh, dear. I was a little afraid of that."

"We got along fine, once she figured out I wasn't going to give up or give in."

Tess flushed. "She is rather strong-willed. I suppose I let her have her own way too often."

"She's spoiled rotten," Stony said flatly. "And she has a temper."

Tess opened her mouth to defend her mothering tactics, then realized Stony hadn't been completely successful in controlling her daughter, either. After all, Rose had ended up sleeping in the same bed with her.

"Perhaps she is a little spoiled," Tess conceded, brushing at the stubborn curl that had found its way back to Rose's cheek. "But she's had to cope with an awful lot over the past year."

Stony shifted from the chair beside the bed to a spot on the mattress near her hips. Tess tensed at the intrusion on her space. However helpful he had been, Stony was still a stranger. And she was in his bed wearing no more than—Good Lord—one of his T-shirts!

"I've been wanting to talk to you about that. I mean, about how you and Rose have been getting by," Stony said.

His voice had that rusty gate sound, as though he hadn't used it much lately. It rumbled over her, sending a shiver up her spine. She wasn't sure whether it was the threat he presented, or the temptation, that had her inching away from him.

"We've been just fine," Tess said.

"Don't bother lying."

"I—"

"I spoke with your landlady."

Tess sighed. "I'm only a month behind on the rent."

"You had to give up your phone two months ago. And I didn't see much in the cupboards to eat. How the hell you two have managed to make it this far, I'll never know."

Tess felt the anger rising and struggled to control it. Rose hadn't learned her redheaded temper; she had inherited it from her mother.

"I'd like to know what your plans are now that you've been fired," Stony said.

"I don't see how my future plans are any of your business," Tess retorted. "I'm sure I'll find something—"

"You can work for me." Stony interrupted her.

Tess was speechless. "Doing what?" she managed to say at last.

He made a broad gesture around the bedroom. "I could use a housekeeper, and I know you can cook. I couldn't pay much, but I could give you free room and board. It would give you somewhere to stay and food in your mouths, at least until your wrist is healed."

Tess took a second look around the room. This time she noticed the layer of dust on the wardrobe, the stack of dirty, rumpled shirts on the rocker, the horse magazines strewn across the floor, the empty beer can on the chest. It was clear the man could use a housekeeper. But if he had really wanted one, he could have hired one long ago.

Her gaze shifted back to Stony's face. "Why are you willing to do this for me?"

He frowned and rubbed his thumb along his lower lip. "I don't have any designs on you, if that's what you're thinking."

She flushed. Because the thought had occurred to her. "I never—"

"Don't bother lying again. You've been itching to get out of here ever since you woke up."

She heard the irritation in his voice. His thumb never stopped that lazy trail from one side of his mouth to the other. She felt a surprising curl of desire in her belly and jerked her gaze away from his mouth back to his eyes. That was no better. They were dark and fierce and feral. They made her feel hunted. She lowered her lashes to hide from him but felt her body quiver in anticipation of the need to fight or to flee.

"The way I figure it, I owe you a job," he continued, apparently unaware of her agitation. "I'm the one who got you fired—even if you should have quit a long time ago."

"And worked where?" she demanded, incensed at the implied criticism. "There aren't too many waitress jobs in Pinedale."

"Couldn't you do something else?"

Her anger died, consumed by frustration at her lack of education. She had a high school equivalency degree, but she had believed that was all she would ever need. She had never considered the necessity of any further formal education because she had been perfectly happy being a wife and mother. She had been very good at her chosen profession.

"I had a job I was happy with, until it was taken away from me."

"Well, there you go. What was it?"

"Housewife."

She saw the stricken look on Stony's face and realized she shouldn't take out her bitterness over Charlie's death against him. "I'm sorry. Ever since Charlie got himself killed, I—" She took a shuddering breath. She wasn't used to speaking aloud about Charlie, and the sudden lump in her throat surprised her. She had believed she had come to terms with Charlie's untimely death. Apparently not.

"Was Charlie your husband?"

"Yes. Charles Lowell. He was a butcher at the local grocery store. Or so I thought. He was caught rustling cattle and was killed in the gunfight that followed."

She looked up and discovered Stony staring at her grim-lipped. His face had paled, and his eyes narrowed to slits. "It's not a pretty story," she admitted. "I was devastated, because I was caught off guard. I had no idea Charlie was involved in theft of any kind. I'm afraid I wasn't myself for a long time after that."

"Didn't you have any family who could have taken care of you?" he asked.

"I'm an orphan. And Charlie's parents are dead. It was—and is—just me and Rose. The sheriff's office collected some money for us. Looking back, I suppose it was strange for them to do such a thing—but it got us through the first few months. When I was myself again, I looked around and realized I would have to get a job. Bud was the only one who would hire me without experience.

"I think he did it because he thought he could pressure me into sleeping with him. I'm sure he had no idea I would resist his advances so long or so completely." Her lip curled up on one side. "I guess he finally ran out of patience."

Stony grunted in sardonic agreement. "Will you take the job I offered you, or not?"

She twisted the sheet in the fingers of her good hand. She didn't have any choice. It was take his job offer or starve. But she didn't like it. Stony made her nervous. He made her skin tingle. He made her feel things she didn't want to feel.

Nevertheless she said, "I'll take the job." And then qualified her acceptance. "But only until my wrist heals, and I can decide what to do with my life."

Or until the day came when it was no longer safe to remain with the lone wolf whose den she had invaded with her cub.

HE HAD KILLED HER HUSBAND.

Stony wished he had inquired about Tess's last name sooner. He had been shocked to hear her husband was Charles Lowell. He had been tracking that particular gang of rustlers for several months before he finally caught them in the act, and he had been forced into the gun battle that ensued. He had performed his job with the ruthless efficiency that had earned him his reputation, and Charles Lowell had died.

His identity as a range detective who hired out to large cattle spreads wasn't generally known, and Stony needed it to stay that way in order to infiltrate the roving bands of rustlers that plagued the vast Wyoming ranges. The police had cooperated and kept his name out of the local paper. For some reason, Tess Lowell had never asked the identity of the man who killed her husband, or she would have known who he was.

Stony knew he ought to confess immediately and give Tess the chance to spit in his face. But she didn't have anywhere else to go, and he was afraid she wouldn't stay if she knew the truth. At least he could give her a place to live until she was well again. She and the kid needed him, and he owed them something because he was personally responsible for the loss of both husband and father, even if the man was a felon.

But he resented the intrusion on his solitude.

He was thirty-three and had lived alone in this five-room cabin, which he had built with his own hands, for the past ten years. He liked the quiet. He had spent many a long winter night before a flickering fire with nothing to disturb his peace but the wind rustling in the pines or the buildup of snow sliding off the steep blue tin roof in thunderous clumps.

When he needed a woman, he sought out one who only wanted the same brief physical satisfaction he desired. Lately he had decided even that sort of relationship wasn't worth the risk it entailed. His isolation had become complete and comfortable.

Until this redheaded woman and her redheaded child had invaded it.

His attention was drawn to the child, who woke suddenly and popped upright in bed like a jack-in-the-box.

"Mama!"

"Don't be frightened, Rose. I'm right here," Tess said, holding out her good arm.

The little girl scuttled across the bed and flung herself across her mother's body as though she were being attacked by ravaging wolves. She peered up at Stony with green eyes a shade darker than her mother's and said very distinctly, "I want to go home."

"I know, sweetheart," Tess replied, brushing at the mass of bright red curls—shades lighter than her mother's deep auburn—that tumbled over her daughter's forehead. "I do, too. But we can't, not for a little while."

The child sat up abruptly. "Why not?"

"Because your mother's arm is broken. She needs to rest and recuperate," Stony said.

"What's reputerate?" the child said, her brows knitted in confusion.

"Get well," Stony amended, amused at the child's mangled effort to repeat the grown-up word.

The little girl's eyes widened, and her gaze slid to the cast covering her mother's arm. She reached out tentatively to touch it. "Mama's hurt bad?"

"The cast is there to protect the broken bone so it can heal," Tess explained.

Tears filled the child's green eyes and spilled over. Her lower lip stuck out, and her chin trembled. "Mama's hurt."

Stony was amazed at the instant transformation. How did the kid do it? He watched her mother fall for the act.

"Oh, sweetheart, I'll be fine," Tess said with a hitching sob as she gathered the child to her breast.

Stony snorted. He meant to convey disgust at the ridiculousness of sentimental tears over something that was done and over. He believed the little girl was simply manipulating her mother, for reasons he couldn't imagine and didn't care to figure out. Two sets of long-lashed, accusing green eyes settled on him, and the sound in his throat changed to something more contemplative.

"Is anybody hungry?" he asked.

"I am," Rose said.

Stony's lips twisted cynically when he saw how instantly the child's tears stopped. One clung to her lashes and skidded down her check when she gave him a wide-eyed blink.

"I'll make some breakfast," he said.

"I'll do it." Tess slipped her legs out from under the covers before she realized the T-shirt bared her all the way from her toes to her hips. She flushed and scooted back under the covers.

"Where are my clothes?" she asked.

"I had Mrs. Feeny put some things in a suitcase for you. It's there in the corner. You can get the rest of your stuff from her later."

Stony was still having trouble catching his breath after the eye-stopping exhibit he had just witnessed. The woman wasn't tall, but she had incredible legs, long and silky and perfectly formed. He fought off the image of those legs wrapped around him. His genitals drew up tight in response to such mental titillation.

"I'll go make breakfast while you get dressed," he said, backing his way out of the room. He felt perspiration dotting his forehead, even though the bedroom was far from hot. It disturbed him that his thoughts had taken such a decidedly lascivious turn. He had cast himself in the role of guardian. So long as Tess was under his roof, he had to resist any temptation to seduce her. He owed Charlie Lowell's widow that much consideration.

The whole wall of the house that encompassed the combined kitchen and living area contained French doors that opened onto a large elevated patio. The view included a forest of evergreen pines and fir interspersed with aspens that had lost their leaves earlier in the fall. The light and empty space immediately brought him comfort.

"Is this your house?"

Stony whirled from the refrigerator door and stared at the sprite who was standing barefoot not three feet away from him.

"You should be wearing slippers," he said to the child, aware of how parental he must sound, when the last thing he ever wanted to be was a parent.

She looked down as she wiggled her toes on the polished hardwood floor. She glanced coyly at him from beneath lowered lashes. "Mama's getting me slippers for Christmas."

Not without money, she wasn't, Stony thought grimly.

"Your feet must be cold," he said, scooping the child up and carting her back toward the bedroom. She didn't weigh as much as a case of beer. "You can wear a pair of socks."

"I'm not supposed to wear socks without shoes," she said soberly.

He met her gaze and frowned.

Her chin trembled. "Mama says so."

"I'm not going to bite you," he snapped.

Rose burst into tears. "Mama!"

"What's going on?" Tess said, hurrying from the bedroom.

Stony was dismayed to see she had left his T-shirt on and merely added a pair of worn jeans. It wouldn't take much to have her naked. She was barefoot, too.

"I told the kid she shouldn't be running around barefoot on this cold floor." He watched Tess's bare toes curl against the wooden floor. His gaze skipped back to her face, and he saw the blush was back in her cheeks.

"I don't have the money for slippers," she murmured.

"Put on a pair of socks."

"I think I'm capable of judging whether my feet are cold," she retorted.

He shifted Rose to one arm and bent down to touch Tess's bare feet. "Your toes are like ice," he said flatly. "Put on some socks."

"I don't wear socks without—"

"Shoes," he finished. "Then put on some socks and shoes."

"Is that an order?" she asked.

He wanted to say yes, but the mulish tilt of her chin advised against it. "A suggestion."

"Very well. I'll be right back."

"Bring some socks and shoes for Rose," he called after her. He looked down at the little girl who was peering at him wide-eyed.

"I don't like you," she announced.

"I don't like you, either," he said.

Rose didn't seem phased by the insult. "I'm hungry," she said.

"So am I," Stony muttered. "That's probably why I'm in such a foul mood." It couldn't have anything to do with the two females who had invaded his lair.

"I can help cook," Rose said.

"Can you now?" Stony set her on the counter beside the fridge so she would be off the floor while he rooted around for breakfast fixings. He set the eggs on the counter while he hunted out the bacon and English muffins.

A moment later he heard a tiny "Uh-oh," followed by the sound of eggs cracking on the floor.

He whipped his head up and caught it on the refrigerator shelf. He grabbed at the painful spot and turned to find the eggs spilled from the carton and creating a gooey puddle on his floor.

The little girl's eyes were wide with fright. "I'm sorry."

Stony fought down the urge to yell at her, remembering how quickly she could summon tears. Besides, accidents could happen to anyone. He was willing to give her the benefit of the doubt. This time.

"Are you going to spank me?" the little girl asked, her chin aquiver.

"I didn't think parents spanked their kids anymore," Stony said. "It's against the law, or something."

"Mama says she's going to spank me. But she never does."

"I'll bet," Stony said. That explained why the kid was spoiled rotten.

"Mama loves me," the little girl said solemnly.

Stony took in Rose's big green eyes, her unmanageable, curly head of hair, the chubby arms and legs, and felt an uncomfortable tug at his heart. Rose was lovable, all right. He had to give her that.

He looked down at the chaos she had created with a box of eggs. Lovable. And messy.

"Oh, no!"

Stony looked over his shoulder at Tess, who was eyeing the broken eggs on the floor with dismay. "I'm so sorry."

"No problem. We can have a bowl of cereal instead. No cooking. Saves on dishes."

"I'll clean up that mess," Tess volunteered.

"I'll do it," Stony said, eyeing the arm she had arranged in the sling the doctor had given her. "You're incapacitated."

"What's 'pacitated?" Rose inquired.

"Means she can't do anything with that broken arm," Stony explained to the child. He caught Rose around the waist and, stepping around the broken eggs, hauled her over to the far side of the breakfast bar, where he sat her on one of the two stools there. He grabbed a handful of paper towels and began sopping up the eggs and dropping the shells into the disposal in the sink.

"You must not get much company," Tess said, settling on the second stool.

"I can stand on this side of the bar," he said, rinsing his hands and drying them. He grabbed some bowls from the cupboard and dropped them with a clatter on the breakfast bar. He only had one box of cereal, a healthy wheat flake, and he began pouring it out into the three bowls.

"I don't like that kind," Rose said.

"It's all I've got," Stony replied.

"I want the kind with marshmallows," Rose insisted.

"Rose, darling—" Tess said.

"Eat it or go hungry," Stony said.

Rose moved her bowl just as Stony began to pour milk, and it spilled across the counter.

Stony set down the milk carton as softly as he could, using his last bit of patience. "It's time we had a talk, young lady," he said to Rose.

"I don't like you," Rose said, her chin tilted in a mulish imitation of her mother.

"I thought we settled that," Stony muttered, glaring back at the little girl. "I don't like you, either."

"Rose—"

"Stay out of this, Tess," Stony said.

"I will not," Tess said, rising from her bar stool, her green eyes flashing. "You seem to be forgetting who you are. And who we are."

"I'm an idiot," Stony muttered. "And you're interlopers."

"What's 'lopers?" Rose asked.

"Intruders," Stony snarled.

"What's 'truders?" Rose asked.

"Unwelcome guests," Tess answered before Stony could speak. "I think we can save you and ourselves a great deal of unpleasantness, Mr.—I don't even know your last name," Tess said, astonished at the realization. "I'm sorry we've intruded on your peace. If you'll allow me to use your phone, I'm sure Harry DuBois will be willing to come and get us."

Stony shoved a hand through his hair, catching the wayward curl on his forehead, which immediately tumbled back down again. "Look," he said. "I don't want you to leave. Besides, you have nowhere else to go."

Tess sighed. "Unfortunately, what you say is true. But I don't think this is going to work, Mr.— What is your last name, anyway?"

"It's Carlton, but call me Stony."

"Very well, Stony. As I said, I don't think this is going to work."

"I'm not used to having people around."

"Especially not children, it seems."

"I don't like kids," he said flatly.

"Why is that?" Tess challenged.

Stony thought of his father and his father's very young new wife and their new family that had excluded him. He had to admit his half brother had been cute. His father had been fascinated by his second son. That kid had gotten all the attention Stony had always craved from a father who had always been too busy working to play with him. Thirteen-year-old Stony had felt sick with guilt and shame at his uncontrollable envy and resentment of the time and attention his father gave his newborn son.

He couldn't tell Tess any of that. "Kids are a lot of bother," he said instead.

"I shall make certain Rose is not a bother," Tess said crisply. "Is there anything else?"

"Just keep her out of my way."

Tess looked around the small cabin. What Stony

asked was unrealistic, considering the size of the place. "I'll do my best."

"I want to go home," Rose said to her mother.

Stony watched as Tess hugged the child. "I wish we could go home, too, Rose. We have to stay here."

"I don't like that man," Rose said.

Stony met Tess's gaze over the child's head. He wasn't proud of his behavior. But he couldn't help his feelings, either. However, there was something he could do to ease the situation for all of them.

"I've got another job up around Jackson Hole," he said. "I'll be leaving this afternoon, so you'll have the place to yourself. I have groceries delivered on a regular basis from town. If you need more, call the supermarket and give them a list."

He hadn't been meaning to take on more work right away, but it seemed best to put some distance between himself and Tess—for whom he felt too great an attraction, and the little girl—who didn't like him.

"What is it you do?" Tess asked.

"I find cattle rustlers. And bring them to justice."

Tess stared at him openmouthed.

He turned on his heel and left the room before she had a chance to ask if he knew the man who had apprehended and killed her husband.

Chapter Three

STONY HAD SPENT most of the past six weeks on horseback or in his Jeep tracking a bunch of winter rustlers that had proved particularly elusive. He hadn't been home once since he had rescued Tess Lowell, spending his time instead at a place he kept in Jackson Hole within sight of the Grand Tetons. It was two days before Christmas, and he wanted to be in his own home for the holiday. Even if he had to share it with strangers.

He wondered if they had already left. Maybe Tess had figured out some other way to support herself, and she and the little girl were gone. Perversely, he found himself wishing they were still there.

Tess had been on his mind a great deal lately.

He figured it was simply that he hadn't had a woman in a long time, and he had found the sight of her green cat's eyes staring back at him from an alabaster face surrounded by wispy auburn curls especially attractive. He couldn't help remembering the look of her long legs slipping from under his covers. Or the soft weight of her breasts beneath one of his worn T-shirts.

He wanted her. There wasn't anything rational or reasonable about his desire. It was purely primitive. Like a male beast in rut. He had to have her.

He planned to have her.

His heart beat a little bit faster when he saw the smoke coming from the chimney of his cabin as he traversed the narrow, winding dirt road lined with ten-foot mounds of county-plowed snow that led up the mountain where he lived.

She was still there.

He left the Jeep outside rather than putting it in the garage and let himself in through the front door, anxious to see her again.

He was stunned when he stepped inside. His place didn't look the same. Not that it didn't look nice. The Western furniture had been rearranged to create a cozy sitting area around the wood stove in the fireplace and everything sparkled with cleanliness. She had brought evergreen boughs inside and strung them across the pine mantel, adding splashes of red with small velvet bows. And she had put up a Christmas tree with homemade decorations and lights. There were even presents beneath it.

It felt like a home. But not his home.

He hadn't celebrated Christmas since he had left his father's house at eighteen. It conjured too many memories of his father and the wife and child who had usurped what little place he had in his father's life. He had decided he didn't need anybody to love him. After college, instead of going into his father's lumber business, he had escaped to this mountain hideaway to be alone, renting a place in town until the house was done.

The Christmas tree brought back painful memories of being shut out, of feeling lonely and alone. Only he wasn't alone this Christmas. Not if the fire in the chimney meant what he thought it did.

His nose led him to the stove, where a savory stew was bubbling, apparently intended for supper later in the day. He used a wooden spoon to take a taste. It was delicious, tangy with sage and bay.

The house was quiet. Normally he liked the quiet. Now it irritated him. Where was she? Where was the little girl?

He went hunting for Tess and found her in the guest bedroom, sitting on the side of one of the twin pine beds, reading *The Three Little Pigs* to her daughter. He stood in the doorway, listening to their laughter as Tess huffed and puffed and blew the house down. It made his chest constrict for no good reason he could discern.

He knew when she felt his presence. Her shoulders tensed, and she stopped reading in midsentence. She could likely smell him, feel his heat. He felt hers.

"Why did you stop, Mama?" the child asked. "Did the big, bad wolf blow the brick house down?"

When Tess turned to look at him over her shoulder he felt a shiver of raw sexual hunger roll down his spine. The hairs stood up on his nape. His nostrils flared, and his body tautened.

She recognized the danger. He saw it in the way her pupils dilated, the way her mouth fell open to gasp a breath of air, the way her body readied itself to fight—or to flee.

She couldn't run from him. Not without the child. And the two of them hadn't a chance of escaping.

He saw the anxiety in her eyes, along with an unnaturally heightened awareness. She moved slowly, cautiously, standing and laying the children's book down on the bed.

He suddenly realized the cast was gone. Her arm was healed. But she was still here. He felt a surge of triumph, almost of euphoria. He had the oddest feeling she was going to walk right into his embrace.

He took a step, opened his arms to her, and found them filled seconds later as an exuberant little girl launched herself at him from the bed. He caught Rose only an instant before disaster.

"You came back!" Rose chirped, clinging to his neck like a limpet. "Mama said you would. Mama said you're a nice man. Mama said you're taking care of us."

He scowled. "I thought you didn't like me."

Her tiny brow furrowed uncertainly, and her worried glance skipped to her mother. "Mama?"

"I believe Rose is willing to give you a second chance," Tess said in a voice that shuddered over him.

He met her eyes. "Thanks to you, I suppose."

She smiled, and a spiral of desire drew his loins up tight.

"I might have had something to do with it."

Her smile faded as sexual awareness rose between them.

Rose grabbed his cheeks between her palms to turn his attention back to her. "I like it here," she said. "I can play in the snow, and chop limbs from trees and stuff. Mama said you might let us stay if I'm a good girl. I'm not supposed to say I don't like you anymore," she added naively.

Stony's glance shot to Tess and caught her blush of embarrassment. So that was how she had gotten the girl to change her mind about him.

"I promise to be good," Rose said. "Will you let us stay? Have you seen our Christmas tree? Mama made some presents for you. Do you want to see your presents?"

"Rose," Tess said, "give Stony a chance to catch his breath."

His breath was caught already—somewhere in his chest.

Rose wriggled to be let down, and he set her on her feet. She grabbed his hand and headed toward the living room as fast as her tiny legs could carry her. He glanced helplessly over his shoulder at Tess, who gave him a winsome smile as he was led away. He held out his hand to her at the last possible moment, and she laid her slight palm in his, allowing herself to be tugged after him.

Electricity shot up his arm as he made contact with her flesh. If it hadn't been for the hold the little girl had on him he would have taken Tess then and there. He flashed her a look that told her his intention and saw the trepidation rise again in her eyes. She recognized the trap too late. She had been caught, and he would not let her go until he had assuaged the powerful need in him to have her beneath him, to put himself inside her and make her his own.

TESS HAD REALIZED the danger too late. She had known Stony was attracted to her, felt it all those weeks ago when she had woken up in his bed. She had assumed he was civilized enough to control his impulses. She should have known better. No man was civilized where sex was concerned.

Harry had warned her. "He's dangerous. Stony Carlton is a lone wolf who doesn't live by anyone's rules. Watch yourself around him."

She had laughed at Harry and reassured him that after a year as a waitress at the Buttermilk Café she was perfectly capable of quelling the pretensions of a too-forward man.

She felt a frisson of excitement skate up her arm as Stony's hand tightened around hers. She had known she would have to deal with the attraction between them sometime. She just hadn't thought it would be this soon.

"Mama made you a—" Rose cut herself off, putting tiny hands in front of her mouth. Wide-eyed she confessed, "I'm not supposed to tell. It's supposed to be a surprise."

Stony led Tess to the sofa she had angled in front of the fireplace and drew her down on it. An instant later Rose was in his lap chattering again. Because her daughter asked a question she wanted answered herself, Tess didn't bother shushing her.

"Where have you been?" Rose asked. "What have you been doing?"

Stony's thumb caressed Tess's wrist. Her blood began to thrum, and goose bumps shot up on her arms. She stared at him, mesmerized, as he spoke.

"I've been chasing some bad men up near Jackson Hole."

"Did you catch them?" Rose asked.

"Not yet."

"Why did you come home?" Tess asked.

"For Christmas," he said simply.

Tess and Stony's gaze met over Rose's head. He might profess not to like children. He might have cut himself off from other people by living on this mountain. But Christmas was a time for families. And he had come back to spend it with them.

"I see you've been busy." Stony gestured with his free hand at the decorations and the tree. "Where did you get all this stuff?"

"The greenery I found on the mountain. The rest is ours," she said. "Harry DuBois brought it out here for us."

He frowned. It obviously hadn't yet occurred to him that she would have had to call someone to take her in to the doctor to have her cast removed. She saw the moment it did.

"I never thought about you needing a way to get around," he said. "I guess I should have."

"Harry was wonderful about helping me out when I needed to run errands. I could have called 911 in an emergency," she said.

His hand tightened on hers. It was an act of possession.

"You're hurting me," she said quietly.

His hold instantly loosened. But he didn't let her go.

"How soon before that stew is ready?" he asked.

"A couple of hours. I was just putting Rose down for a quick nap before supper." She smiled ruefully. "I'm afraid that's out of the question now."

He arched a dark brow. "What if I read to her? Do you think she'd lie down then?"

"You'd do that?"

He gave her a roguish grin. "How long does it usually take Rose to fall asleep?"

She realized suddenly why he wanted Rose in bed. So he could take her to his.

"How would you like for me to read to you?" he asked Rose.

"Will you be the big bad wolf?" Rose asked.

"How's this?" Stony growled menacingly in his throat.

Rose shrieked in mock fright and raced for the bedroom.

Stony winked at Tess and headed after the little girl. "I'll see you in a few minutes."

Tess suspected Stony's estimate was optimistic. As excited as Rose was, it would be a little longer than a few minutes before he returned. But she had better use whatever time she had to decide how she was going to handle the situation once she and Stony were alone.

She chewed on her thumbnail worriedly. She didn't believe Stony would force his attentions on her. Unfortunately he wouldn't have to use force. She had felt her body respond to his mere presence in the bedroom doorway, to the heat of him, the scent of him, the predatory look in his dark brown eyes.

To be honest, she had fantasized over the past

weeks, as she had slept in the twin bed next to her daughter, what it would be like to spend the night in Stony's arms. If he beckoned, it would be difficult to refuse him.

But they would be two strangers having sex, not two lovers making love. It was tempting to imagine herself lying beneath Stony in his bed, but she wasn't sure she would be able to face herself in the morning. Her husband had been the only lover she had ever had. And though they hadn't been married when they made love for the first time, she had been deeply in love with him.

It had happened on a hot summer night, on a blanket laid out on the prairie grass with the sky and stars above them. She had been so frightened and so very excited, because she loved Charlie so much. She had trusted him not to hurt her. Only, it had hurt that first time, and it had never been as good for her as it was for him. But she had wanted to please Charlie, wanted him to love her as nobody else ever had. He had been a cowboy for one of the ranches in the area, much older than her—twenty-three—and, she had thought, much wiser.

But Charlie hadn't used any protection, not that first time, and not later. She was equally responsible for what had happened. She accepted that now. But her foster parents had been sorely disappointed in her when she told them she was pregnant and had kicked her out of their house. If Charlie hadn't married her, she didn't know what she would have done.

She understood the male need for sex because her husband had possessed it. She had not understood that a woman could feel the same...hunger. That was the only word that described what she was feeling—had been feeling over the past six weeks—for Stony Carlton. She was surprised because she knew she couldn't possibly be in love with him. She hardly knew him. But she was attracted to him in a way she had never been attracted to any other man, even her husband.

She had heard it said that for each person there was a perfect mate, that somewhere in the world the other half was wandering, waiting to be found. She felt that way about Stony, that he was her other half, and that she had to fit herself to him, make him a part of herself, or she would never be complete.

Yet she shied from joining herself with a man she didn't love. It seemed...ruthless, heartless, unfeeling.

Not unfeeling. She was feeling entirely too much. Her body sang with excitement. Her skin tingled. Her breasts felt achy. Her belly curled with desire.

She stood and paced the living room, like a mountain lion in a cage. She wanted him. But she would be damned if she would give in to such animal urges. She was a rational human being. She should be able to act in a cool and rational manner.

She would tell him no. And she would mean it.

She turned abruptly as Stony appeared in the hallway that led into the living room. He stopped where he was, and she had the sense of being prey, of being hunted. She looked around and realized there was no escape. She had to go through him to get to the front door of the house. Not that she could leave without Rose. And he knew it. Knew she was trapped. She saw it in the merciless smile that curled his lips.

"Hello, Tess," he said.

His rumbling voice skittered over her spine and made her shiver. "No," she said.

He quirked a dark brow. "I haven't asked for anything. Yet."

She shoved a wayward curl behind her ear and huffed out a breath of air. Her palms were damp, and she rubbed them down the sides of her jeans, then curled her arms around herself protectively.

"You feel it, don't you?" he said.

"No."

His eyes crinkled at the corners as his smile broadened. "I can hardly believe it myself," he confessed. "I swore off women a while back. You've made me rethink my decision."

"We're strangers," she said pointedly.

He shook his head slowly, the smile suddenly gone. "We've never been strangers, Tess. We've known each other forever."

So he felt it, too. Whatever it was. That strange connection between them, urging their bodies together, promising a wholeness, a joining of souls.

Yet, she fought it. Because it couldn't possibly be right to have sex—it could only be sex—with this man she hardly knew.

"I want you," he said as he took a step toward her.

She held her ground.

"I haven't been able to think of anything but you." He took another step.

She searched for an escape route, a means of avoiding him. There wasn't any. Her body quivered as she stood still, waiting.

"I need you," he said, his voice guttural, animal. His eyes were lambent, lit by a fire that heated her inside. He took the last step that brought them into contact. "I have to have you."

She moaned as his arms slid around her and pulled their bodies together. She felt her breasts crushed against his hard chest even as his palm curved around her buttocks and lifted her until her hips fit into the cradle of his, against the hard, thick length of him.

Her hands rested on his shoulders, yet she couldn't summon the strength of will to push him away. It felt so good to be held by him, so impossibly right!

"This is crazy," she said at the same time she laid her head back so he could more easily kiss her throat. His lips and teeth and tongue feasted on her flesh, sending shivers of sensation shuddering through her body.

She grasped his hair, intending to free herself, but clung to him as his mouth captured hers, his tongue probing until she let him inside.

And then she was lost.

His hips thrust against her in time with the movement of his tongue in and out of her mouth. She groaned and arched her body upward, needing to be closer, resenting the layers of denim and cotton that separated them. His hand slid between her legs, and he lifted her nearly off the ground. His thumb caressed her until she gasped, as he found the spot he had been seeking.

She reached for him with her mouth, needing to be

closer, to be connected to him. Then her tongue was in his mouth, tasting him, teasing his inner lip, biting at his lower lip until he growled deep in his throat.

They began tearing the clothes off each other, couldn't get them off fast enough. Buttons popped, clattering across the hardwood floor, zippers came down, T-shirts were ripped off until they stood naked before each other.

His eyes were heavy-lidded, his gaze feral, the pupils huge, making his eyes dark black pools into which she might fall and never return. His body was surprisingly tanned, lean, but muscular, with sinews visible in his arms and shoulders. His belly was flat, his chest furred with black hair that became a narrow black line leading to the curly bush that surrounded his genitals.

Her gaze rose to his. She was panting, unable to catch her breath. Frightened. And exhilarated.

It was going to happen. He was going to claim her. He was going to make her his.

She felt her knees weaken, nature's way of making sure the female was prone, so the male seed could take root. He caught her before she fell and lifted her into his arms, holding her tight against his chest.

She hadn't given a thought to where they were, the fact that her daughter could waken and come upon them.

He carried her to his bedroom, to the king size bed that hadn't been slept in since he had left. He pulled down the covers and laid her on the cool sheets, following her down until he lay atop her. He nudged her legs apart with his knees and put his hand between her thighs to touch her.

She flinched at his touch, though it was gentle. It was almost embarrassing how wet and ready she was. His touch made her even more so.

She stared up at him, wondering what it was about this particular man that made her so vulnerable to him. He reached into the bedside table and found the protection she hadn't thought about.

He really doesn't like children, she thought.

But she was grateful he was taking the precautions that had been the farthest thing from her mind. She knew better. She knew the consequences of being foolish and in love.

Well, she was certainly foolish, anyway.

He spread her hair on the pillow around her face, playing with it, caressing it between his fingertips.

"It's softer than I thought it would be. Because of all those curls," he explained with a smile that made her heart beat faster.

She slid her hands through his hair. "Yours is soft, too." She tugged his head toward her, wanting his mouth on hers.

The kiss was long and slow and deep. Her body arched upward into his, an itch seeking to be scratched.

His hand curved around her breast, and she made an animal sound at the feel of his callused fingertips on her flesh. He cupped the soft mound and held it steady for his mouth. He sipped at her, licked and bit and licked again. Then he suckled her, drawing her nipple into his mouth.

She nearly came off the bed.

He spread her legs with his knees once more and placed himself at the entrance to her. She expected him to thrust quickly, but he took his time, entering her a little way and then backing off, only to return and probe a little deeper, until at last she reached up with her legs around him and urged him inside to the hilt.

He gave a satisfied sigh as he sank into her that was matched by a guttural sound of her own.

Then he turned her face up, so she would be looking into his eyes and began to thrust, in and out, slow at first, and then faster, as his thumb played with her between their sweat-slick bodies.

She began to writhe beneath him, and her eyelids floated downward. She had never felt like this. She couldn't seem to control her body. It began to contract, to spasm in a way that was both frightening and immensely pleasurable. She fought the lack of control, fought the loss of self.

"Look at me, Tess," he commanded. "Come with me," he urged.

She opened her eyes and met his gaze, fierce and intense, deep and dark as a well. She began to slide into the darkness where there was nothing but joy, the two of them no longer separate but joined as one euphoric being.

"You belong to me," he said triumphantly. "You'll always be mine."

It was the last thing she heard before the darkness consumed her.

Chapter Four

THE LOVEMAKING Stony had just experienced far surpassed anything he had ever known with a woman. But he had no idea what had possessed him to utter those unbelievable words at the moment of climax.

"You belong to me. You'll always be mine."

He had to be out of his mind. For years he had been a loner who didn't need anyone. He had no reason to marry, because he never intended to have children. What had made him stake his claim on Tess Lowell—a woman who came packaged with a three-year-old imp?

He hardly knew the woman.

He felt like he had known her all his life.

It had to be lust that had prompted his behavior. He had desired her, so he had taken her to bed. Now that his need was slaked he would be fine.

Only, he wanted her again already, and they had just finished a bout of lovemaking that was indescribably satisfying. He couldn't imagine not wanting her tomorrow and the day after that. So maybe it was something more than lust. But what?

He raised himself on his elbow so he could watch Tess while she slept. The curls around her face were damp with sweat, and her lips were swollen, pouty from his kisses. He had left a love bruise on her throat. He slowly trailed the sheet away, so he could look at all of her.

It was, after all, only another female body. He had seen his share of them. Why did he find this one so exquisite? Nipples the pink of prairie roses. Breasts full and exactly the right size for him. A slightly rounded stomach. The deep russet curls between her legs. And, oh, those legs! He liked the way she had wrapped them around him, her heels digging into his buttocks, demanding to have him inside her.

He was aroused again merely looking at her.

He wasn't sure what he should do about the situation. He had never wanted anyone to love him because he had no intention of giving love in return. Loving left you vulnerable. He had vowed when his father abandoned him never to give anyone the chance to hurt him that way again. It was safer not to ask for love. It was safer to be alone. Even if it was occasionally lonely.

Good Lord! Did he want her to love him?

No, of course not. Though she didn't yet know it, he was the one responsible for making her a widow. Better not to let his thoughts wander in a hopeless direction.

But he had no intention of letting Tess go anytime soon. Even though he could never let himself love her. Even if all they could ever have together was fantastic sex.

Her eyelids fluttered open, and he watched her eyes fill with tears. He kissed away the first salty drop before it could reach the pillow. "What's wrong?"

"I...I don't understand what compelled me to do

such a thing. I hardly know you." She suddenly realized she was naked before him and scrambled to cover herself.

"Don't," he said, catching her wrist and preventing her from drawing the sheet back over her. "I like looking at you. You're beautiful."

"I'm not. I have stretch marks. And my legs—"

"Are perfect." He smiled. "All of you is perfect." He hadn't noticed the stretch marks. He searched for them and found them along her hips, silvery lines where her flesh had stretched to accommodate a baby. He had a fleeting picture of her grown huge with his child and brushed it away.

"We have to get dressed," she said. "Rose will be waking soon."

"Don't worry. I locked the door. She can't get in."

A rueful smile appeared before she said, "You don't know Rose. She'll stand at the door and yell until we let her in."

"All right. We'll get up. Soon."

She started to rise, but he levered himself over her and kissed her deep and hard. It only took a moment before he was protected and inside her again. He saw her flush and realized she had been wet and hot and ready for him.

She had wanted him again, too.

He threaded his fingers through hers and held her hands prisoner above her head as he slowly thrust into her. He stared into her eyes, willing her to accept his claim. Her chin trembled, and her eyes grew liquid with feeling.

"This was meant to be," he said. "The two of us together. Don't fight it, Tess."

She groaned and arched upward, raising her breasts to him, an offering fit for the gods. He supped, drinking the heady wine she offered him.

"Please," she begged. "Please."

He knew what she wanted. He gave it to her.

Himself. All of himself, enough to make two halves into one whole. Enough to fill them both full. Enough to take them to paradise again.

I NEED HIM. I want him. I never want to leave him.

They were the first thoughts Tess had when she surfaced from a deep well of pleasure for the second time in as many hours. They frightened her.

All she had ever wanted her whole life was to be loved, to belong to someone who would need her as much as she needed him. She had needed and loved each set of foster parents who had taken her in. But the most she had ever received in return was adequate care. She had never been mistreated; but she had never been loved, either.

She thought she had learned her lesson: not to give her love where it wasn't wanted, not to lay herself open to the pain that came inevitably when she had to acknowledge she wasn't loved in return. Even with Charlie—heaven forgive him—she had known her love was not returned.

He had wanted her body, and he had been honorable enough to marry her when she had gotten pregnant. But Charlie had never loved her. He had been incapable of the emotion.

Here she was making the same mistake again. She didn't want to feel what she was feeling. But she didn't know how to stop. She turned and stared at Stony, who was sleeping beside her. She had to get out of here before she let this man sneak past her guard and into her heart.

He didn't like children. He liked living alone. He had no room in his life for her and her child. She would be a fool to trust another man, to give her heart to him. Especially this one.

She had asked Harry about Stony Carlton and gotten few answers. Stony wasn't a lawman, yet he hunted outlaws—rustlers—for a living. She wondered if he knew all about her husband's activities. Her thoughts shied away from contemplating such a possibility. It was better not to know.

Theirs was clearly a relationship doomed at the start. Yet she had let it start. Better to end it now, before she got hurt. Although, there would be hurt, even now. Because, though she wouldn't have wished it, would never have dreamed it, this lonely man already possessed a part of her soul...the part that had been missing all her life.

Tess dressed quickly and left quietly, closing Stony's bedroom door behind her. She was relieved that Rose wasn't yet awake and took advantage of the slight respite to spend some time alone in the living room.

She sat cross-legged on the comfortable sofa in front of the wood stove and watched the flames flickering inside the glass door.

She should leave.

Only, where would she go? Her situation hadn't changed one iota since she had accepted Stony's charitable job offer. She didn't want to continue imposing on him now that she was well. But she had tried to find a job in town once the cast was off her arm and discovered there was no job to be had until the season began. She was stuck here until spring.

She felt Stony's presence before she heard him. She supposed a man used to sneaking up on rustlers had to be able to move quietly. It irritated her nonetheless that she hadn't heard him coming. Although, when all was said and done, there was nowhere she could run.

She turned and found him standing right behind her dressed in nothing more than a pair of jeans. He had left the top button undone, and it was plain he wasn't wearing anything beneath them. The aged denim hugged his body like a glove, revealing the vivid outline of his arousal.

She wrenched her gaze away and turned to stare at the fire.

"We have to talk," he said, vaulting over the couch and settling softly beside her, his legs crossed Indian style.

She was aware of him, the heat of him, the musky male scent of him. "I have nowhere to go—"

"—or you'd leave," he finished for her.

"Yes, I would," she said, her chin jutting. "This…thing…between us is…disturbing."

"What if I said I understand what you're feeling?"

She glanced at him quizzically. "You do?"

"Something…unusual…has happened—is happening—between us."

"Something magical," she said quietly, almost wistfully.

His gaze softened as he met her eyes. "You felt it, too?"

She nodded, then ruffled her hair with her hands. "It doesn't make sense."

"All I know is I don't want you to leave right now," he said.

Her lips twisted cynically. "Lucky for you, I can't get another job until the season begins in the spring."

He smiled. "That settles it, then. You'll stay."

"But this…thing…between us… What are we going to do about it?"

"If this is something we both want, I don't see why we can't enjoy each other—take physical pleasure from each other—without letting it go any further than that. I don't want a wife."

"Or kids," she reminded him.

"Or kids," he agreed. "But I do want you."

"And I want you," she admitted. "So we merely take what physical pleasure we can from each other for a few weeks or months without any other commitment between us?"

"I don't see why not," Stony said.

Tess saw more than a few pitfalls in his plan, but she looked at him and realized she wanted to feel again the wholeness she experienced when he held her in his arms. "All right," she said. "Until spring. Agreed?"

"Agreed."

She held out her hand, and he took it. Electricity arced up her arm. She tugged her hand free and stood, needing to put some distance between them before they ended up in bed again.

"When's supper?" he asked. "I'm hungry."

"I'm hungry, too," Rose said, appearing in the doorway to the kitchen.

"You're barefoot again, young lady," Stony admonished.

Rose yelped and raced back toward the bedroom.

"Where's she going?" Stony asked.

"To get socks, I imagine," Tess said with a smile.

"Can she get them on by herself?"

"I'll have to help her. The sock drawer's too high for her to reach."

"You're busy," Stony said, rising from the sofa. "I'll do it."

Tess arched a disbelieving brow. "You don't like kids," she reminded him.

"Yeah, well, I'd like it even less if she got sick. Besides, I'm hungry, and you're putting supper on the table." He winked, a charming gesture that made her heart flutter. "I think I can handle it."

It was impossible not to smile back at him. "Be my guest," she said.

Stony didn't hurry down the hall because he knew Rose would be there waiting for him. He hadn't counted on the little girl's resourcefulness. She had pulled out the bottom drawer of the chest and was standing on it in order to reach the top drawer of the chest, which she had managed to open. The whole chest was in danger of tipping over onto her.

"Rose!" he said, his voice harsh with fear.

She leaned back, startled. Her weight, added to that

of the open drawers, was all it took for the chest to begin its tumble.

He snatched her off her precarious perch and caught the falling chest with his hip. He grunted in pain as everything on top came thumping down onto the braided rug.

"What's going on in there?" Tess called from the kitchen. "Is everything all right?"

"Everything's fine," Stony called. "Hunky dory," he muttered under his breath. He clutched Rose tight while he gave his adrenaline-laced heart a chance to slow down. His hip throbbed where the chest had caught on the bone. He leaned his weight back to force the chest upright.

"What's hunk-dory?" Rose asked, apparently oblivious to the danger she had been in.

"It means you nearly got killed, but you didn't," Stony retorted as he shoved in the bottom drawer of the chest with his bare foot. He shifted her onto his arm so he could look her in the eye. "You should've asked for help. You could've been hurt."

"I was getting socks," she said in a small voice, "like you said."

Which made the whole thing his fault, he supposed. It surprised him to realize he cared enough about her to be worried that something might happen when he wasn't around to keep an eye on her.

She pointed to the mess on the floor. "Everything fell down," she said, her chin trembling.

"Yeah, well, nothing's broken," he said gruffly. "We can put it all back again." He knew he was an idiot to be trying to placate a three-year-old, but there wasn't anyone around to catch him at it, so he could do as he pleased.

She wriggled, her sign to be let down, picked up a pewter bookend and handed it to him. "Here," she said. "I can help put it all back."

They worked together over the next several minutes. He picked Rose up at her insistence so she could rearrange everything to her liking on top of the chest. By the time they were done, she was smiling again. Seeing that smile made him feel ten feet tall. It was ridiculous to let her under his skin. Especially when she wasn't going to be hanging around very long. But he didn't call Tess to come get her kid. Hell, he was enjoying himself.

"You still need socks, young lady," he said, folding his free hand around her ice cold toes.

She giggled. "Can you do piggies?"

"Do what?"

"You know. Piggies."

He was afraid he did know. It sounded like fun. But he wasn't going to let her make a substitute father out of him. "You need socks," he repeated.

He opened the top drawer and pulled out a pair of pink socks.

"Not those," she said firmly.

"What's wrong with these?"

"I want the ones with Mickey Mouse."

Stony started to argue with her, saw the mulish cast of her mouth and changed his mind. Tess would be wondering what had happened to them. He searched through the whole drawer and came up empty.

"There are no socks in here with Mickey Mouse on them."

"Where are they?" she demanded.

"How should I know?" Frantic to avoid the tantrum he could see coming, he grabbed a pair of socks with white lace and pink bows along the edge. "How about these?"

Her eyes widened, and she said with three-year-old reverence, "Those are only for Sunday school." And then, "They're my very favorite."

"You want 'em, you got 'em, kid." He sat down on the bed and tugged the socks on, despite the resistance of her curling toes.

Rose looked first at the lacy socks and then up at him with something akin to awe. He felt absurdly delighted to have pleased her so well. He took her hand and headed back down the hall. "Come on. Let's go see your mom."

The first words out of Tess's mouth when she saw the two of them was, "Those are her Sunday school socks. She'll ruin them if she walks around in them without shoes."

"I'll buy her another pair," Stony said, exchanging a glance with Rose, who beamed back at him.

"I don't want you spending your money on us," Tess countered.

"It's only a pair of socks," he argued.

"Maybe to you it's only a pair of socks," Tess said, meeting his gaze. "To me it's an hour of work behind a counter." She turned to Rose and said, "Go put on a pair of shoes. Now."

Rose turned to Stony. "Do I have to?"

Stony saw the alarm on Tess's face at this clear sign of rebellion in the ranks. His own mother had died when he was very young, so his father's word had always been law. Now he saw what might have happened if his mother had lived. When there were two adults in a child's life, there was room for appeal. Only, Rose wasn't his daughter, and he had no right to be making decisions that affected her life.

"Do as your mother says, Rose. She's the boss."

To his surprise, Rose didn't argue, just stomped her way back to the bedroom.

He let Rose go, then had an awful thought. "Where do you keep her shoes?"

"On the floor of the closet," Tess replied.

He heaved a sigh of relief. At least she couldn't knock anything over. He realized he was worrying about her—as if she was his responsibility or something. Which she wasn't. And never would be.

But he was plagued with guilt at the thought of how dire Tess's circumstances must be if she had to be careful not to ruin a pair of child's socks. It was small solace that her husband would probably be in jail now, if he weren't dead. Perhaps a good lawyer might have gotten Charlie Lowell off with a short sentence. Perhaps he would already have been out of prison and back helping his family.

They needed help from someone. For a while, so long as Tess and Rose stayed, it might as well be him.

IN THE MONTHS that followed, whenever he went cut hunting the ever-elusive rustlers, Stony wore the navy

blue mittens and scarf Tess had knitted and given him
for Christmas. When he was home, he spent his days
playing in the snow with Rose, and his nights loving
Tess.

If he let himself think about it at all, Stony had
supposed Tess would have less time for him because
of the child. It had been that way with his father. Time
and attention given to his new family had taken away
from time and attention given to him.

Somehow, Tess managed to make him feel a part
of the time the three of them spent together. Her
warmth and joy enfolded both him and the child. The
jealousy he had expected to feel toward Rose—akin
to the shameful resentment he had felt toward his
halfbrother—never materialized. He wondered if it
was because he didn't want or need Tess's attention
as much as he had wanted or needed his father's love.

Actually the opposite was true. What he needed
from Tess far exceeded the care and respect he had
wanted from his father. It dawned on him as he lay
in bed with her spooned against his groin, his arm
under her breasts, that he wanted her love.

The thought terrified him.

What if Tess was like his father? Would he always
come second behind the child? Would he always end
up with whatever love—and time—was left over after
she had given to Rose first. It was selfish to want
Tess's love all to himself. But he did.

He was unaware he had made a disgusted sound in
his throat.

"What's wrong?" Tess whispered into the darkness. She turned in his arms and pressed herself against him. His body instantly hardened.

"Don't, Tess." He didn't want to need her any more than he already did.

"What's wrong?" she asked.

He heard the caring in her voice. She had plenty of time for him now. Rose was sound asleep. "I don't want to talk about it."

She sat up. "You've been moping around for the past three days. You might as well tell me what's troubling you. Neither of us is going to get any sleep until you do."

"It's nothing," he insisted.

"Fine," she said turning her back on him. "Keep it to yourself."

When he tried to put his arm around her, she shoved him away and said, "Leave me alone."

Here at last was the rejection he had expected from her all along. He refused to accept it.

"Don't turn away from me, Tess."

Tess heard the longing in his voice and recognized the need for what it was.

"Oh, Stony." She turned back into his waiting arms, pressing herself against him. And felt the fire ignite between them as it always did.

She tried not to let her love show, tried not to give too much of herself. When Stony thrust inside her she arched into him. When his mouth captured hers, she surrendered to his passion. When their bodies joined at last, she knew her soul was lost. To a man who didn't want to love her, a lone wolf who couldn't be caged.

Chapter Five

STONY HAD REALIZED over the course of the winter that he couldn't live without Tess. He resented the time he had to spend away from her hunting down rustlers. He was ready to admit he needed her in his life. However, he had some daunting hurdles to get over before that was possible.

He had to tell Tess that he was the man who had killed her husband. And he had to come to terms with the fact that he would always have to share her with Rose, in the same way he had been forced to share his father with a half brother. Both obstacles loomed, seemingly insurmountable, before him. The need to resolve them consumed his waking moments and haunted his dreams.

He knew Tess was aware of his distraction, yet she didn't confront him about it. He was glad, because he had no idea how he could explain why he had kept his part in her husband's death a secret from her all these months. He was living a lie. Unfortunately he knew exactly how Tess felt about lies.

The second time he had returned to his cabin, having left it to return to Jackson following his brief Christmas holiday with Tess and Rose, he had found things achingly familiar, even to the savory stew bubbling on the stove.

At supper he had said, "I don't know when my house has ever seemed so much like a home. Thank you, Tess."

She had blushed, those marvelous roses appearing in her cheeks. "Do you mean it, Stony? Really?"

"I don't lie. Especially about important things."

"That means a lot to me," she said, her eyes downcast. He thought she wasn't going to explain herself, but the rest of it came tumbling out. "I was devastated when I found out that Charlie had been lying to me—about the rustling, I mean. To this day, it's the one thing I can't forgive him."

He had felt a pang of remorse at the lie of omission he was perpetrating. *Tess, there's something I have to tell you. I killed your husband.* The words were on the tip of his tongue. He could hear himself saying them. They remained unspoken.

Surely, when the time came to tell Tess everything, he would find a way to make her understand why he had kept the truth from her. Fear of what she might say and do when she learned his part in her husband's death upset his stomach. He had laid down his fork, the pleasant meal abruptly ended.

During the past four months, the right time had never come to confess. The longer the lie lay between them, the more difficult it became to tell her the truth.

He was running out of time. The snow was melting off the mountain. It was already gone in town. Soon the tourists would begin to arrive, and Tess would leave him to return to her life in town.

Unless he could make things right about what had happened with her husband. Unless he could offer love, even when it meant accepting second place to someone else in her life.

Stony turned on his side in bed and stared at Tess in the early golden light of morning. She was more beautiful to him than ever. And infinitely precious. He should wake her up and confess the truth.

Now was not the right time, either. He had gotten a call last night, a lead on the rustlers who had proved so elusive all winter. He was closing in on them. He had to leave this morning and return to Jackson. He didn't know how long he would be gone.

He lay back down and folded his hands behind his head, staring at the ceiling. He was going to lose her. Deep in his gut he knew it, and he was bone-deep scared.

One second the room was silent. The next, a tornado of energy came whirling in. Rose's pajama-clad behind plopped down on his stomach, and her hands landed flat against his bare chest. He gave a *"woof"* as the air in his diaphragm was pushed out by the weight of her. She rubbed her nose against his and said, "Good morning, Stony."

Her visits had become a morning ritual. After the first nearly embarrassing episode several months ago, he had stopped sleeping naked. It was a small enough sacrifice to enjoy the light she brought with her each morning.

"Hi there, little bit," he said. "What's up?"

"Is it spring yet?" she asked, glancing out the window.

Snow from an early March storm was melting from

the tin roof, dripping off the eaves. "Almost," he said.

"You promised to let me ride a pony when spring comes."

"So I did." He rubbed his morning beard. There was no putting it off. "I have to leave for a while, Rose. I have to go chase the bad men again."

She frowned, a ferocious glare worthy of the vilest villain in a penny dreadful. "I don't want you to go."

A sudden lump formed in his throat. He didn't want to go, either. How had Rose become so dear to him when he harbored such resentment against her for the place in her mother's heart she stole from him? It was hard not to be enchanted by Rose, who gave love freely and demanded nothing in return.

She bounced up and down on his stomach. "Don't go. Don't go. Don't go," she chanted.

He grabbed her hips to save his solar plexus. "I won't be gone long. And when I come back, it will be spring."

"Promise? And I can ride a pony?"

"I promise. And you can ride a pony."

"Yippee!" The bouncing started again, as though she were already on the horse, a wild bucking bronc.

"Whoa, there, cowgirl! Wait until you have the horse under you." He slid Rose onto the bed between them, tickling her once he had her down. She giggled delightedly. It was all part of the game between them.

Rose turned to Tess, who by now was always awake and leaning on her elbow with a grin on her face, watching their antics.

"I'm hungry, Mama," Rose said.

"Breakfast will be ready as soon as you put on the clothes I left at the foot of your bed last night," Tess said.

Rose hugged her mother and got a kiss on both cheeks and the tip of her nose before she disappeared into her own bedroom to dress.

Stony proceeded with the next part of the ritual, which involved him and Tess and a few drugging early-morning kisses that occasionally turned into hard, fast and unbelievably satisfying sex. But not this morning.

Tess leaned back and searched his face, looking for something.

"What is it?" he asked.

"Remind me what it is, precisely, that you don't like about kids," she said.

His eyes shuttered immediately. This was forbidden territory, and she knew it.

"Don't shut me out, Stony. Talk to me."

"What is it you want me to say?"

"Explain why you profess not to like kids when I can see with my own eyes how good you are with Rose."

He sat up against the headboard and shoved an irritated hand through his hair. He couldn't tell her about the lie. Maybe he could tell her about this. "It's not something I'm proud of," he admitted, hoping that would be enough to placate her.

"Can you tell me what it is? Will you?" she persisted.

It came out in a rush, before he could stop himself. "My mom died when I was little, and it was just my dad and me. He must have missed my mom a lot, because after she was gone, he lost himself in his work. He never had any time to spend with me. So I spent my time alone.

"When I was thirteen, my dad remarried and started a second family. He changed his priorities. My half brother, Todd, suddenly got all the attention I'd been yearning for ever since my mother's death." He shrugged. "That's it."

He was amazed at her perception when she said, "I see. Oh, I see. Why you profess you don't like children, I mean. You resented sharing your father's love with a baby."

"I don't want to share you," he said, the words torn from him almost against his will.

"Oh, Stony." Tess slipped her arms around Stony's waist and laid her head against his chest, where she could hear his heart madly thumping.

"Don't you know love is boundless?" she said quietly. "It doesn't have limits. I can love Rose and still have more than enough left over for you."

It was an admission of love, of sorts. Even that was more than Tess had intended to say. Yet, she knew Stony had needed to hear her say it.

"Leftovers," he grumbled, pulling her tightly, possessively, against him.

She hesitated only a second before plunging even farther into dangerous waters. "No. Not leftovers. I love you differently than Rose. She's my own flesh and blood. I feel responsibility and delight and devotion when I look at her.

"But you, Stony. You're the other half of me. I've

been looking for you all my life. I love you with every particle of my being.''

His arms tightened until she thought her ribs would crack. She waited to hear the words from him, needed to hear them. She silently begged the wary wolf to take the few steps necessary to reach the hand she had held out to him.

"God, I love you, Tess."

She felt her nose burn and tears sting her eyes. She clutched at him, a sob of joy clogging her throat. "Oh, Stony. I love you so much."

"What about me?" Rose demanded. She stood beside the bed fully dressed, her shirt on inside out, tugging at the sheet that covered them.

Tess looked at Stony, and they grinned at each other. He reached down and scooped Rose up in one arm and pulled her close to include her in their hug.

"I love you, too, Rose," he said, his dark eyes focused on Tess.

Tess knew what it meant for him to make such an admission. Knew it was only the beginning for them all. There would be no need for her and Rose to leave now. The future loomed before them, bright and shining.

"Are you going to be my daddy?" Rose said.

Tess looked to Stony for his answer, her heart in her eyes. *Say yes,* she willed him. *We come together as a package. It won't mean leftovers. I have plenty of love for both of you.*

He cleared his throat before he spoke, prolonging the moment, a wary wolf until the very end. Then he surprised her, because she had really thought he was going to say yes.

He said maybe.

"We'll see, Rose," Stony said. "We'll have to see."

Tess was startled—almost alarmed—at how quickly Stony extricated himself from their cozy cuddle. "What's the hurry?" she asked.

"I've got to get going," he said. "I have to be in Jackson by noon."

Since it was early morning and Jackson Hole only an hour's drive away, his excuse didn't make much sense. Maybe everything was moving too fast. Maybe he didn't trust her not to give him leftover love. Or maybe he was being forced into a commitment he didn't really want to make. Whatever it was, she felt the lone wolf retreating from her.

"Why don't you go into the kitchen and get out the orange juice," she said to Rose. "Then wait for me, and I'll help you pour it into the glasses."

"Okay, Mama," Rose said.

Tess heard her trotting down the hall. "Can you drop me off in town before you leave?" she asked Stony. "I have some errands to run. I can get a ride back from Harry."

"Why is Harry so willing to give you all these rides?" he said, stepping out of bed and yanking on a pair of jeans.

"Because he's my friend," she said. "Why else?" She got out of bed herself, because that was no place to argue with a man.

"I don't know," he said, plainly irritated as he buttoned up his fly. "Why don't you tell me?"

"Are you trying to start an argument?" she asked, fisted hands perched on her hips. "Because if you are, I'll be more than happy to give you one."

"Am I about to see that famous redheaded temper of yours?" he snarled. "I've been waiting four months for it to erupt. I knew it was only a matter of time."

He was purposely provoking her, but she couldn't seem to stop herself. "I suppose you don't have any foibles."

"My foibles never bothered anybody when I lived alone."

"That can easily be arranged again!" She shot the words back. She was heartsick, listening to herself. She didn't want to leave him. She loved him. But he must want her to leave. Otherwise, he would never have started this argument. Unless there was something else.

"What's wrong, Stony? What is it you aren't telling me?"

Tell her now! Dammit, tell her.

He couldn't. He was too scared. Happiness of a kind he had never imagined was in his grasp. He couldn't take the chance of losing it.

"Dammit, what do you want from me?" he raged.

"I want an answer!" she retorted, easily as infuriated as he was.

He grabbed her arms and pulled her to him, capturing her mouth with his, his tongue thrusting possessively between her teeth. His palms cupped her buttocks, and he dragged her up the front of him until his hard length was pressed against her. She wasn't nearly close enough. He jerked her panties down, tore open the buttons of his jeans and shoved down his underwear until he was free.

He lifted her legs around his hips and thrust inside her, deep and tight. He gripped her buttocks as he drove into her, hard and fast, reaching a climax only seconds later.

He felt the weight of her as his senses returned. She was trembling in his arms. Her breathing was as ragged as his, and he could see the rapid pulse pounding in her throat.

He eased her legs away from his sides and disengaged them, because his knees were threatening to buckle.

It was only then he realized he hadn't used a condom.

He always used a condom. Because he didn't want kids, didn't like kids. Only, Tess had made him realize that was another lie. One he had told himself for years.

"Tess, I…"

"Don't say anything."

"I'm sorry," he said anyway.

Her eyes slid closed, and she clung to him. It took him a moment to realize her knees were threatening to buckle, too.

"Sit down before you fall down," he said, urging her onto the bed. He rearranged his clothing and picked up her silky underwear from the floor where it had fallen and handed it to her. When she didn't take it, he dropped it on the bed beside her.

She sat unmoving. Silent.

He didn't know what had come over him to make him take her like that, without warning. Her continued silence scared him even worse than her anger. "Tess, we'll talk about this when I get back, all right?"

She didn't answer him.

He gripped her chin and forced her to look at him. "You'll be here when I get back." It was an order. One he was afraid she would defy.

She remained mute.

He let go of her chin, and paced before her like an animal in a cage. "Look, I couldn't stand the thought of Harry DuBois pawing you like your boss."

She looked up at him, her brow deeply furrowed. "Harry is nothing like Bud. He's my friend. That's all we are to each other."

"Then you'll come back here and wait for me after you've finished your errands in town?" he asked anxiously.

"You'll have to give me a ride into town first," she said with the beginning of a smile.

"About…about what happened," he said, his hand plowing its way through his hair. "I…I don't know what came over me."

She glanced up at him coyly. "If I didn't know better, I'd think you were jealous of Harry DuBois."

He grabbed at the excuse she had given him for his behavior and managed a sheepish grin. Maybe he had been a little jealous. "You belong to me," he said.

"Be here, Tess."

"I'll be here when you get back," she promised.

TESS HAD fully intended to keep her promise to Stony when she made it. She hadn't counted on finding out the dreadful secret he had kept from her for more than four months.

Stony had killed Charlie.

She had gone to Harry's office to ask for a ride home, and he had seen the love bruise on her throat that Stony had put there during their tempestuous lovemaking that morning.

"Why do you stay with him, Tess?" Harry demanded. "I've told you time and again the man's dangerous."

"Not to me," she replied with a smug smile. "Come on, Harry," she said, slipping her arm through his. "Have a piece of pie with me at the Buttermilk Café before I pick up Rose from Mrs. Feeny. Then you can drive us home."

"All right, Tess. Against my better judgment, I'll give you a ride back up to his place."

They were settled in a booth with a slice of the buttermilk pie for which the café was famous in front of them when Harry said, "How soon do you think you'll be coming back to town? There's an apartment coming available in the complex over by the hospital next week."

"I don't think I'll be coming back to town," Tess said.

"You'll have to, once you get a job."

"I don't think I'll be looking for a job in Pine-dale."

"What are you talking about?" Harry asked. "What's going on, Tess?"

"I think I'll be staying at Stony's cabin. With him."

"You'd actually consider living with him indefinitely? When you won't even consider a marriage proposal from me. Explain that to me, Tess."

Tess flushed. "He loves me, Harry. And I love him."

"You know nothing about the man!" Harry snarled, keeping his voice down to avoid being overheard by the growing lunch crowd in the café.

"I know everything that's important to know about him."

"Like the fact he killed your husband?" Harry snapped.

Tess's heart actually stopped beating for an instant. "That's…" She started to say impossible, but she had known for months that Stony hunted rustlers for a living. She settled instead for, "Unbelievable."

"Believe it," Harry said. "I don't understand why he never told you himself. I didn't think he had, or you wouldn't be in love with the man."

"He…he was only doing his job." She hated herself for defending Stony, when what she wanted to do was rage at him. She closed her eyes and gritted her teeth to try to stop her chin from trembling.

Why hadn't Stony told her? He couldn't care for her feelings very much, or he would have confessed his part in Charlie's death long ago. He had said he loved her. Had he stretched the truth about that, too?

More likely, he just liked sleeping with her, making love to her.

"Stay in town with me, Tess. Don't go back to him. I'll take care of you. You won't have to worry about anything. You can stay at my place and keep house for me."

"Rose doesn't like you, Harry."

Harry snorted. "Rose is stingy with her favors, Tess. Tell me, does she like Stony?"

She hadn't, at first. She loved him now. The thought of how disappointed, how utterly heartbroken her daughter would be if she never saw Stony again, made Tess's throat constrict. It was painful to swallow the bite of pie in her mouth, but somehow she managed it. A tear scalded her cheek as it slid free. She brushed it angrily away. She wasn't about to cry over any man who could so callously lie to her.

She had been a fool again and given her trust to yet another untrustworthy man. Only this time it was infinitely worse. This time the man who had betrayed her held more than her heart. He possessed the other half of her soul.

"Tess, let me comfort you," Harry urged. "Let me take care of you."

"No!" she snarled across the table at him. "The last thing I'd ever do is put my life in another man's keeping. Take me back to Stony's cabin, Harry."

"What for?"

"I want to pack mine and Rose's things."

"Then what?"

"I have a little money saved—my salary for the past four months," she said with a cynical twist of her mouth. "I plan to use it to buy us tickets on the first bus that passes through town."

"Where will you go, Tess?"

"Anywhere that takes me away from here."

Chapter Six

HARRY WAS INCENSED at the way things were turning out. Not only had he lost his chance of getting Tess Lowell into his bed, but it was likely Stony Carlton was going to show up in the wrong place at the wrong time and spoil a real sweet thing. Damn Charlie Lowell for getting himself killed. The replacement Harry had been forced to hire to run his rustling operation wasn't nearly as reliable or as accessible. Every time he had to make contact with the man it increased the danger of getting caught himself.

It had been damn handy over the past four months having a spy in the enemy camp. Not that Tess had known the role she played. But every time she called on him for a ride into town he had known for sure that Stony was out in the field. He had promptly gotten his band of rustlers out of harm's way.

Only, this time, Stony had left home the very day Harry had scheduled a tractor trailer pickup of stolen beef. Harry wasn't sure he could get in touch with his henchman in time to warn him. He had tried phoning his contact in Jackson, but there hadn't been an answer, and he refused to leave an incriminating message on an answering machine.

Harry had no choice except to drive to the rendezvous point himself and warn his man off before it was too late. He didn't want things spoiled too soon. A few more good runs, and he would have all the money he needed to buy himself a ranch someplace nice and warm, like Arizona.

When Harry arrived at the rendezvous, he saw the trailer was already there being loaded. He watched for a long time from seclusion, making sure there was no sign of the range detective before he drove down into the valley.

"Hey, boss," his contact said. "What are you doing here?"

"There's trouble," Harry said. "Stony Carlton is on the prowl. Take what you've got, and you and your men get out of here."

"There's only a dozen more head to load, boss. Then we'll go."

"I said now, and I meant now."

The man opened his mouth to argue before he caught sight of Harry's hand resting on the butt of his police revolver. "Sure, boss. Whatever you say."

It wasn't as simple as it should have been for the truck to make its escape. The rear wheels had stuck in the mud caused by melting snow. Harry had only stayed to make sure the men didn't disobey him, and he was furious when he realized they were going to have to unload the cattle already in the truck in order to break it free.

"Get the damn chute back in place," he shouted into the truck window. "And get those cattle out of there!"

"Not so fast."

Harry whirled and uttered a string of foul expletives.

Stony arched a brow. "Very inventive. Too bad you couldn't have used a little bit of that intelligence to avoid getting yourself into this situation in the first place."

Harry started to reach for his gun.

"I wouldn't do that if I were you," Stony said. "I've already had to kill one man in the past year. I'd hate like hell to make it two."

Stony had to keep an eye on the men in the truck, which caused his gaze to waver from Harry for an instant.

"Don't, Harry!" Stony said as Harry reached for his gun.

"I'm not going to jail," Harry said as he drew.

Stony shot to kill. It was what he had been taught. A wounded man with a gun could still shoot back. Harry grabbed his chest as he fell backward, the gun flying from his hand. Harry's bullet caught Stony's sleeve and ripped through a quarter inch of his arm.

Stony ran up to Harry, to kick the gun out of his reach and to see if there was anything he could do for the man. From the corner of his eye he saw the two men in the truck take advantage of his distraction to shove open their doors and run. They wouldn't get far. Help was already on the way.

"Damn you to hell," Harry muttered, clutching at his chest.

Stony knew the wound was serious. He did what he could to staunch the bleeding, but it didn't look good. He saw from the resignation in Harry's eyes that he knew he wasn't going to make it.

"There's an ambulance standing by," Stony said. "The police will call it in as soon as they get here."

"How did you find us out?" Harry asked.

"I've been hunting you for months, watching your patterns. I took a guess where you would hit next." He shrugged. "I was right."

"How did you know to wait for me?" Harry insisted.

Stony's eyes narrowed. "I didn't. If you hadn't shown up when you did, we would never have known about you. Unless your men gave you up."

"Charlie threatened to do that if I didn't give him a bigger share," Harry said. "That's why I had to kill him."

"What?"

"Shot him with a rifle from the hill behind you."

"But I—"

"Your bullet only wounded him. Mine killed him."

"I don't believe you," Stony said.

"Why would I lie?"

"Why would you tell me the truth now?"

"Because I'm dying. Because I owe Charlie Lowell something. Because I like Tess. Ask the coroner, if you need proof. He'll tell you what kind of bullet killed Charlie Lowell."

Stony's eyes narrowed. "You think this will make a difference to Tess?"

Harry tried to laugh, but coughed blood instead. His voice was weaker, and he had to pause often to catch his breath. "I told her you killed Charlie. She hates your guts. Good luck."

"Damn. Oh, damn."

"She leaving you, Stony. She's taking the next bus out of town."

They could hear police sirens in the distance. But the light was already dimming in Harry's eyes.

"Tell Tess I'm sorry," he gasped.

They were the last words Harry said. Stony closed Harry's eyes and stood to wait for the Jackson police to arrive.

It took an interminably long time to point out which way the two rustlers had gone on foot, get his arm bandaged and explain the circumstances of Harry's death. He excused himself as quickly as he could, pleading a family emergency.

It was an emergency. If he didn't hurry, he wasn't going to have any family. He drove like a crazy man along the treacherous curving roads that followed the Hoback River through the mountains from Jackson south to Pinedale.

Stony was glad he hadn't turned out to be the one responsible for Charlie Lowell's death. It would make it easier in later years when Rose was old enough to be told how her father had died. But he had a feeling his innocence wasn't going to help much where Tess was concerned. He had lied to her. Even though he hadn't known it at the time.

He skidded his Jeep to a stop in front of the Buttermilk Café, where the bus that was headed north from Rock Springs along U.S. Route 191 would stop.

She wasn't there.

For a panicked moment he thought the bus had already come and gone. Then he saw a couple of people with traveling bags drinking coffee and realized he had arrived in time.

Except, if she wasn't here, where was she?

He tried several other restaurants within sight of the Buttermilk Café, figuring maybe Tess hadn't wanted to wait there because of Bud. She wasn't in any of them. He thought of Mrs. Feeny's place, but the elderly woman said Tess had picked up Rose around noon. She had no idea where Tess had gone from there.

Stony was getting frantic. Maybe Tess had hitch-hiked, caught a ride with some tourist passing through town. Didn't she realize how dangerous that was? Surely she would have rejected such an idea, in consideration of Rose. He felt like going from door to door through town looking for her, but he knew the futility of that.

He realized there was one other place she might be.

As he made the last turn up the winding road to his cabin he saw the smoke coming from the chimney and felt his heart begin to pound.

Let her be there. Let her be waiting to hear my explanation. Let her be understanding.

There was no one in the living room when Stony stepped inside. There was a stew bubbling on the stove with the familiar scents of sage and bay filling the room—and making his senses soar.

He followed the hallway to Rose's room, where he found Tess reading *Little Red Riding Hood*. He saw the moment she realized he was there. Her body tensed, and she hesitated ever so slightly before she continued reading.

"What big teeth you have, Grandma," Tess said.

"The better to eat you with," Stony finished in his best big-bad-wolf voice.

"Stony!" Rose cried.

He opened his arms, and she threw herself into them.

"You're home! You're home! I want to go ride a pony. You promised."

"Yes, I did," Stony said. "As soon as you wake up from your nap, we'll go." He paused and added, "If that's all right with your mother."

"Please, Mama. Oh, please," Rose begged.

Tess kept her back to Stony as she put the book between the pewter bookends on top of the chest. She turned to him at last, and he saw the damage his lies had done.

"Stony and I have to talk, Rose. You take a nap, and we'll decide later whether there's still time for a ride before...dark."

Before...they left?

So she hadn't forgiven him. This was only a respite. His work was still ahead of him, convincing her that she belonged with him. That she could trust him with her life.

And with her love.

Rose started to whine. "I want to ride now."

"Do what your mother said, Rose. Lie down and go to sleep," Stony ordered in a voice the little girl immediately obeyed. He couldn't promise her the ride would come later. He had no idea what Tess would do or say. He had no idea whether the two people he loved most in all the world would still be here at the end of the day.

He followed Tess into the living room and sat with her on the couch. The wood stove was lit to take the chill from the room. They watched the flames through the glass door in silence.

"How can I make you believe you can trust me?" Stony asked at last.

"Why, Stony? Why did you lie?"

He took a breath and let it out. "I was afraid of losing you."

She turned to stare at him. "Did you really kill him, then?"

He shook his head, unsure what to say. "I thought I did. It turns out Harry DuBois actually killed him."

"What?"

"I caught the rustlers I've been hunting since the fall. It turns out Harry was the brains of the outfit. Charlie worked for him. He killed Charlie because Charlie asked for a bigger piece of the action."

"Oh, Charlie. Oh, no," Tess moaned.

He reached for her but she jerked herself out of his way. "Please, don't touch me. Not yet."

He had the terrifying feeling she wasn't going to let him back in, that she was going to shut him out. He kept talking. So long as they were talking nothing was settled.

"The rustlers were so successful eluding me because Harry was informing them every time I came hunting for them. Harry knew what I was doing because whenever I was working you asked him to give you a ride back and forth from town.''

"Oh, no!"

"Pretty nifty work on his part, I have to admit.''

"I'm sorry if I was responsible—"

"If he hadn't been using you, he would have figured out some other way to keep tabs on me. It's harder to catch the bad guys when the good guys are the bad guys.''

She shook her head. "I think I know what you mean.''

"About us—"

Tess interrupted him. "I want to believe you lied to me because you were afraid of losing me. I want to forgive you.''

"But..."

"But I'm afraid, Stony. I gave you my trust, and you let me down. Just like Charlie.''

"I'm not at all like Charlie,'' Stony countered. "I would never purposely do anything to hurt you. I love you, Tess. I want to marry you.''

She gasped and turned wide eyes toward him.

He hadn't known he was going to propose until the words were out of his mouth.

"You must be desperate,'' she said, the hint of a smile teasing at her lips.

His features remained grim. He wouldn't believe she belonged to him until she said yes. "Will you marry me, Tess?''

"I have a daughter, Stony.''

"I know that. I love her, too, Tess. Will you marry me?''

Tess had done a great deal of thinking in the hours since Harry had given her and Tess a ride to Stony's cabin. It was a known fact you could never really tame a wolf. Stony Carlton had been a lone wolf for a very long time.

Still, he had come a long way in the months she had known him, from the man who wanted no commitments, the man who wanted no children, who had rescued her in the Buttermilk Café, to the man who had proposed to her and waited now for her answer.

The truth was, there was a great deal of risk involved in loving any man. She had to choose between loving Stony, and spending her life without him. Given those two choices, she knew what her answer had to be.

"I love you, Stony."

Stony let out a whooshing breath and scooped Tess into his lap. "Lord, woman, don't ever leave me in suspense like that again!"

Tess tunneled her fingers into the hair at his nape and pulled his face down for her kiss. "Love me, Stony."

"I do, Tess. More than life."

His mouth came down hard on hers, and Tess willingly surrendered to his strength.

"Are you going to marry me?"

"Anytime you want," she said with a grin.

A small head popped up behind the sofa. "Are you going to be my daddy?" Rose asked.

"Rose!" they both exclaimed together.

Rose stood her ground. "Does it?" she demanded.

They looked at each other and grinned. She was a proper wolf's cub, all right—all spit and fight.

Stony grabbed Rose by the arms and dragged her over the top of the sofa into Tess's lap, so he was holding both of them. "Yes," he said. "I'm going to be your daddy. Is that all right?"

"Do I still get to ride a pony?" she asked.

Stony laughed. "Yep. You might even get one of your own."

"Yippee," she said, bouncing up and down. "I'm gonna have a daddy *and* a pony!"

"You have a nap to finish first, young lady," Stony admonished. "And where are your slippers?" he asked, catching her bare feet in his hands.

Rose slipped out of Tess's lap. "I'm gonna go take a nap," she said. "So I don't need any slippers."

She was gone an instant later.

"Good Lord," Stony said. "Do you suppose they'll all be like that?"

"All? How many did you have in mind?" Tess asked.

"At least one more," he said. "If that's all right with you."

"I'd love to have your baby—as many babies as you'd like."

"Come here, Tess. I want you."

His eyes were feral, dangerous. The predatory beast was back, wanting her, loving her, a lone wolf who had finally found his mate. Some other woman might have tried to tame him, but Tess was perfectly satisfied with the wily rogue who had claimed her for his own.

Single in the Saddle
Vicki Lewis Thompson

Prologue

"STONY'S GONNA fire us for this, if he don't kill us first." Ty Eames looked at the cowpokes gathered around the bunkhouse table. "Am I right?"

"No, you ain't. You're just playing Chicken Little, as usual." Officially, Jasper Ingram was foreman of the Roughstock Ranch and rode herd on its four wranglers. Unofficially, he'd become a father figure for all of them, including his boss, Stony Arnett. Jasper held both positions with pride. "Fact is, Stony's gonna thank us. Eventually. This is no time to panic."

Glancing at the watch he seldom wore, Jasper pushed back his chair. "I gotta leave if I'm going to make San Antonio by the time Daphne's plane lands. You boys do like we planned, and take Stony into town later for a couple of beers. Then tell him."

"I still say all hell is gonna break loose," Ty grumbled.

"Not if you present it right." Jasper had expected this from Ty, who never failed to spot a dark cloud in every silver lining. "Let Ramon explain it to Stony," Jasper said, gesturing to a short Hispanic man on his left. "He's the slickest talker we've got."

Ramon preened. "I'll handle it, Ty. Just leave it to me, amigo."

"What I don't understand is why you didn't tell him

before this, Jasper?" Big Clyde asked. "Sending his picture to that magazine was your idea."

Jasper smoothed his mustache as he searched for a good excuse. Big Clyde had a way of putting his finger on the most sensitive part of an issue. "I just haven't found the right moment, is all," he hedged, knowing Big Clyde was right. "And as I recollect, y'all thought advertising for a wife was a fine idea. Y'all helped me cut Daphne out of the herd and we answered her letters together."

"Mostly Ramon did," said Andy, the youngest wrangler and the biggest prankster of the bunch. "Ooh-la-la, what a Romeo."

"You might want to pay attention and learn a few things," Ramon said.

Ty shifted in his chair. "Letters don't mean all that much. She's probably all wrong for ol' Stony."

"She fits all the specifications I've ever been able to worm out of him," Jasper said. "Reddish hair, nice figure, pretty smile, likes horses."

"It's mighty suspicious that she left Texas and moved to Hawaii," Ty said. "Why would anyone leave Texas? We should've asked her about that."

"It's probably because of that interior decorating she does," Jasper said. "There's more call for that kind of stuff in Hawaii. Besides, Stony might want her to give that up, once the babies come."

"We could use some interior decoratin' around this place," said Big Clyde, surveying the ragtag collection of bunks and scarred furniture. "The ranch house ain't much to look at, either."

Andy leaned back in his chair, a mischievous grin on

his face. "How do you figure she does interior decorating with that feng shui? We never did ask her to tell us what that was. Maybe she leaps into a room and starts breaking up the old furniture with karate chops. Stony might not go for that."

"I don't know about Stony, but I sure ain't messing with her," Ty said. "I've seen those Steven Seagal movies, and I don't hanker to get one of those fancy kicks aimed at me."

Jasper started toward the door. "Nobody's messing with her, because she's gonna be Stony's wife."

"I still think you're the one to tell him," Big Clyde said. "You've known him the longest."

"Get a couple of beers in him and he'll take it better," Jasper said. "Ramon can explain that we all think he's been working too hard—"

"Just how drunk do you want us to get him?" asked Andy, who looked more than ready to party.

"I don't want him *drunk.*" Jasper sent a stern glance around the table. "Just loose. Happy. I don't want any of you cowpokes drunk. Big Clyde's gonna make sure of that and bring you boys home afterward, just like we've always done. Now I hafta go. It's more'n an hour to the airport and I'm late."

1

THROUGHOUT THE LONG flight from Honolulu, Daphne Proctor kept *Texas Men* magazine handy, so she could look at Stony Arnett's smile whenever she felt nervous butterflies in her stomach. The rest of the time she studied her favorite reference book on feng shui.

The Oriental philosophy had already changed her life. After discovering feng shui, she'd experimented by redecorating the love-and-marriage corner of her Honolulu apartment. Boy, had that worked a miracle. With breathtaking speed she'd found a discarded *Texas Men* magazine on a bus, written to Stony and fallen in love, long distance.

Flushed with success, she'd explained feng shui to her boss, hoping he'd let her use the principles with clients. He'd listened carefully to her description of how the right placement of furnishings could potentially affect health, happiness and prosperity, and then he'd appropriated her ideas, claiming them as his own. Daphne took his betrayal as a clear sign to start over in Texas with the man who was fast becoming the center of her world.

Stony hadn't actually proposed in his letters, but he'd come close as he described long, lonely nights and the desire to share his life with someone. No doubt he wanted to propose in person, which was the way she'd prefer accepting his proposal, anyway.

Through his letters, she'd learned that his mother had died in a barrel-racing accident when he was only nine, and that he'd grown up on the rodeo circuit, learning bull riding from his rodeo clown father. He hadn't complained about his rough-and-tumble childhood, but Daphne could read between the lines. He was thirsting for security and a deep, abiding love.

He'd scrimped and saved to buy the Roughstock Ranch, and now he needed a good woman by his side. Daphne prayed that she'd be all that he wanted in a wife. He definitely was all she wanted in a husband. As the plane neared San Antonio, she abandoned her feng shui book and stared at Stony's picture nonstop, because her stomach suddenly felt as if a whole flock of butterflies was loose in there.

Daphne's seatmate, a slim older woman, put aside the book she'd been reading most of the flight and glanced through her granny glasses at the magazine Daphne held. "Nice-looking cowboy. Someone you know?"

"Yes." Daphne smoothed the picture with her hand. Stony had sent the magazine a candid shot, which she liked better than a studio portrait any day. He was leaning against the top rail of a corral, probably watching something going on inside just as the photographer asked him to look around. His over-the-shoulder glance gave her a good view of those shoulders, the kind a girl could lean on. His dark Stetson hid most of his hair, but she knew from his letters that it was coffee brown and he liked wearing a hat because otherwise he was forever shoving his hair off his forehead.

He was squinting slightly in the picture, but she could still make out the kindness in his blue eyes. Yet it was his easy grin that had captured her interest and made her decide to write to him. Well, that and his cute buns. A girl had to be excused for having some weaknesses.

Daphne started to tuck the magazine away as the plane began its descent.

"What's that magazine? I've never seen it before."

"It's...um...called *Texas Men.*"

"You mean like pinups?"

"Not really." Daphne still felt self-conscious telling people she'd hooked up with a mail-order man, but at least these guys had all their cards on the table. "It advertises bachelors looking for a committed relationship."

"Really?" The woman perked up. "Anybody in there over sixty?"

"I didn't notice. Would you like to take a look?"

"Absolutely! What a dynamite concept." The woman adjusted her glasses more firmly on her nose and flipped through the pages. "I get so sick of these old farts who want to play footsie with every woman in the retirement village."

"The young guys are just as bad." Daphne remembered walking into her apartment eighteen months ago and finding her steady guy in bed with her best friend.

"So my granddaughter tells me. Whatever happened to monogamy, anyway?"

"My thoughts, exactly," Daphne said. "That's why I decided to become a born-again virgin."

The woman put down the magazine and stared at Daphne over the top of her glasses. "Excuse me?"

Daphne blushed but held her ground. This was a philosophy she believed in, after all, and the more people who heard about it, the better. "It just means that whatever experiences you've had with men in the past don't count anymore. You make a decision to keep yourself pure, and so you're a virgin from that moment on, until you find the man you intend to marry."

"This is fascinating. I wish now I'd spent the flight talking to you instead of keeping my nose in a book. For one thing, my granddaughter could use this information."

"You could become a born-again virgin, yourself."

The woman laughed. "I think I already am, by default. I require a romantic approach, and most of the men I meet in my age bracket are pretty clueless on that score." She turned back to the picture of Stony. "Is he your guy, the one you're going to marry?"

"Well, we haven't specifically talked about marriage because we haven't met, but yes, I believe he is."

"And you're going to meet him now? How exciting!"

Daphne gazed at the picture. "I'm a wreck, to be honest. I'm sure I'll be fine once we're together, but in the meantime, I'm really stressed."

The woman held the magazine up and studied the picture more closely. "And how long have you been a...virgin?"

"Seventeen months and twenty-six days."

The woman nodded, an appreciative smile on her face as she continued to look at Stony's picture. "What a terrific way to break your fast."

RIDING IN THE FRONT passenger seat on the way back to the ranch, Stony wondered if he could have done anything to prevent the bar fight. Fine time for Jasper to be visiting a sick cousin in San Antonio, right when he could have helped Stony keep the wranglers in line. They should've celebrated Andy's twenty-first birthday the following night, when Jasper could have been there, but Andy had acted like he'd die if they didn't party tonight.

Although Stony's cheek throbbed from connecting with a chair leg, he felt he had to tend to his men first. He'd had plenty of practice with this routine after all the times he'd dragged his father away from similar drunken brawls. Opening the bag of ice between his feet, he pulled a plastic bag from the box on his lap. "Who needs an ice pack back there?"

"Ramon needs one for his lip," Ty said from the back seat. "He's bleeding like a stuck pig. I'll bet Elmer's gonna soak us for the damage to his place."

"Oh, who cares?" Andy said, grinning despite a chipped tooth. "We whupped them boys! The Roughstock Ranch rules! Did you see how Big Clyde held that cowboy over his head and just dropped him on the table? And then Stony punched that other guy just when he was swinging a chair at Ramon. And I got in a good right hook, but I'm not sure who I hit, so—"

"You hit me, Rambo," Ty said. "I need an ice pack for my eye, Stony. I doubt I'll be able to see out of it by tomorrow. I warned y'all that Andy's practical jokes would go too far one of these days."

"Aw, heck," Andy said. "I was just having fun. A little mayo on that cowboy's chair seat. So what?"

"I guess you picked a cowboy with no sense of humor." Stony hated fights, but once this one started, he'd had to help his men. He turned to Big Clyde, who as the only nondrinker was driving the ranch van. "You okay?"

"Just my knuckles. They'll heal. Put something on your cheek, there, boss, so it don't swell up on you."

Stony filled another plastic bag and winced as he pressed the ice pack to his cheek. Now that the physical problems were under control, he felt as if he should say something to his cowhands. He tried to think of what wisdom Jasper might offer in this situation. "Well, Andy, this time you had some friends to wade in and help you out of a jam. Next time you try one of your tricks, you might not be so lucky." There, that sounded like something Jasper would say.

"I wouldn't call Andy lucky," Ty said. "Now Ramon can't talk, and that's a big ol' problem, right, Andy?"

"Uh, yeah. Guess so," Andy said.

"A hell of a problem," Ty continued darkly. "Now I don't know what we're gonna do."

"I guess you'd better talk, then, Ty," Big Clyde said.

"I *knew* it would land on me to do the dirty work! Always does!"

Stony gazed back at Ty. "What in blazes are you jabbering about, cowboy? Why does anybody have to talk?"

"Just because. So here goes nothin'." Ty cleared his throat. "Boss, we need to talk to you about somethin'."

"So it seems. Shoot."

"We think we need a woman around the ranch."

Stony frowned. "You mean a cook? I don't know if I can afford one. I expect y'all must get tired of fixing your own meals down there at the bunkhouse, but—"

"We don't need no cook," Andy said. "But you might."

"Me? You're sick of me coming down there to eat with you? I can take a hint. I'll buy a microwave."

"That's not what Andy means, boss," Ty said. "We all think...you've been working way too much."

"A cook won't help my workload much, boys."

"Forget the cook thing," Ty said. "We just think you need to relax, have some extracurricular activity. You never take no breaks."

"I thought that's what tonight was all about, taking time out to have a few beers and celebrate Andy's birthday," Stony said.

"You're leading him off into a ditch, Ty." Big Clyde took a deep breath and clenched the wheel tighter. "We think you need a...a girl to have some fun with once in a while."

Stony chuckled and pushed his hat back with his thumb. "You boys are concerned about my love life?"

"That's the point. You don't have no love life to be concerned about," Ty said.

Stony grinned and shook his head. "Look, I appreciate the thought, and I'll consider it, once the drought eases up and there's more time to think about such things. Just my luck, the minute I buy a ranch, the Hill Country gets its driest summer in fifty years."

Some indistinct murmuring among Andy, Ty and even Ramon aroused Stony's suspicion. Something was going on, and he wasn't at all sure he was going to like it.

Finally Ty spoke up. "Here's the thing. We could tell you didn't have no time to look for a girl, so we...well, we thought it might be a good idea if we sort of..."

"You'd better get it all out, and quick," Andy said. "We're almost there. He has to know."

"Know what?" Stony was surprised to see Jasper's pickup truck parked under the security light near the bunkhouse, and a horrible possibility dawned on him. He turned toward the back of the van. "When is your birthday, Andy?"

"Technically?"

"Yeah, technically. Is it even this month?"

"Well..."

"Uh-huh. And I don't suppose Jasper has a sick relative in San Antonio, either, does he?"

Ty cleared his throat. "Well, no. You see, Jasper went into San Antonio to pick up—"

"My God. You boys have hired a hooker."

AFTER SEEING THE INSIDE of Stony's ranch house that evening, Daphne concluded that he needed her desperately. The furniture was what some called "cowboy oak," rugged pieces with clean lines, but the wood's beauty was covered with layers of dust. The arrangement was haphazard, and yellowed newspapers and catalogs littered most of the surfaces. Not a curtain fluttered at a window, not a flower poked out of a vase. The friendliest thing about the room was the golden retriever who greeted them with tail wagging.

"And who's this?" Daphne asked.

"Dog."

"I figured that out. What's her name?"

"Just Dog." Jasper scratched behind the retriever's ears. "That's the only name Stony'll give her. She wandered onto the ranch last winter and has been here ever since. She dotes on Stony, but he claims she's not really his dog, because he don't want a dog. But, personally, I think he's kinda attached to her." Jasper looked around the room. "Whatcha think of the place?"

The weathered cowboy seemed so eager for her to be happy here that she disguised her dismay and smiled. "It's just fine, Jasper. Very nice. Where shall I put my things?" She figured Stony would initially house her in a guest room, although she didn't expect to be there long.

Jasper's color heightened and his mustache twitched. "Uh, Stony's room, I reckon. I didn't—that is, *he* didn't say nothing different."

So her man was ready to start playing house right away, was he? Knowing his ultimate goal was marriage, Daphne didn't mind a bit. With a sense of anticipation, she rolled her suitcase down the hall as Jasper led her to the master bedroom. Maybe Stony had spent some time preparing this room, at least.

"Stony, he's been real busy," Jasper said over his shoulder. "We're in a drought, and we've spent most of our time moving the herd so they get enough grass. Not much time for housekeeping chores."

Apparently not, Daphne thought as she surveyed the unmade bed. Stony probably didn't care that it was an elegant four-poster crying out for a lace canopy. Then she reminded herself that Stony had grown up without a mother and probably didn't put much importance on dusting and making beds, let alone decorating. She could hardly wait to turn this place into a welcoming home, something Stony apparently never had.

She propped her suitcase in a corner of the room and turned to Jasper. "How about if you find me some clean sheets and I change the bed for him?"

Jasper looked uncomfortable. "Oh, I could do that, ma'am. Let me rustle you up a sandwich in the kitchen and then I'll straighten up in here."

"Jasper, I didn't come here to be waited on. I'm too excited to eat, and this will give me something to do while I wait for Stony. When do you think he'll be back from town?"

Jasper's mustache twitched. "That's hard to say, exactly. Most any time, I guess. Or could be later. I hope you're not too disappointed that he's not here, but the boys thought a couple of beers would help calm his nerves."

"Believe me, I understand. I'm a little nervous myself." Understatement of the year, she thought. "If you don't mind, I'll probably feel better if I can spend some time alone settling into the house before Stony comes back."

"I think Stony keeps some Jack Daniel's in the cupboard, if you want a shot of whiskey," Jasper offered.

Daphne wasn't a whiskey drinker, but she was

sorely tempted. She shook her head. "Thanks, anyway."

"Then I'll get you those sheets."

Moments later she bid Jasper goodbye with a sense of relief. He took the dog back to the bunkhouse with him, and although she wouldn't have minded the retriever's company, she decided the dog might be an unnecessary distraction once Stony arrived.

After making up the bed and turning back the covers, Daphne considered tackling the mess in the living room, but she'd hate for Stony to show up in the middle of the process. A cleaning woman wasn't the image she wanted to project. She and Stony had sent each other sentimental love poems and confided their innermost dreams to each other. This first moment needed to be something special, a fantasy that matched the romance of their courtship so far.

Fortunately she'd brought some candles along in her suitcase. With the lights off and candles lit, the dust and clutter faded into the background. She found an old radio on a table in the corner and turned it on. Country-western music, turned low, added another layer of atmosphere. Now she was getting somewhere.

For the first time, she allowed herself to imagine this place as her future home and admitted to herself how important that was to her. Even her career choice of interior decorating had blossomed from her longing for a home of her own. Stony wasn't the only one who wanted to create a safe haven after being bumped around in a turbulent world.

Daphne's mother was on her fourth husband, and the only time Daphne remembered feeling as if she belonged was on a ranch not so far from here owned by husband number three. That happiness had lasted until she turned eighteen and her stepfather had tried to seduce her. Unwilling to tell her mother, she'd accepted a scholarship in Hawaii, because it seemed like the only place that would put her truly out of harm's way.

But she'd missed Texas. Now her mother was in Michigan with her fourth husband, and Daphne, at long last, was back in her beloved Hill Country. She felt sorry for her mother, who believed so fiercely in happy endings but lacked the patience to wait for the right man. Daphne had noticed that same flaw in herself. *Texas Men* had seemed like the perfect solution, because she'd had to save the money for the plane trip before she could fly to meet her new love. And now her patience was about to pay off.

"You've GOT IT WRONG, boss!" Ty said as Big Clyde eased the van toward the front of the ranch house. "You see, Jasper, he heard about—"

"So Jasper hired her, then. Same thing!"

"No, really," Big Clyde said. "It's not what you—"

"Is there or is there not a woman waiting for me in that house?" Stony thundered as the van stopped by the front gate.

"There is," Ty said, "but she—"

"This puts all of Andy's little practical jokes in the shade." Stony threw open the door. "Well, she'll just have to leave. I sure as hell don't want a hired woman in my bed!"

All the wranglers started talking at once.

"Y'all just hush!" Stony glared at them. "I'll get Jasper to take this woman back and then we'll have a talk. A long talk."

"We're dead men," Ty said with a groan.

"That could well be," Stony said, slamming the door of the van.

"Her name's Daphne!" Big Clyde called out the window after Stony. "Daphne Proctor!"

"Sure it is," Stony muttered as he swung open the gate and strode down the walkway. "As if she'd give out her real name." He'd never been with a prostitute, but he knew a lot of guys who had. The idea had never appealed to him. After two years of working with these guys, he'd expect them to understand him better than this.

The porch steps squeaked loudly as he took them two at a time. "I'm gonna kill Jasper," he vowed as he flung open the door and stepped into...candlelight.

Not a light bulb burned in the living room, but candles flickered everywhere. He never lit candles, not even when the electricity went out. Then he used a battery-powered lantern. He was stopped in his tracks by how different the room looked in this light. The flickering glow picked out the good points—the rock fireplace and oak furniture—and disguised the worn cushions and the layer of dust covering everything. Soft music played in the background, and for the first time since he could remember the place looked inviting.

"I...brought the candles from Hawaii," said a soft, musical voice.

Damn, but she sounded nice. Sweet. But of course

she wasn't. She apparently made enough as a hooker to afford trips to Hawaii. He shuddered to think what Jasper and the boys had paid for her to come here. He looked in the direction of the voice and saw her standing in the shadows.

"It's good to meet you at last," she said, stepping toward him.

As the light fell on her face, he caught his breath. Damned if she wasn't the most beautiful woman he'd seen in a coon's age. And if he could park his pride for the night, she was all his.

2

SHE WASN'T QUITE what Stony had expected. No wonder she made so much money at her trade, looking like she did. The candlelight picked out the red highlights in her shiny hair and put a gleam in her brown eyes. Her skin looked smooth and warm, her full mouth tempting. He realized just how long it'd been since he'd held a woman. Sending this one away would take a powerful effort.

To make matters worse, he didn't feel in complete control of himself. The beers had sabotaged his famous discipline and the bar fight had pumped him full of adrenaline. The combination put him in the mood for exactly what the lady was offering.

"You're...Daphne," he said, his vocal cords feeling rusty.

"Yes." She cleared her throat. "That's...that's me."

He'd always thought call girls were more polished than this. Daphne, or whatever her name was, seemed jumpy and unsure of herself. God, what if she was a beginner and he was her first customer? What if he rejected her and she started to cry? Her floral scent reached out to him, teasing him with the thought of making love to her. Despite his angry statement to his cowhands, despite his reluctance to engage in hired sex, he was becoming aroused.

Then he realized something was missing. "Where's the dog?"

"Jasper took her down to the bunkhouse. She's a very nice dog."

"Yeah, she is." His pulse jumped with excitement just hearing her voice. "So Jasper picked you up."

"Yes, and I understand completely why he came to San Antonio instead of you. It gives us both a chance to...get used to the idea."

That really confused him, unless she actually was trying this for the first time. Poor girl, maybe she was in a bad way financially. Maybe she'd decided the only answer was to put her terrific-looking body on the block. She wore a classy outfit, which surprised him, considering her profession. A knit top draped nicely over her breasts and tucked into a garment he hadn't seen much lately, a skirt. The skirt came to just above her knees, giving him a glimpse of leg and a whole lot of ideas he shouldn't be having.

"Jasper told me you went into town to have a few beers with your wranglers," she said. "I don't blame you for being nervous. I've been a bundle of nerves myself."

"Really?"

"Really. But I shouldn't be. And you're just the way I imagined you," she said, venturing a little closer. "Am I the way you imagined me?"

"No," he said.

Hurt flashed in her large eyes.

"I mean, you look better," he said. "Lots better."

"Oh." She smiled.

The smile just about finished him. When she smiled,

she looked fresh, and almost *innocent*. That was a laugh. But an innocent look on the face of a woman who traded sex for money sure made things more interesting.

He gestured to the candles. "You went to a lot of trouble."

"I thought it was important."

He felt his resolve slipping away. She was either a beginner or she loved her work enough to really put some effort into it. How many men could turn away from that prospect? If he'd found a hardened professional in this room, he could have sent her packing without a second thought. But this one was so into the romance of it, almost as if they were soul mates instead of two people conducting a business transaction.

She came closer, then gasped. "You're hurt! Did something happen?"

He shrugged. "Just a bar fight." This latest development had made him forget all about it. "It was nothing, really. I'm okay."

"That bruise looks painful." Her breasts nearly touched his shirtfront as she reached up and brushed her fingers lightly over his cheek.

He couldn't seem to stop looking into her dark eyes, so filled with concern, as if she really did care what happened to him.

She trailed her finger down his cheek. "With you going into town for drinks to shore up your courage, and with me anticipating this moment for so long, it almost feels like..."

He found breathing difficult. "Like what?"

"It'll sound silly."

"That's okay."

"It feels like a wedding night."

His heart went out to her. Poor kid, she'd probably given up hope of the real thing, so she had to fantasize about the experience when she was with a customer.

"Would you like to kiss me?" she murmured.

She had to be unusual, he decided. He'd heard that hookers didn't like to kiss their clients. They might do everything else in the book, but no mouth-to-mouth contact. He faced the fact that he wanted to kiss her, badly. He imagined sinking into that velvet fullness, tasting lipstick-flavored excitement as he explored the sweetness of her mouth with his tongue. But as turned on as he was right now, if he kissed her it would all be over. He'd take her back into that bedroom and love her all night long, assuming Jasper had paid for that amount of time.

She placed her hand gently on his chest and gazed up at him. "I've been saving myself for you, Stony."

Oh, she was good. If she was half as good in bed as she was delivering these virginal-sounding lines, he'd be passing up a real treat. A treat the boys had probably paid for out of their hard-earned wages because they thought he should stop living like a monk. They'd obviously searched carefully before choosing a woman like Daphne to ease this ache he'd pretended didn't exist. They'd gone to a heap of trouble, and so had this woman, with her candles and all. He'd be an ungrateful saddle tramp to refuse what had been so generously offered.

Maybe he needed to take the night off in more ways than one. Maybe the boys were right, and he needed to relax and enjoy the pleasures of the flesh for a change. It had been a very, very long time.

Slowly he cupped her face in both hands, and her skin felt just as delicious beneath his fingers as he'd expected. "I've been saving myself for you, too, Daphne," he murmured. Then he closed his eyes and touched his mouth to hers.

DAPHNE HAD IMAGINED this moment at least a million times. Winding her arms around his neck, she packed weeks of anticipation and longing into her kiss. She wanted Stony to know how deeply she cared for him, how glad she was to find a man who believed in lifelong commitment. After all the written words that had passed between them, at last they could communicate in the ageless way designed for lovers.

On the plane, she'd wondered if they'd spend hours talking before they finally found the courage to touch each other. But when she'd realized he intended for them to share a bed tonight, when she'd heard him pounding up the steps, so eager to see her, she'd known they'd be in each other's arms in no time. Finding out he'd been hurt in a fight had awakened her nurturing, protective instincts. She would gladly give up her virginity to this special, caring man.

Tossing his hat aside, he groaned deep in his throat and pulled her close. At last she could experience what she'd dreamed of for weeks—his strong arms wrapped around her, his broad chest pressing with exquisite force against her aching breasts, his mouth seeking the heat within hers. They'd never discussed the physical side of their relationship in their letters, but they were discussing it now in the only way that counted. His obvious arousal sent the message that this was a union of body and soul.

He was wild for her, and she loved every frantic movement as he tugged her knit top from the waistband of her skirt and slid his hand up her back to unhook her bra. Later they could take their time, but now desperation drove them both to seal their bargain in an elemental way.

Skimming the top over her head and taking her bra with it, he tossed the garment over a nearby chair and cupped her breasts in both hands. "So perfect," he murmured, his gaze sweeping back to her face. "You seem...untouched."

"Because that's the way I feel." She covered his hands with hers. "For me the past is wiped away, and you are the first man I've ever known." She tilted her head back and closed her eyes. "Teach me about pleasure, Stony."

His breath caught. Then the air stirred above her puckered nipples as he leaned down and gently swirled his tongue over each one.

She trembled. "I like that."

Stroking her nipples with his thumbs, he kissed the hollow of her throat. "You're bewitching me, lady."

"You forget. I don't know how to bewitch a man."

His laughter had a ragged edge to it. "Right." He kissed his way downward until he reached the tip of her breast. As he drew it slowly into his mouth, she moaned and her knees threatened to buckle. She grasped the front of his shirt with both hands, and he slid an arm around her waist to steady her as he continued the sweet assault.

And it truly seemed like the first time a man had caressed her in this way, as if her breasts had never known the swift tug of desire that traveled downward, settling in the deepest part of her. Her body tightened and quivered, preparing for the welcome invasion to come. The lovemaking would be incredibly powerful, she knew, because Stony wasn't interested in a plaything to amuse himself with for a few hours. He wanted a wife.

He kissed his way back to her mouth. "I'm taking you to bed, little darlin'," he murmured against her lips.

"Just remember," she whispered between kisses, "that this...is my first time."

He chuckled and swung her up in his arms. "Mine, too."

HE WASN'T LYING, Stony thought as he carried her into the bedroom, dark except for a shaft of pale moonlight coming through an uncurtained window. It was his first time with a call girl. And he'd been operating under some misconceptions about what the experience would be like. He'd thought that professionals would be sort of impersonal, maybe a little mechanical in their actions. He wouldn't have expected such fantastic chemistry. This woman seemed as eager for him as he was for her.

Even her virgin-for-a-night routine intrigued him. Damned if he didn't want to play along. He'd made love to a few women in his time, but none had ever claimed to be a virgin, for which he'd been grateful. Seducing a virgin usually meant a wedding was supposed to follow, and he didn't ever expect to take that walk down the aisle. Pretending someone was a virgin, though, was just about perfect.

And Daphne was just about perfect, he thought as he laid her on the bed. Except for her calling in life, she was his dream girl—although he'd run like hell if he actually found his dream girl, for her sake as much as anything. He wasn't any good at the hearts and flowers routine. He'd had no practice in it and he didn't intend to start at this late date. His father had been destroyed by losing the love of his life, and Stony never intended to let himself in for that kind of heartbreak.

As he gazed down at Daphne, he saw that the sheets weren't messed up the way he generally left them each morning. "Did you fix the bed, too?" he asked, slipping off her shoes and tossing them to the floor.

"Do you mind?"

He braced his hands on either side of her head and leaned down to nibble on her full bottom lip. "Sweetheart, I haven't minded a single thing about this night so far."

"I got Jasper to find the clean sheets. I didn't rummage around without permission."

He lifted his head and gazed down at her, barely able to make out her face, yet knowing how earnest she must look, how concerned that he wouldn't think she'd been pawing through his stuff. "You really are an unusual girl."

She reached up and combed the lock of hair that fell across his forehead. "Just right for an unusual man," she said, running her fingers through his hair.

He liked the feel of that and held still so she'd do it some more. "It's no use trying to make it stay put. Without my hat it just won't."

"I know."

"You do?"

"Sure." She cupped the back of his head and urged him closer. "You told me."

He wasn't making sense of the conversation, but that wasn't surprising, considering the state he was in.

He started to kiss her again, wanted to kiss her again, but first he had to make sure he had birth control. If not, he'd have to ask if she'd brought any, and he hated doing that. If she'd brought some, that would be a sign of her professional behavior, and he liked pretending she wasn't being paid for this, just as she was pretending.

"Don't go away." He gently disentangled himself and went into the bathroom to check the cabinet under the sink. He was in luck, as long as the darned things didn't go bad. The unopened box had been sitting there ever since his first shopping trip after buying the ranch. He'd had some idea he'd be using them, but the ranch had taken all his time and energy for almost two years.

Remembering something else, he walked into the living room and blew out all the candles. He and Daphne might be about to set each other on fire, but he had no desire to burn down the house he'd worked so hard to buy. It was a sweet thought, though, bringing those candles. He'd always remember how she'd looked standing there in the glow of them.

When he returned, he found her still in bed, but she'd climbed under the covers, moved to the far side of the bed, and pulled the sheet up to her chin. "What's this?" he asked, smiling.

"Modesty."

"Oh, right." His smile widened. "You would be modest, being a virgin and all."

"I *am*."

She said it with such conviction that he laughed with delight. "Thank you for being here tonight, Daphne." He set down the box and started taking off his clothes. "You're exactly what I needed."

"I know."

"You certainly do know a lot." He continued to undress and wondered if she'd taken off her skirt and panties before she slid under the sheet. Shortly he'd find out. And whether she claimed modesty or not, that sheet would soon be history. "You must be a very wise young lady."

"About a few things."

He pulled off his boots and shucked his jeans. "But not what happens between a man and a woman when they lie in bed naked together, right?" He noticed the moonlight washed over her side of the bed in particular, which was good. It would give him light to love by.

"You'll have to show me."

Finally his briefs joined the pile of clothes on the floor, freeing his erection. "I'll be only too happy to do that, sweetheart." There was just enough light on her face that he could see her eyes widen, which was a very gratifying reaction, indeed.

He walked to the bed and pushed back the sheet on his side as he lay down beside her. Damned if he didn't enjoy the idea that she wanted him to coax her a little, like a new bride. Propping himself on one elbow, he looked into her eyes as he ran his finger along the edge of the sheet. "We don't want any secrets between us, now, do we?"

"No," she said softly, with a trace of shyness.

"Then let me see you," he murmured, drawing the sheet down gradually over the slope of her breasts. As he uncovered the dusky tips, his mouth moistened with need. He paused to lean down and taste her, all the while listening to her breath quicken and thinking what a wonderful thing it was to make a woman gasp with pleasure. He'd missed that.

Easing the sheet down a little more, he kissed his way down the valley between her ribs. The sweet scent of desire greeted him as he traveled farther down to her flat stomach and discovered nothing covering her but the thin sheet.

But as he tried to venture deeper into blissful territory, she pulled the sheet tight across her hips. Ah, she was a coy one.

He slid back up to cup her face in one hand. Then he kissed her, long and thoroughly, using his tongue in a suggestive rhythm until she whimpered and her grip relaxed on the sheet. He pushed it gently down to her knees, then stroked lightly up the inside of her thigh, stopping just short of his goal.

Lifting his lips a fraction from hers, he whispered his request.

"Yes" came the trembling response.

As he covered her mouth with his, he almost believed he was the first man to slip his hand into her moist curls and begin the intimate journey that would bring them both so much joy. She was drenched with passion and moaned as he carried out his slow exploration.

Raising his head to look into her eyes, he rubbed her tender flashpoint. His touch registered in her eyes, and he savored the heady feeling that she was ready to explode. "Lesson number one," he murmured, stroking her quickly and surely until she cried out and arched against his hand.

He felt her climax in every nerve and ached for his own completion with a fierceness that stole his breath. When the next explosion took her, he needed to be deep inside her, absorbing her convulsions and letting them sweep him into the mouth of the volcano with her.

Speechless and panting, she lay trembling on the bed. With a soft kiss he eased away from her and rolled over to get the condom box. It seemed an unnatural thing to do, as if he should just enter this woman and spill his seed, taking her virginity and creating new life. He must have gone crazy to be thinking things like that. This was nothing but sex for hire.

But as he turned back to her, he couldn't accept that. The notion didn't square with the way she looked at him, or the welcome in her expression as she held out her arms. A tiny thrill of fear pierced the red haze of desire in his brain. But to pay attention to that fear would mean leaving this bed. And he couldn't do that.

The sheet slid to the floor as he kicked it aside and moved between her thighs. As he gazed down at Daphne, he was startled by how right, how natural it seemed to be making love to her. It was as if he'd been waiting for this woman, this moment, all his life. Yes, he was definitely going crazy.

She smiled up at him. "I've dreamed of this for so long."

Maybe she was the crazy one, he thought. Maybe this gorgeous, sexy woman was missing a few spokes in her wheel. All he knew was that a woman who looked like

Daphne and made love like Daphne was his fantasy, so he might as well enjoy the evening's surprise gift. "So have I."

He entered her gently, allowing her to adjust to him. When her eyes glistened with tears, he stopped. "Am I hurting you?"

"No." Her voice was choked with emotion. "But Stony, it really does feel like the first time for me. And it's...so beautiful that I'm...crying."

"Oh, sweetheart." Tenderness for her overwhelmed him and he leaned down to kiss the tears that slid from the corners of her eyes.

"D-don't stop," she said, sniffing. "Don't stop because I'm crying. Please. Oh, please."

She hardly had to beg, he thought. The hot sheath of her body tempted him beyond enduring, despite his concern about her tears. Closing his eyes, he surrendered to the needs driving him and shoved deep. He groaned at the intense pleasure.

"Who are you?" he whispered.

"Silly man. You know who I am."

He opened his eyes to gaze at her. "Just tell me again."

"Why, Stony, I'm the love of your life."

3

THEIR LOVEMAKING was all Daphne could have hoped for. True, they hadn't said those three important words to each other, but that would happen soon, when the time was right. Meanwhile she was curled inside Stony's protective embrace, and her world was about as perfect as it could be. Excitement had kept her from sleeping well recently, and that, combined with a long day of traveling, sent her quickly into a deep slumber.

Sunshine falling on her face and the chirping of a robin outside the window finally pried her awake the next morning. After a moment of disorientation, she remembered where she was and what had happened the night before. With a smile she rolled over and found the other side of the bed empty.

Hoofbeats sounded outside. She tumbled from bed, grabbed up the discarded sheet to cover herself and hurried to the window just in time to see Stony canter out of the yard on a big bay, his golden retriever running to keep up with him. *And the cowboy rides away.*

She battled disappointment, telling herself this was a working ranch where people got up at dawn. The routine couldn't stop around here just because she'd arrived. They were fighting a drought, and no doubt Stony had to check on the herd, just like Jasper had said. In his typical considerate fashion, he'd let her sleep in, allowing for jet lag.

He'd learn soon enough that she didn't expect that sort of mollycoddling. Maybe she hadn't emphasized enough in her letters how much she'd loved ranch life and ranch work during the few years she'd been able to enjoy it.

Stony, the horse and dog disappeared from view over one of the many undulating hills she could see from the bedroom window. She'd arrived in the dark, and this morning was her first chance to drink in the welcome sight of Texas Hill Country since she'd left eight years ago.

Even though the area wasn't quite as green as she remembered due to the drought, it was still one of the prettiest places in the world, in her opinion. She could hardly wait to get on a horse and explore the Roughstock. In his letters Stony had told her about a small lake on the property and the cypress-lined stream that fed into it.

Eager to begin her new life, she turned from the window, laid the sheet over the bed and started toward the bathroom. Then she saw the note on the nightstand anchored by a box of condoms. She picked it up, and underneath lay a hundred dollar bill.

Puzzled, she read the note.

Dear Daphne,

I figure you've made arrangements for Jasper to drive you back to San Antonio. I don't know what he paid you, but this is from me, in gratitude for making this cowboy a very happy man last night.

Help yourself to coffee and toast before you go.

                              Sincerely, Stony Arnett

Daphne sat on the bed and read the note again. And again. Her stomach twisted with anxiety. Surely there was some mistake. Some horrible mistake. He was writing to her as if she were a prostitute hired for the evening instead of the woman he planned to marry.

And there was something else that bothered her about this note. He'd always typed his letters, saying his handwriting wasn't very good. That was true enough, she thought, looking at the scrawled message, although he wrote as legibly as most men.

Still holding the note, she walked over to the suitcase she'd left in the corner of the room. She pulled out the thick packet of letters from a zippered compartment, unfolded the top one and held it beside the message she'd found on the nightstand.

The signatures were similar. She looked more closely, hoping against hope that she was wrong and the same man who had written the note had also signed those letters. She was no handwriting expert, but she'd had plenty of art classes while she studied interior design, and her eye for detail was pretty darned good.

At last she had to face the ugly truth, one that made her feel as if she'd just swallowed a large chunk of cement. The signatures were not the same.

STONY'S SELF-ASSIGNED chore this fine morning was to repair a section of fence along the east boundary of the ranch. It wasn't one of his favorite jobs, but even mending fence didn't seem so bad today, considering the treat he'd had during the night.

He'd enjoyed himself so thoroughly that he'd considered waking her up at dawn to have another round. Then he'd thought better of it. There might be some awkwardness this morning, especially when he gave her the extra money, which he felt she certainly deserved.

No, better to let her leave in a dignified way when he wasn't around. Once she was safely back in San Antonio, he'd ask Jasper about her. Maybe next time he'd just drive to the city, get a hotel room and invite her to come there. Yeah, that was a better plan.

He hadn't thought he'd ever be interested in such a setup, but a woman like Daphne could change a guy's mind. Lord, was she terrific. He couldn't remember when he'd had a better time.

"Hell of a beautiful morning, Dog!" he called out to the retriever, who barked happily in response.

As Stony neared the spot where he'd noted the bad section of fence two days ago, he recognized Jasper's buckskin ground-tied beside it. Sure enough, there was Jasper tackling the job Stony had assigned himself for the day.

Jasper glanced up from his work as Stony dismounted and dropped his horse's reins to the ground. The retriever trotted over to Jasper for some attention. Jasper scratched behind the dog's ears, but the foreman looked worried, and his mustache twitched as it usually did when he was nervous. "Howdy, boss."

"Howdy, Jasper. Did you ever see such a pretty morning as this?"

"Could use some rain clouds on the horizon, I expect."

"You know, Jasper, I have a feeling that rain is coming. Yep, I think the drought's about over."

"You're mighty cheerful this mornin'," Jasper ventured.

"Good lovin' puts a smile on a man's face."

Jasper shook his head in wonder. "Then you ain't upset with me? I mean, after I found out about the bar fight, and the fact the boys didn't really explain it very well, I thought you'd be steamed, for sure."

"Well, I was, at first. I'm sure the boys told you that."

"Yep. Sort of expected you to show up at the bunkhouse with my walking papers. Didn't sleep so well last night."

"I'm sure you didn't. That was quite a thing to pull, Jasper."

"I know it." Jasper set his tools on the ground and took off his hat to wipe a sleeve over his forehead. "And I know it was low-down."

"I'm impressed with all the planning it took. I didn't think you were that interested in my love life, Jasper."

Jasper's gaze grew more intense. "I take interest in everything about you, Stony. Always have, ever since your mom died and your dad...well, your dad's never been the same, and it always seemed like you could use some extra looking after."

Stony was touched. "I guess I've always known that."

"I hated tricking you like this, but it was the only way I could figure you'd go for such a thing, if it was sprung on you kind of sudden."

Stony laughed. "It was sudden, all right. But I guess you and the boys knew what you were doing, after all. I had a great time."

Jasper relaxed enough to grin at Stony. "When you didn't show up at the bunkhouse last night, I figured things had gone passable well. I was hoping you'd sleep in a little and enjoy yourselves. That's why I came out here to work on the fence."

"I thought about staying with her a little longer, but I decided against it, all things considered. But she's quite a girl, Jasper. I don't know what you paid her, but I left a little extra on the nightstand. I'll take over here if you want to get back and drive her into San Antonio."

Jasper's grin faded. "What in hell are you talking about?"

"Somebody's got to take her back, and I think it would be a lot better if you did it. But if you'll give me her phone number, I just might call her again some time. And I guess you ought to tell me what she charges, so I can save up. She was sure worth whatever you paid her, though. She's—"

"Hold it." Jasper stared at him in horror. "You think Daphne's a hooker?"

"Of course she's a hooker!" Stony returned Jasper's stare, and gradually all the goodwill he'd been feeling curdled in his stomach. His throat constricted with dread. "Isn't she?"

BY THE TIME DAPHNE heard hoofbeats in the yard, the tears were all gone and she was fighting mad. She'd quit her job, given up her apartment and spent her savings on a plane ticket to Texas, supposedly to meet the man she was going to marry. After seventeen months and twenty-six days of virginal behavior, she'd eagerly given herself to that man, only to discover he thought she was a prostitute.

She'd played by the rules, trying to be so careful so she wouldn't end up with another jerk in her bed, but somebody else obviously thought that rules were meant to be broken. Once she found out who that was, there would be hell to pay.

After showering, she'd forced down some toast and coffee as a practical measure. No telling how soon she'd eat again. Then she'd repacked what few things she'd removed from her suitcase, all the while nursing her anger. Now she stood in the living room and faced the front door as three miserable-looking cowboys and Stony's dog walked silently into the room.

The men whipped off their hats immediately, and the dog flopped to the floor and put her head on her paws.

Daphne crossed her arms and waited. Jasper looked the most dejected, wincing each time Stony, who stood in the middle, sent him another angry look. Watching Stony and remembering their lovemaking made Daphne's insides quiver.

With his hat off, his hair kept falling over his forehead as it had last night when she'd tried to gently finger-comb it into place. Her fingers still remembered the texture of his hair. But today there was no tenderness in Stony's expression as he angrily shoved his hair back and glared at his foreman.

Contrasting Stony's cold behavior with his sweetness of the night before upset Daphne even more, so she concentrated on Jasper and the other man, a sandy-haired cowboy who kept clearing his throat. He had a shiner on his left eye, obviously from the same bar fight that had given Stony the bruise on his cheek.

Then all three men started talking at once.

"Stop!" Daphne held up one hand. "Before you make things worse, I want to know one thing. Who's been writing to me all these weeks?"

Jasper looked up at the ceiling, down at the dog, over at the window as his mustache twitched. "I have, ma'am," he said at last. He took a deep breath and met Daphne's gaze. "This whole thing is my fault. I'm the ringleader, so I want to make things right."

"It's not all his fault, ma'am," said the sandy-haired cowboy, squaring his shoulders. "And if I may say so, you're even prettier than your picture. And if I may also say so, I was against this whole thing from the start."

"And who are you?"

"Ty Eames, ma'am. And as the senior wrangler here, I'm ready to take the blame along with ol' Jasper. Of course technically it's Andy's fault. If he hadn't started the bar fight, then Ramon would've been able to talk, and he can talk the horn off a saddle, if I may say so. And I wouldn't have messed up like I did. And now I suppose you'll use one of them feng shui moves and take us all out at one whack. I knew this would turn out bad."

"Excuse me?" Daphne frowned as she tried to make sense of Ty's little speech.

Jasper elbowed Ty in the ribs. "They use it for defense, straw-brain. She won't just whack you while you're standing there."

Stony glanced at Daphne. "What're they talking about?"

"In one of her letters, she told us she used feng shui in her decorating business," Jasper said. "We're not exactly clear how that works, but this is one woman who can take care of herself, boss."

Daphne started to explain that feng shui was a philosophy of arranging space, not a martial art, then changed her mind. Let them think she could crush their windpipes with a single blow. Served them right.

"So all of the hands worked on the letters?" Daphne asked.

"Jasper typed, but we all made suggestions." Ty twisted his hat in his hands. "Ramon was in charge of the poetry. He knows about words."

Daphne closed her eyes. All those tender little verses she'd thought Stony had sent, verses she'd taped to her bathroom mirror so she could see them first thing in the morning, hadn't had anything to do with the man she'd made love to last night.

She opened her eyes and glared at them. "Am I part of some elaborate joke, then?"

"It's no joke, ma'am," Jasper said, glancing sideways at Stony. "We had the best of intentions. Stony, here, just won't slow down, so we thought—"

"You thought you'd find me a *wife*?" Stony was rigid with fury. "And you tricked this poor woman into flying all the way from Hawaii thinking I was in *love* with her? It's unforgivable." The dog at his feet whined.

No matter how much Daphne tried to harden her

heart, pain sliced through her each time she was reminded that all Stony's tenderness the night before had been directed at a woman he thought was being paid for her services, not the woman he planned to spend a lifetime loving.

"So all the letters were just a pack of lies," Daphne said.

"Of course they were," Stony said. "And I—"

"No, they weren't," Jasper interrupted.

Stony rounded on him. "How can you stand there and deny it, after admitting you rented a P.O. box just so I wouldn't know what you were up to?"

"I figure I'm getting fired, anyway, so I might as well tell this young lady exactly what we done." Jasper stood up a little straighter. "We put the truth about Stony in them letters. I've known him since he was born, traveled the circuit with him and his folks, then him and his pa. The boys and me didn't make up nothing. All we said about him is right."

"Even the poetry," Ty said. "Ramon found a book of Stony's and took bits from it."

Stony whirled in Ty's direction. "Ramon swiped my mother's poetry book?"

"Ramon didn't swipe nothing, boss. He just went in there one day and copied all sorts of pretty things out of it, things he thought Daphne would like."

"I did like them." Her dreams were in ashes, yet Daphne felt her anger ebbing away as she pictured a bunkhouse full of cowhands gathered around an old typewriter while they gave tips to Jasper on what to put in each letter. She blushed to think how lovingly she'd written back to Stony, especially there at the end, when they'd begun openly talking about sharing a life-time.

She'd thought those letters were just for Stony's viewing, when in fact they'd probably been passed among the wranglers. Still, the cowboys had obviously treated this project with respect. It was crazy and na-ive, but not malicious.

"I still think it might've worked," Jasper said, his jaw tightening. "If somebody had told Stony the truth before he walked in here last night."

"We *tried*," Ty said, his expression agonized. "But we were counting on Ramon, and then his lip was all busted, so Big Clyde said I was the one who had to do it, but I didn't have a speech ready, so it came out wrong. He told us to shut up and went barreling into the house, saying he'd send Daphne straight home. Andy was sure she'd clear up the misunderstanding herself, first thing, as soon as he tried to send her home, but I just knew it would turn out terrible. I've always known it would turn out terrible. I—"

"Hush your mouth," Jasper said.

For the first time, Stony looked uncomfortable.

"You shoulda told him, even when he told you to shut up," Jasper muttered.

"You shoulda told him earlier," Ty shot back.

But Daphne was still stuck on the point that Stony hadn't meant to make love to her, after all. She glanced at him. "You'd planned to send me home?"

"It crossed my mind." He rubbed the back of his neck and looked away. "I don't...I've never paid for...that is, it's not my way to—"

"Then why didn't you just tell me so and have Jasper

drive me back last night?" Fascinated, she watched the flush rise from his shirt collar. "That would have saved us both a lot of grief."

"You're right. I should have done exactly that. And I apologize." Still he wouldn't look at her.

Daphne felt her first moment of triumph since she'd found that demoralizing note. Stony had never been with a prostitute, yet he'd been so attracted to her that he'd made an exception in her case. He'd even been impressed enough to leave her an extra hundred dollars, which in her rage she'd ripped into little pieces and flushed down the toilet.

She wouldn't have been able to accept that money in any case, but unfortunately she was in a bit of a financial bind. Being totally on her own again hadn't figured into her plans. She'd have to ask Jasper to drive her back to San Antonio and then she'd take a bus up to see her mother in Michigan. Her mother was always good for thinking up ways to look on the bright side.

She mustered all the dignity she possessed. "Well, then. If someone can drive me back to San Antonio, I'll be on my way."

Stony nodded. He'd didn't plan to stop her, she realized with a fresh pang of sorrow. He might have enjoyed their interlude, but he obviously wasn't interested in continuing the association.

Jasper seemed to be busy watching Stony. Then he turned back to Daphne. "Where are you headed? Back to Hawaii?"

"I don't think that's any of your business."

"I don't feel right sending you off like that," Jasper said. "In your last letter you said you were quitting your job and giving up your apartment. You ain't got nothing to go back to, looks like."

Stony gave her a sharp glance. "Is that right?"

"Don't worry about it. I'll manage."

He stared at her and shook his head. "I don't operate that way. I was planning to repay you for the plane fare, at least, but if you don't even have a job anymore…could you get it back?"

"I don't want it back, not that it's your concern. We're nothing to each other, as it turns out, Mr. Arnett."

"Um, I wouldn't say that, exactly." To his credit, he did look worried about her.

"I would. I'm all packed. If you can spare somebody to drive me, that's all I'll ask of you." She started from the room.

"Hold on a minute," Jasper said. "Let's not be hasty."

"I think hasty is just what we should be," Daphne said, continuing toward the bedroom where her suitcase stood ready. She paused and glanced back at them. "I shipped a box of my work-related materials here. When I'm relocated, I'll send you the address so you can forward the box to me."

Jasper snapped his fingers. "I clean forgot. You planned on startin' your own business here."

"Obviously I won't be doing that." She'd counted on living here with Stony and gradually building her list of clients in her spare time whenever he didn't need her help with the ranch. She'd liked the idea of creating a design center in a small town rather than battling the competition in a big city. She'd even dreamed of opening a small mail-order shop selling items geared to the principles of feng shui. Twenty-four hours ago, anything had seemed possible. Now nothing did.

"You wanted to go into business in Rio Verde?" Stony asked.

Tears threatened to overwhelm her again, and she knew she'd better retreat and get herself in hand. "I might consider San Antonio, instead," she said, to save her pride. "Give me a minute to freshen up and I'll be right with you." Choking back a sob, she walked into the bedroom and closed the door firmly behind her.

4

JASPER CLAPPED HIS hat back on his head. "The way I see it, we got one chance to make it up to her for what we done."

"What *you've* done," Stony corrected him. "And let's get one thing straight. I'm not firing you. I couldn't run this ranch without you, and you damn well know it. Obviously I can't keep you on and fire everybody else who was involved, so y'all still have a job."

"That's a relief," Ty said, putting on his hat. "I only got about forty bucks to my name."

"But," Stony added, pulling his hat low over his eyes, "once this is over, we need to talk about who's in charge around here."

"Stony, I know I'm just your foreman," Jasper said. "But danged if sometimes I don't feel like you're the son I never had. The actions I took were more like a father might take, like your father might take, if he ever hung around long enough to notice how lonely you get."

"Dammit, I am not lonely!" Even if that wasn't quite true, he'd a darn sight rather be lonely than heartbroken.

The dog whined again and slapped her tail on the floor.

"I say you are, and I say that what happened last

night is living proof. Now, I hope you'll take this comment in the spirit of fatherly advice. I think you owe that little gal some consideration after taking what she offered last night."

Embarrassment heated Stony's cheeks. "You know what I thought she was."

"And you could have turned her down, like you apparently intended, instead of going ahead with things and making it all worse. From the way she looks at you, I'll guarantee you're part of her misery right now."

"So what can I do about that? I'm not marrying the girl, just to make her dreams come true."

"Then make her business dream turn out the way she hoped," Jasper said. "She used to live around these parts, and she told us how nice it would be to be back in the Hill Country again."

Stony blew out a breath and shoved his hands in his back pockets. "You boys stirred up a pile of mischief, didn't you."

"We can fix some of it," Jasper said. "Just give her a roof over her head while she prospects for customers and gets herself established. The boys and I will call in a few favors and get her some decorating jobs. Pretty soon she'll be able to set up in town, and we can all feel better about this."

"That ain't gonna work," Ty said. "Nobody in Rio Verde would think to hire a decorator, and you know it, Jasper."

"That's because they ain't never had one to hire before! There's some folks who could use the advice, and a few who have the money to spare. We'll just talk it up."

"I still say it won't work," Ty said. "But listen, Stony, if you don't want her, do you care if I swing a rope in her direction? I'm not getting any younger, and all this talk about wives and such has got me to thinking."

Stony glared at the wrangler, irritated beyond reason, considering he wasn't interested in Daphne. "I think it's best if you stay away from her."

"But why? She's a fine-looking woman, and somebody's bound to—" He glanced down at his leg. "Quit kicking me, Jasper!"

"You got horsehair for brains, cowboy," Jasper said. "We're talking about the lady's business prospects, not her marriage prospects at the moment. And you ain't set to be no bridegroom with only forty dollars in your pocket."

With a final snort of disgust for Ty, Jasper turned to his boss. "So what do you say, Stony? That girl needs somebody to stake her a room and three squares a day so's she can get on her feet again. Seems like the least we can do."

Stony felt control of his life slipping away. But Jasper was right, he *had* been a part of this disaster by taking Daphne to bed last night. He didn't want a wife, didn't even want a steady girlfriend, but that didn't justify sending Daphne away without a job or a place to stay. He'd treated the dog better than that.

"I'm not set up for guests," Stony said.

"You ain't just whistling Dixie," Ty said, glancing around at the scarred and dusty furniture, the curtainless windows, the stacks of yellowed newspapers and catalogs. "Smells nice, though."

"She lit a bunch of candles last night. I threw the stubs in the trash, but you can still smell them, I guess."

"Candles, huh?" Ty rocked back on his heels as he gazed longingly at the closed bedroom door.

Jasper whacked him upside the head with his hat. "Get your mind back on the business at hand, boy. Seems to me there's an iron bedstead in the barn. Ty, you can clean it up while I head into town today and pick up a mattress for it. You got four bedrooms in this place, Stony. One of 'em will surely do."

"Yeah, I guess." This would be tricky, Stony thought. Every time he looked at Daphne, he remembered the taste of her, the pleasure of sinking deep inside her, her eager response as he made love to her. He hoped that reaction would wear off quick, because he didn't dare make love to her again. Not when he knew she was in the market for a husband.

"Here she comes," Jasper said as the bedroom door opened again. "Do you want to do the talking, or should I?"

"I'll do it." Stony glanced at Jasper. "Assuming I am still running this outfit."

Jasper raised both hands. "Abso-damn-lutely. Just call me the idea man."

Stony grimaced. "And you do get some doozies, don't you?"

Daphne walked into the room pulling her wheeled suitcase. When the accusations were flying around, Stony hadn't really noticed what she was wearing today, but now he did—white slacks and a green blouse the color of granny apples. Stony liked the way the color went with her reddish hair. She didn't wear much makeup, which was nice because then he could see the dusting of freckles across her nose. He liked the way the slacks fit her, too. The blouse was buttoned to just above the top of her bra. He remembered exactly what her breasts looked like, and what—

"Stony?" Jasper said. "You maybe had something to say to the lady?"

Stony coughed into his fist. "Uh, yeah. Daphne, we were talking, and we figure you can just stay here and set up your business in Rio Verde like you planned."

"No, thanks."

"And Jasper's going to get a mattress for the—" Stony paused. "What did you say?"

"Thanks, but no thanks. I don't accept charity."

"This ain't charity," Jasper said. Then he glanced over at Stony. "Is it okay if I say something, boss?"

Stony waved a hand in the air. "Go ahead." Damned if he was going to plead with this woman.

"We thought you might think this was charity," Jasper said to Daphne.

"We did?" Ty asked.

Jasper shot him a glance.

"Oh, yeah, we did," Ty said. "So I guess you're not interested, huh? I told them this would never work, but they—"

"Button your lip, cowboy," Jasper said. "Ma'am, here's what we figured would take care of the charity angle. To earn your keep, you can start decorating right in this here house." He swept an arm around the room.

Stony's gaze swung to Jasper. "Hey, we didn't—"

"I reckon you'd find enough to keep you busy making this pigsty look nice," Jasper said, ignoring Stony.

"It's not a pigsty!" Stony said. "And it's...it's practical!"

"It's a nightmare," Daphne said. "If things had turned out differently, I was planning to start on this room immediately."

"And do what?" Stony asked, looking around.

"Break up the furniture, probably," Ty said. "You know, take that rickety table over there and whap! Right through it with the side of her hand. I've seen it on TV. One minute it's furniture, the next it's kindling."

Daphne seemed to be trying not to laugh. "That's not a bad idea. Whoever designed that table should be shot." She grew solemn again. "But I really can't stay, guys. Sorry. Jasper, will you be the one taking me back?"

Maybe it was the laughter that sparkled briefly in her brown eyes. Stony thought of how she must have started out on this trip full of high hopes for a new life. He remembered how terrific he'd felt when he left the rodeo for good and bought this ranch. She'd felt that way yesterday. Today her dream was gone, and she was facing her loss with great courage.

She couldn't have the home and husband of her dreams, but the business part was possible, with a little help from his friends and neighbors in Rio Verde. Stubborn pride was keeping her from accepting his offer. He recognized that easy enough, having a generous dose of the problem himself.

"Please stay," he said, looking directly into her eyes. "We've made a mess of your plans. Jasper tells me you grew up in this area, and you were looking forward to moving back."

Her expression shifted from stubborn to uncertain.

Stony pressed his advantage. "And Jasper's right about this house. It needs a lot of work. I wouldn't know where to start." He wondered if he was consigning his furniture to the woodpile. "I'd like you to fix it up. I'd consider it a big favor. There's plenty of room in this house, and you don't look like you eat much."

"Real smooth, boss," Ty said, turning to Daphne. "Look, if he don't feed you right, come on down to the bunkhouse. We all take turns cooking, and most of us are a pretty fair hand with a stove."

"She'll eat up at the house," Stony said, with a warning glance at Ty.

Daphne looked around at each of the three men. Then she surveyed the living room. "What sort of decorating budget would I have?"

"Whatever you need," Jasper said.

Stony made a choking sound.

"Within reason, a'course," Jasper added.

"Of course."

Stony wasn't sure he liked the gleam in her eye when she said that.

"All right," she said. "I'll accept your offer."

Dear God, what have I let myself in for? Stony thought just as the toe of Jasper's boot jabbed his ankle. "That's great," he said, mustering a smile.

"Real fine," Jasper added.

"I hope you won't be sorry," Ty said. "Personally, I don't think—"

"That's for sure," Jasper said. "Maybe you and me should be moseying along, Ty."

"I have a couple of conditions," Daphne said. "I know how small towns are, and I don't think I'd have much luck starting a business if everyone thought I was Mr. Arnett's mistress."

Stony felt warmth climbing into his face as he realized that's exactly what folks around here would think.

"So I want everyone to say I'm Mr. Arnett's cousin from Hawaii."

"We can do that," Jasper said. "Right, Ty? Right, Stony?"

"Sure thing," Ty said.

Stony merely nodded, not trusting himself to speak. The idea of having Daphne as a mistress was a damn potent one.

"The second condition is between Mr. Arnett and me, if you wouldn't mind excusing us for a minute."

"Like I said, Ty and I have things to do. Let's go find that bedstead, boy."

"I'll bet it's too rusty to use," Ty said.

"Yeah, you would." Jasper grabbed Ty by the arm and headed out the door. Just before they left, Jasper paused and whistled for the dog, who trotted out with them.

Stony watched them depart and longed to follow. He'd rather not face Daphne alone just yet, which was why he'd hauled Jasper and Ty in on the discussion in the first place.

He was all jumbled up when it came to Daphne. If

he'd been told the truth about her he would never have made love to her, knowing she was just the kind of woman he didn't dare get too close to because he might begin to care too much and wind up like his father. But he hadn't known the truth, and he had made love to her, and damn it, he wanted to do that again. He couldn't allow himself to, of course. It wouldn't be fair to her. But that didn't stop the ache he felt every time he looked into her eyes.

With a sense of foreboding, he turned back to her and touched the brim of his hat. "Ma'am."

"First of all, I want you to know I tore up that hundred dollar bill you gave me."

Stony winced. "Did you put it in the trash can? Maybe I can—"

"I flushed the pieces."

"Oh." He sighed. That hundred bucks was probably only the tip of the iceberg as far as what this rodeo was going to end up costing him. "I guess you were pretty mad, and I can't say as I blame you. We need to get something straight, though. Jasper may have put stuff in the letters about me that was true in its way, but anything he said about my needing a wife was all in his head. I'm not interested in getting married. Not now, and not in the future."

She lifted her chin and her dark gaze snapped. "Don't worry, Mr. Arnett. I'm not going to try and trick you into matrimony. The man I marry will consider it an honor and a privilege, not the jail sentence you seem to think it would be."

"You got me wrong." Stony rubbed the back of his neck. "I'm not saying anything against you. I'm sure being married to you would be an honor and a privilege...for somebody else. I'm just not cut out for all that happily ever after stuff. Jasper was way off on that estimation."

An emotion flickered in her eyes and disappeared. "Apparently so. And because of that, I deeply regret what happened between us last night."

"You do?" His ego began to smart. "Was I...I mean, it wasn't so bad, now, was it?"

"That's not the point. You took my virginity."

Stony's mouth dropped open. "You mean that was for real? But..." He sorted through his limited information about virgins. "It didn't seem like...isn't there supposed to be blood or something?"

"Not in this case. I was a born-again virgin."

"Huh?" Stony wondered if his original thoughts about this woman were correct, and she was crazy as a bedbug.

"Seventeen months and twenty-seven days ago I took a personal vow of celibacy, not to be broken until I met the man I intended to marry. I made love to you because I thought you were that man."

Stony let out his breath in a long sigh of relief. "So you weren't *really* a virgin. Just on the wagon, so to speak."

"No, I was *really* a virgin. And the only reason I'm telling you this is that this morning, I took that vow again."

Stony blinked. "Just like that, you can call yourself a virgin again?"

"I can, and I do."

"Yeah, but Daphne," he said, chuckling, "last night

we...I mean, you can't really call yourself a virgin after what we...considering how much we...well, you know."

Her gaze was icy. "As far as I'm concerned, last night never happened. The slate's been wiped clean. It's as if you never touched me. As if no man ever did."

He wasn't sure he cared for that. He liked to think a woman couldn't erase the memory of his loving quite that easily.

"Although we'll be living under the same roof, and that might seem like a tempting situation, it won't be for me," she said. "I intend to stay pure until my marriage, which will obviously be to someone else. Do you understand?"

So she was making herself off-limits. That was a good thing, he thought, because he shouldn't have anything more to do with her, anyway. "It's fine with me," he said. And the minute the words were out of his mouth, he knew they were a lie.

"Good. Now, if you'll excuse me, I'll go pick out which room will be mine." Grabbing her suitcase handle, she started down the hall.

He watched her go. Her every movement teased and tantalized him. She might have put temptation behind her, but there it was running straight at him, ready to play. He groaned, pulled his hat low over his eyes and headed outside.

DRESSED IN CUTOFF JEANS and an old T-shirt, Daphne swept cobwebs from the corners of her little bedroom. As she cleaned, Stony's retriever stayed underfoot and made the job tougher, but she appreciated the company. Finally she put aside the broom and crouched down to scratch behind the dog's ears and ruffle her fur. The retriever licked Daphne's face, obviously overjoyed with the attention.

She looked into the dog's brown eyes. "You're way too nice to go without a name," she said.

The retriever panted happily and licked Daphne's face again.

"Stony can call you whatever he wants, but I'm giving you a name. And I have the perfect one. I'll call you Chi, which in feng shui represents life force. How do you like that? Wag your tail if you like it."

The dog's tail thumped so enthusiastically on the wood floor that a cloud of dust made Daphne sneeze.

"God bless."

She glanced toward the doorway and saw Jasper standing there balancing a mattress.

"Getting along with the dog, are you?" Jasper said.

"She's a great dog." Daphne gave Chi a final pat and went over to help Jasper with the mattress. "Did Stony ever try to find her owner?"

"Yep. Put notices up around town, but nobody claimed her. Best we can figure, somebody let her out on the highway, figuring she'd find a home."

"That's criminal." She took one end of the mattress and Jasper, the other, as they lifted it onto the springs of the old iron bedstead Ty had brought in earlier.

"Yep. But the thing is, she's been real good for Stony. He might not've wanted her at first, but now he'd be lost without her."

Daphne gave the mattress a final shove into place. "If that's a not-so-subtle message that I should worm my way into his good graces so he'll get used to the idea of having me around, forget it."

"I was just talkin' about the dog." Jasper gave the mattress a pat. "I never asked if you liked firm or soft."

"Firm."

"That's how I puzzled it out. I said to myself, A gal with backbone will want firm."

"A gal with backbone would be on a bus out of San Antonio by now." Daphne dusted off her hands and glanced at him. He was the source of her troubles, but she had a hard time staying angry with such a nice old guy. Meddlesome, but nice.

"Personally, I figure it takes more courage to stick around," Jasper said.

She propped her hands on her hips and blew her hair out of her eyes. "Look, Jasper, you'd better give up on this little scheme of yours, because even if I wanted to, which I don't, your boy Stony is totally against the institution of matrimony."

"I s'pose he told you that."

"Yep."

"And I s'pose you believed him."

Daphne threw up her hands. "You *do* still think it will work! Is that why you came up with plan B? You're beating a dead horse, Jasper. I'm happy to be back in Texas and I'd love to establish a business in this area, but that's all that's going to happen, believe me."

Jasper just smiled and walked over to the doorway, where he picked up a large plastic bag. "I got you a couple of pillows and some sheets, too. Stony don't have any of them double-size, just the king." He tossed the bag onto the mattress.

"I appreciate that." Daphne opened the bag and took out a package of sheets patterned in violets. She'd told Stony in a letter—no, she'd told the boys, it turned out—that she loved violets. A lump rose in her throat as she remembered one of her fantasies, that Stony would meet her at the airport with a bouquet of violets. She gazed at Jasper. "This whole thing is a stupid idea and it just isn't going to work. Why don't you just drive me to San Antonio this afternoon and we'll call it quits?"

He sat on the edge of the bed and patted a space next to him. "Come and set a spell, Daphne. You been working hard and you need a break."

"I don't need a break." Daphne went over and sat down, anyway. In spite of herself, she just plain liked Jasper. "You just want to brainwash me." She stroked Chi, who had positioned herself so she could lean against Daphne's knee. "Just like you did with those letters, making me think Stony was some sentimental guy who longed for the love of a good woman."

"He is."

She glanced at Jasper and rolled her eyes. "Ha."

"He just don't know it yet."

"Hey, that's my dream. To hook up with a guy who's totally clueless about himself. Sorry, but you'll have to get some other woman for the job."

Jasper didn't seem the least put off by her protests. He just kept looking at her with that same little smile on his face. "I'm plum amazed each time I set eyes on you."

"I know. It's hard to imagine somebody could be as gullible as I am, isn't it? But those days are over."

"I knew you'd be a good one, but I didn't know how good." He nodded. "This is all gonna work out fine. Hey, I nearly forgot." He unsnapped the pocket of his western shirt and pulled out a scrap of paper. "I rustled you up a couple of possibilities in town while I was in buying the mattress."

If that was Jasper's idea of bait, it was working, Daphne thought. She took the paper with growing excitement. If she could interest these people in her services, they would be the first clients who were exclusively hers, the first time she wouldn't have to share the commission or the credit with anyone. Boy, did that feel good. Maybe she shouldn't be so hasty to throw away a business possibility. "Thanks, Jasper."

"You're more'n welcome. Guess I'd better quit jawin' and get back to work." He patted her shoulder and stood. "Oh, and you gotta promise me you won't break up none of the furniture in these folks' houses. That good stuff was bought at a big store in San Antonio, not like Stony's old hand-me-downs."

Daphne looked up from the paper with a smile. "Actually, I don't..." She stopped herself from confessing the truth. The misunderstanding about her martial arts skill might still come in handy in the next few days. "I don't think Stony's furniture is all that bad," she finished. "It just needs some TLC."

Jasper gazed at her and slowly nodded. "Yep. And that about describes Stony, too."

5

STONY HAD SUFFERED through one hell of a day, not even counting the opening sequences with Daphne. Sure enough, a few head of cattle had worked their way through the break in the fence that would have been repaired that morning if it hadn't been for the interruption in routine. Rounding up the strays had turned into a major hassle, especially after a calf somehow got separated from its mother. Stony had spent two hours of hot riding finally getting them back together.

And then the fence had to be repaired, plus another section Big Clyde discovered was down in the process of looking for the missing cattle. To make matters worse, they were shorthanded. Jasper spent most of the day fetching a mattress for Daphne, and Ty was out of commission while he cleaned the iron bedstead and set it up in her room.

All this, Stony thought as he put up his horse and walked toward the ranch house, because the boys thought he needed a woman around. He needed a woman around like a fish needed a bicycle. Things were going along pretty damned good until Jasper got this fool idea into his head, turning Stony's predictable little world ass over teakettle.

He'd missed lunch, and he was starving. Ordinarily

he'd clean up a bit and head down to the bunkhouse for some grub, but he remembered telling Daphne they'd eat up at the house. Now that suppertime was here, he wondered how in hell he'd manage that. He didn't think there was anything in the kitchen except maybe a can of beans and a few slices of bread.

By the time he walked through the front door he'd worked himself into quite a mood. With daylight savings time there was plenty of light to see without any lamps being turned on, so he had no problem noticing that the living room was completely rearranged and all his magazines and catalogs were missing. All his weary frustration settled on one available target.

"Daphne!" he bellowed.

No answer. But the dog came trotting down the hall and over to him, tail wagging.

Patting the dog absently, he called Daphne's name again, and still got no answer. He knew she had to be here. She had nowhere else to go. He began to panic. What if something had happened to her? She'd stayed alone in the house most of the day, and maybe she'd fallen and hit her head, or been bitten by something she was allergic to. Damn, he should have sent somebody back to check on her during the day, to make sure she was all right.

Heart pounding, he started checking every room in the house. Finally he made it to the last bedroom down the hall on the left, and there she was, propped up on pillows, reading. Perfectly fine. He wanted to wring her neck for scaring him so bad.

She glanced up at him. "Hello."

"What do you mean *hello*? Didn't you hear me call you?"

"Yes."

"Then why didn't you say something?"

She regarded him quietly. "I may be enjoying your hospitality in exchange for my decorating services, Mr. Arnett, but that doesn't mean I have to come running just because you shout my name as if you were calling the hogs."

He was trying to follow what she was saying, but with her propped on a bed like that, he kept remembering how she'd been propped in his bed the night before. And last night she hadn't been calling him *Mr. Arnett*, either. "Could you go back to calling me Stony? It sounds a whole lot friendlier."

"That depends. There was nothing friendly about the way you yelled out *Daphne* at the top of your lungs when you first came in the door."

"I was afraid you'd been hurt or something."

"Really? That first shout sounded more like a wounded bear than a worried man."

He had been upset, but one look at her in those cut-off shorts and he couldn't for the life of him remember why. "Yeah, well, I probably shouldn't have yelled like that. I'm not used to...to having someone else around. You'll have to excuse my poor manners."

"Apology accepted." The set of her shoulders relaxed a bit.

He glanced around the spotless room, which contained only the iron bedstead with its mattress and some flowery sheets on it. "So this is the place you picked."

"I thought under the circumstances it would be best for both of us if I stayed as far away from your room as possible."

"Don't worry. I won't bother you." But she was going to bother him, he had a feeling. He might be wise to start sleeping in the barn. He'd put in a long, tough day, and he shouldn't have any energy left, but the longer he stood in the doorway of her room, the more he wanted to join her on that bed.

She put aside her book. "What's the plan for dinner?"

"To tell the truth, I don't know."

"We can just have whatever you usually have. I'm not picky."

He rubbed his chin and noted that he could use another shave. "I usually eat down at the bunkhouse with the boys."

"Oh." She swung her legs over the side of the bed.

He caught himself watching the way the fringe of the cutoffs moved against her thighs and he looked away again.

"Why don't you go ahead and eat down there, then?" she said. "If it's okay with you, I'll just poke around in the kitchen and see what I can find."

Guilt washed over him. "I'll bet you didn't have any lunch."

"Well, no, but that's okay. I just didn't want to go through your cupboards without discussing it with you first."

"Aw, Daphne, admit it. You're starving to death."

She met his gaze. "Okay, I could eat an entire

Thanksgiving meal, start to finish, by myself. I thought I'd keel over from hunger before you got home."

He grinned. "That's more like it. Let me clean up and feed the dog. Then we'll go into town for dinner."

"But—"

"You could poke around in the cupboards for a week and not find anything but bread and coffee, and maybe a can of beans. I don't know about you, but I'd rather have a steak."

Her eyes began to sparkle. "You're on."

"Good." He turned away. "I'll be ready before you know it," he called over his shoulder.

"I think I'll change, too."

He turned back to her. "No need. It's not a fancy place, and you haven't been out on the range all day. You're fine the way you are."

"Thanks, but I still think I'll put on something a little nicer."

"Hey, it's not like we're going on a date. You look fine."

The sparkle left her eyes.

He cursed himself for being an insensitive fool. Being tired didn't excuse being an idiot. "I'm sorry. I didn't mean it the way it sounded. I only meant—"

"I know exactly what you meant." All the pleasure had left her expression. "And you don't have to take me out at all. Go down to the bunkhouse. If you'll loan me your truck, I'll drive to the grocery store and stock up on a few things for myself."

"The store's not open this time of night. You're in the country now." He sighed and repositioned his Stetson.

"Daphne, we're in what you'd call an awkward situation here," he said.

She crossed her arms over her chest. "You could say that."

"It seems to be causing me to act like a first-class jerk."

"You could say that, too."

He hoped the little lift at the corner of her mouth was the hint of a smile. "I think we need to talk a few things out," he said.

"Maybe so."

"I think a lot better with a good meal in my belly."

"So do I."

"I'd like to take you to dinner, Daphne, if you're willing to go with a guy who has a bad case of hoof-in-mouth disease. I'll be ready in about fifteen minutes." He decided to leave her on that note. In fifteen minutes he'd know whether she'd accepted his invitation, such as it was. Ordinarily he was a lot smoother with women, but ordinarily both he and the woman understood the rules—fun and games, no entanglements. In this case there didn't seem to be a single rule worth using.

DAPHNE'S STOMACH was rumbling by the time she climbed into Stony's battered but serviceable pickup truck. She hadn't changed clothes, but vanity had tempted her to put on a little makeup, comb her hair and spritz some of her favorite cologne at her wrists and throat.

Stony smelled darn good, too, sort of a minty scent overlaying the aroma of clean male. Unless she missed her guess, he'd shaved in addition to showering. Both his white western shirt and jeans were freshly washed, and his hat was a newer, nicer version of the brown Stetson he'd worn out on the range today. He was one yummy cowboy as he steered the pickup down the dirt lane leading to the paved road into town.

Not that it seemed to matter to her libido whether he was grimy or clean. What he'd never know, because she'd never tell him, is how attracted to his range-weary look she'd been when he'd appeared in her bedroom doorway this evening. She'd longed to hold out her arms and welcome him home, smooth the frown of concern from his forehead and comfort him with kisses. As an added temptation, she knew how satisfying those kisses could be.

The sun dipped below the hills as they proceeded toward town, and the afterglow tinged the landscape rosy orange. She remembered checking the calendar before she'd left Hawaii. A full moon was on the way. Try as she might, she couldn't eliminate the wrench of disappointment every time she thought of how things might have been tonight if Stony had truly been the author of those letters.

Of course, if she just wanted sexual satisfaction, she'd bet good money Stony would agree to an affair with no strings attached. He'd apparently had a great time last night, and if she told him she'd changed her mind about being chaste until she found a marriage partner, he'd probably think that was a terrific idea. But tempting as Stony was, she refused to compromise her belief in meaningful lovemaking. She would wait for the love of her life to come along before giving up her virginity...again.

She opened her window and let the summer breeze flow in, bringing with it the scent of woods and wild-flowers. The rusty screech of a barn owl came from a thicket near the road. Hawaii was beautiful, no doubt about it, but she'd missed the familiar sights, smells and sounds of home. She took a deep breath and leaned her head back against the seat. She had a place to sleep, potential clients, and was about to have a good old-fashioned Texas beefsteak. Life could be worse.

"By the way, what did you do with my magazines and catalogs?" Stony asked, his voice casual.

She heard the careful tone of his voice and knew he was making an effort. No doubt his bellowing when he first came home had to do with her rearranging the living room this afternoon. "I stacked them, by date, in a box I found. I put the box in the front hall closet."

He let out a little sigh. "That's good."

"You don't really want me to redecorate the ranch house, do you?"

"Now, I didn't say that."

"You didn't have to. I can see you tense up each time you think I'm going to mess with something of yours. Jasper found me a couple of clients today. If I can get my business going, I'll be out of your hair in no time."

"I admit I tense up, but that doesn't mean I won't like what you do, once I get used to it. When I walked back through the living room tonight, I had to admit the furniture looks better the way you have it. You can move around the room easier."

Hearing that was gratifying, considering that was exactly what she'd been trying to accomplish. The ranch house would be a fun challenge if she didn't think he'd come in bellowing every evening when he discovered the latest change she'd made to his environment.

"You have to understand that I've never lived in a real house before," Stony said. "I bought this place as is, with the furniture and everything. The house seemed like a luxury hotel after being on the road all my life. It didn't occur to me to change anything. I just left it the way it was when I moved in."

She found herself watching the motions of his hand on the steering wheel. He drove with the practiced ease of someone who'd spent hours on the road. The tilt of his wrist and the flex of his fingers reminded her of the way he'd touched her while they'd made love. Damn him for being so good at it. "I can't imagine living the way you did, all those years," she said. "Keeping all your belongings in the back of a pickup as you traveled from one rodeo to another, sleeping in the truck so you could save the cost of a motel."

He glanced at her. "How'd you know I slept in the truck?"

"From your—from Jasper's letters."

He was silent for a while. "Where are they? The letters, I mean."

"In my suitcase. I thought of burning them today, considering they're all fake. But I'd already cleaned out the fireplace and I didn't want to fill it with new ash."

"You cleaned out the fireplace? You didn't need to do that."

"Oh, I especially needed to clean out the fireplace, to protect your reputation. Otherwise, everyone might not believe that I'm your cousin from Hawaii."

"I'm not following this. What has the fireplace got to do with my reputation?"

"According to the principles of feng shui, it happens to be located in the fame and reputation sector of your house. I think I'll make some sort of dried flower arrangement to perk it up. For the time being, your reputation and mine are linked, so I'm protecting my interests, too. At the very least, the ashes needed to be cleaned out so—"

"Hold it. My house has sectors? What in tarnation are you talking about?"

"If you're going to use that belligerent tone, I'm not going to explain it to you."

He took a long, deep breath. "I don't know what it is about you that gets me agitated so fast. I'm usually a very calm guy."

The darkness hid her smile. "Really. In the past twenty-four hours you've been in a bar fight, violated your principles and slept with a woman you believed to be a prostitute, nearly fired all your wranglers and started yelling at me the minute you came home. This is calm?"

"My routine's shot to hell, is all. And now you're telling me that cleaning out my fireplace is going to keep the town from talking behind our backs. It's too much for this ol' country boy, Daphne. All I want is a simple, peaceful existence. No frills. No hysterics."

She gazed at his profile in the light from the dash. After weeks of gazing at a photograph of him, she was fascinated by the play of different emotions over those familiar features. She'd fallen in love with a lie, but she was having a hard time convincing her heart of that, especially when he said things that echoed phrases from the letters. "Jasper must know you pretty well," she said. "He and the boys wrote something like that, about wanting a peaceful life."

Stony was silent for a while. "When we get home, I'd appreciate having those letters to read, if you don't mind. Might as well know what I was supposed to have said."

"You can just have them, period. I certainly don't want them anymore." Daphne hadn't been entirely truthful when she'd told him why she didn't burn the letters. In actuality she'd been unable to destroy them, although logically she knew that keeping them was only prolonging a fantasy that should be allowed to die a merciful death. If Stony took the letters, that would be the end of that, which was probably a good thing.

"Daphne, for what it's worth, I wish I could be the man you thought I'd be. But I'm just not."

"Of course you're not. How could you be?" Yet deep in her heart nestled a thought that wouldn't die, a belief that despite the evidence, he could be that man.

STONY HADN'T TAKEN a woman out for a meal since he'd moved to Rio Verde, so he should have figured it would cause comment among the residents. The steakhouse was the only one in town, so of course he saw lots of folks he knew. Each time, he introduced Daphne as his cousin from Hawaii who would be staying with him for a while. He was pretty sure they didn't buy the story.

After the fourth person had left their table with that information, Daphne giggled. "I remembered small towns were nosy, but this is ridiculous."

"Apparently I've been more of a topic of discussion than I thought," Stony said as their meal arrived.

"They don't believe this cousin stuff?"

"Nope." Stony cut into his meat. "Even if you did clean out the fireplace. But I imagine they appreciate that we came up with the story, instead of acting as if we don't give a hoot what people think."

"Do you?"

He paused with the fork poised in midair. "Do I what?"

"Give a hoot."

"Not really. But you do, so we'll do our best to make them believe us." He took a bite of his steak and had to admit it was better than any of the boys could cook up. And sitting across a restaurant table from Daphne was a sight more pleasant that eating in the bunkhouse with his wranglers.

Daphne plunged right into her meal without preliminaries, and he got a kick out of the obvious enjoyment she took in her food. Come to think of it, this might be the first decent meal she'd had since she arrived in Texas. Under the circumstances, she probably didn't have much of anything last night, either.

She paused for a moment and glanced up at him. "What are you smiling at?"

He hadn't realized he'd been smiling. "I guess because I haven't shared a dinner with a pretty woman in a long time, and I'd forgotten how nice it could be."

"Thank you." Her eyes took on that inviting sparkle again. "I haven't been very good at creating stimulating dinner conversation, I'm afraid. I was very hungry."

"That's okay. I like a woman who appreciates her food."

Daphne pointed at her plate with her fork. "This is one of the things I was looking forward to—top sirloin, Texas-style."

"Then go for it. Don't let me interrupt."

"Thanks. I believe I will. This is excellent."

It was excellent, Stony thought as he started in on his own meal again. The food didn't absorb all his attention, though. He couldn't help noticing how the candle in the red glass container sent flickers of light over her hair, the way the candles had done last night when he'd first walked in. Every time he thought about her lighting all those candles and carefully making the bed in preparation for his return, his heart ached for her. Jasper had really set her up for a fall, one she obviously didn't deserve.

Finally she nudged back her plate with a sigh. "That was wonderful. I think I'll live."

"Dessert? I hear they make good homemade pie here."

"You're going to think I'm a pig, but I'd love that."

"I don't think you're a pig. You probably haven't eaten in two days. Besides, you'll be keeping me company. I'm having some, too."

After their plates were cleared and they were waiting for the pie to arrive, he leaned his elbows on the table and gazed at her. "Jasper and Ty showed me the magazine with my picture in it."

She met his gaze. "And you're wondering why I wrote away to a mail-order magazine."

"Not really. It's not so easy to meet the right person, and from what I hear, you don't find them hanging around the bars. Writing to someone for a while, you'd get to know them before you got in over your head."

"Well, it was supposed to work that way."

"But you had to pick the ringer in the group. I was actually wondering why you wrote to me instead of the guy on the next page, who had a lot more muscles." He had an unsettling thought. "Or did you try him first and I was second best? God, maybe I was at the end of the line. Don't tell me if I was."

She laughed. "Goodness, you have got your ego involved with this, haven't you?"

"I didn't know I had until this minute. Forget it, you don't have to tell me anything. It doesn't matter, anyway."

"I guess not." She propped her elbows on the table and rested her chin on her hands.

He couldn't stop looking into her dark eyes. "Will you...write to somebody else in the magazine now?"

She shook her head.

"Why not?"

"At the risk of giving you a swelled head, I'll tell you that you were the only one I wrote to, the only one I planned to write to."

That made him feel way too good. He wanted to ask why but didn't dare, for fear he'd show how interested he was. Then their dessert showed up, and the subject got shuffled to the side while they both dove into melt-in-your-mouth apple pie with ice cream dripping over the sides.

It was possibly the most perfect dinner Stony had ever had in his life. Daphne was so easy to be with that he felt as if he'd known her forever. As he paid the check and held the door for her, he caught a whiff of her cologne. That sweet scent reminded him of what would make this evening even more perfect. Unfortunately, that was out of the question.

6

SURE ENOUGH, a full moon lit their way home. In Daphne's fantasy, she'd pictured them snuggled together on the front porch of Stony's house looking at that moon and planning their future together. It looked as if the atmosphere would go to waste.

"Beautiful night," Stony said.

"Uh-huh."

"Okay, I just have to ask. What's all this born-again virgin stuff? What made you get into that?"

She almost laughed. Obviously he was wishing they could go home and repeat last night's events, and this was the obstacle in the way. "A man," she said. "I met a guy in college, and I always assumed we'd get married some day. We decided to live together, to save money as much as anything, but of course we were... intimate."

"Of course. You can't expect a man and a woman to live together and not have sex. That would be weird. Well, except in our case," he added quickly.

"It turned out that all we were having was sex," Daphne said. "There was no love, at least not on his part. That became obvious when I got off work early one day and found him in bed with my best girlfriend. He said he had the right to do that, because we didn't have any piece of paper saying he couldn't."

"That sucks."

"I was pretty devastated." But perhaps he'd hurt her pride more than her heart, she thought.

"I'll bet. The guy was a jerk."

She appreciated his indignation. In fact, with every comment Stony made, he was endearing himself to her. She wondered if he realized how accurately Jasper had portrayed him, except, of course, about his wanting a wife. That was a huge exception, however.

"Anyway," she continued, "I took stock and realized that a lot of women I knew thought they were making love to the man in their life, when in fact the man considered it just convenient sex. We weren't valuing ourselves enough to save that important act for marriage, when you both promise to love, honor and cherish."

"Getting married doesn't guarantee the guy won't mess around on you."

"I know. And when you're with someone you get carried away by hormones and kid yourself this is a trustworthy person. That's what I liked about *Texas Men* magazine. Through the letters you could find out a lot about a person before sex scrambled your brains."

He blew out a breath. "It scrambled mine last night. I shouldn't have done what I did, Daphne."

She closed her eyes as she remembered exactly what he'd done. A wave of longing swept over her, making her skin tingle and her body ache for him. Opening her eyes again, she forced herself to make a rational comment. "Not many men would have turned away, all things considered." She swallowed. "I made it very easy for you to say yes."

"But now you've wiped it out of your mind, as if it never happened?"

"I...I'm working on it," she admitted.

"If you figure out how to do that, let me know. I could use some help."

She risked a glance in his direction. His hands were clutching the wheel for dear life, as if he had to hold on to something to keep from reaching for her.

"I understand your reasoning," he said. "And I respect it. But now that we've...been together, I just naturally find myself wanting to repeat the experience." He took a deep breath. "And we'll be living under the same roof, so that makes things even tougher."

She was really being tested, she thought. She was the one who'd put the restrictions on herself, and no one would know or even care very much if she lifted them. But then she'd be doing the very thing she'd vowed not to do again—make love to a man when all he wanted was simple sex. At least Stony hadn't pretended to be in love with her in order to change her mind. She valued that about him.

"Maybe I can afford a room in town," she said.

"I don't think there's much available. Besides, the shenanigans of my men got you into this, and as the boss, I'm responsible for what they do. No, I want you to stay. I even want you to fix up the place while you're there. I'm just asking if you'll...be careful. Try not to walk around in your nightgown in front of me, stuff like that."

"I might ask the same of you."

He gave her a sideways glance. Then he concentrated on the road again, but a smile twitched the corners of his mouth. "Are you saying I appeal to you some?"

"I picked you out of the magazine, didn't I?"

"Yeah, but you might have been disappointed by the real thing."

"Did I act disappointed last night?"

Stony glanced at her again. "You could have been putting on a show. Women do that."

"I don't."

He groaned softly. "You know, Daphne, I think we'd be wise to change the subject."

SOON AFTER THEY GOT BACK to the ranch house, Stony asked for the letters and said he was turning in for the night. He hoped the letters would put him right to sleep. Reading about himself would undoubtedly be a very boring subject. He bid Daphne good-night, whistled low to the dog, went into his room and closed the door.

He'd no sooner undressed and settled in to read than the dog scratched at the door. "You would pick tonight to want out," he grumbled, pulling on his jeans and opening the door. He started down the hall, expecting the dog to follow him, but instead she turned right and headed for Daphne's room. Once there, she whined and scratched at Daphne's door.

"Oh, for God's sake," Stony said. "Okay, stay with her, then." He refused to get his feelings hurt because the retriever had always preferred his company and now seemed to want Daphne's instead.

Daphne poked her head out of the door.

"She wants to sleep with you," Stony said. Then he

chuckled and shook his head. So did he, but he was too civilized to go whine and scratch at her door.

"That's fine," Daphne said, opening her door wide enough that he glimpsed satin, lace and bare shoulder.

He turned and started down the hall to keep himself out of temptation's way.

"Come on, Chi," she said.

That made him turn back. "What did you call her?"

Daphne stood half in and half out of the door, revealing just enough of herself that he noticed her blue nightgown was one of those shorty types he was partial to. His body reacted.

"I called her Chi," Daphne said, stroking the dog's head. "I know you didn't give her a name, but I...did."

He watched her fondle the dog and desire raged in him. When he spoke, his tone was harsher than he intended. "So you won't poke through my cupboards without permission, but you'll name my dog."

"It's just my name for her, because I didn't like saying 'Come here, Dog' all the time."

Come here, Daphne. Please.

"Dogs should have a name, just like people," she said. "But you don't have to pay any attention to this one."

I'm paying attention to you. I want you so much I can barely breathe. He cleared his throat, fighting for control. "What—what does that name mean?"

"In the Oriental culture, it stands for life. She gives this house life, so I thought it fit."

"Well, at least it's short."

"Yes. Good night, Stony." She slipped back inside her room and the dog followed her. She closed the door with a gentle click that seemed to echo down the hall.

He'd never wanted a woman so ferociously in his life. He weighed the option of walking down the hall and opening that door. She might protest. She might even resist when he first took her into his arms. But he remembered how she'd responded last night, and she wouldn't resist long.

But then where would they be? She'd have violated her code, and he'd feel like a jerk for taking what she wanted to save for her future husband. No, he couldn't give in to this punishing need. Jasper had a hell of a lot to answer for already, and the list was growing.

Inside his room once more, he closed the door, took off his jeans and climbed back into bed. Reading the damn letters should take care of his problem. His mind would be so occupied with Jasper's devious ways that he wouldn't have any room left for thinking about Daphne's sweet body.

The plan sort of worked. As he read, he fumed at all the details of his life that Jasper had revealed to Daphne. Jasper had painted a picture of a poor motherless boy raised by a grieving and drunken father, a boy who had grown to manhood starving for affection. What a line of bull.

True, Abe Arnett was drunk a lot, but he'd done his best to raise his son, teaching him everything he knew about riding bulls. He'd provided food and shelter, and that showed how much he cared, didn't it? Life was tough, and Abe had prepared Stony to handle that. He hadn't needed someone to fuss over him. He'd survived just fine, no matter what conclusions Jasper wanted to draw.

In fact, Stony hoped that one day his dad would decide to settle down on the ranch with him. It would be a way of paying him back for all he'd done over the years, and it would get him out of danger. At his age he shouldn't be dressing in a clown suit and dodging bulls, in Stony's estimation.

Last winter he'd talked Abe into paying him a visit, but he hadn't stayed long, claiming he was too restless to make his home there with Stony. After Daphne's reaction to the ranch house, Stony wondered if maybe it hadn't been welcoming enough to tempt his dad to stay. When Daphne was finished redecorating, he'd invite Abe back, maybe for Christmas, and try again.

Daphne. He wondered if she was asleep yet in her virginal bed sprinkled with little purple flowers. How he would love to make the springs of that old iron bedstead sing tonight. With a sigh he returned to the letters.

Before he could get into them again, he heard scratching at his door. The dog was back.

"Tarnation, Dog," he mumbled. "Or Chi, or whatever your name is." He threw back the covers and got up. As he opened the door to let her in, Daphne's voice floated down the hall.

"I think she wants the freedom to go back and forth between our rooms," she called softly.

That makes two of us, he thought.

"I'm leaving my door open so she can do that," Daphne said.

Great. Now he'd be able to walk down there without open-

ing any doors. She sure knew how to make things tough on a guy. "Okay," he called back. He wondered if he walked in his sleep. He almost wished he did and could claim that he'd been totally unconscious when he crawled into her bed and made passionate love to her all night.

"Good night, Stony."

"Good night, Daphne." He looked down at the dog, who definitely seemed to be smiling as she wagged her tail and gazed up at him. "You're causing trouble, you know."

The retriever shoved her nose against the palm of his hand.

Stony realized just how much trouble the dog had caused when he heard the creak of the iron bedstead as Daphne climbed between the sheets. With both doors open, he'd know every time she moved.

He got back into his own bed and tried to focus on the letters, but every squeak of Daphne's bed reminded him that she was lying awake only steps down the hall. His pesky imagination played with images of her in the satin and lace that barely covered the body he'd explored so thoroughly the night before. His only consolation was that every creak of the bedstead springs told him she wasn't having any better luck forgetting that than he was.

THE NEXT MORNING, DAPHNE stayed in her room until she no longer heard Stony rustling around in the house. After a night of frustration and vivid dreams, she didn't trust herself alone with him in the early morning hours, with two beds so handy. Better to let him get on his way before she appeared.

After she heard the front door close behind him, Chi came trotting into her bedroom.

"What? You didn't get to go?" She ruffled the dog's golden fur.

Chi just sat looking at her, panting and grinning.

"Okay, you're right. We're burning daylight." She showered and dressed, taking one forbidden moment to take the cap off Stony's after-shave and breathe in the minty scent that reminded her of being close to him. He kept the bathroom reasonably neat, but a peek into his bedroom revealed that he'd left the covers as tousled as they'd been when she'd first seen the room.

She fought an almost irresistible urge to fling herself into that tousled bed and wrap herself in the memories of loving Stony. But it was high time to get over the fantasy and on with reality.

In the kitchen she found a note propped against the coffeemaker, which was filled with freshly brewed coffee.

Daphne,
I'll be back by about noon so we can go into town. I'll give you a quick tour so you'll be able to find your way around by yourself later, and we'll pick up some groceries.

Stony

P.S. I left the dog with you. If you need me, send her to get me.

Daphne glanced down at the dog sitting by her feet. "Well, I do need that cowboy, but not in the way he means," she said. "So I guess we'll leave him alone this morning. After I have some coffee and toast, you and I will measure this house and start making some real improvements."

Shortly before noon Daphne stopped working and changed into a skirt and blouse, just in case she met any potential clients while she and Stony were in town. She was pleased with what she'd managed to achieve in a few short hours. An arrangement of wildflowers and dried grasses decorated the fireplace, and containers of flowers were scattered throughout the house, even in Stony's bedroom. Consulting her reference book, she'd determined the boundaries of the nine principle feng shui areas.

She'd concentrated most of her efforts on her room, figuring that was the safest area in which to give her creativity free rein until Stony got used to her embellishments. Moving furniture by herself wasn't easy, but she managed to angle the head of the bed against one corner. Then she hauled in a lamp table from the living room and set a candle, a vase of wildflowers and a couple of books on it. Next she positioned an oak dining chair next to the window. Finally she knotted two of her silk scarves together and draped them around the window frame with a sprig of flowers tucked into the knot.

After she finished dressing she started out of her room and turned back for one last appreciative look. Her sprig of flowers was slipping out of the knot, and her perfectionistic tendencies wouldn't let her leave it that way. Climbing up on the chair she'd used as a ladder in the first place, she reached up to fix the arrangement.

It was almost out of reach, and the slim skirt she wore wasn't as easy to maneuver in as her shorts had been. She stood on tiptoe, pressing her lips together in concentration as she stretched upward to adjust the flowers. Chi lay quietly nearby, watching her.

Then, without warning, Stony's voice came from the doorway behind her. "Looks nice."

With a gasp of surprise, she lost her balance. In the split second she knew she'd fall, she half turned and flung herself toward the bed. She kicked over the chair in the process, which knocked into the lamp table, sending the vase of flowers, books and candlestick crashing to the floor.

She heard Stony curse, her skirt rip and Chi yelp in pure terror as she hit the mattress so hard she bounced. Luckily the old iron bedstead held.

"Are you okay?" Stony hovered over her as she gasped for breath.

"Yeah," she panted.

"Good. I have to go after the dog. I'll be right back."

Still breathing hard from the shock, Daphne pushed herself up on her elbows and surveyed the disaster. The vase and candlestick were broken, and water was seeping toward her books. She leaped up and rescued them. Then she ran into the bathroom for a towel to soak up the water. She'd righted the chair and was picking up pieces of broken pottery and tossing them in a wastebasket when Stony came back.

"I got her," he said, crouching down to help her pick up the pieces. "Luckily she hadn't gone too far by the time I chased her down. Last time it took me an hour to find her."

Daphne glanced over at him. "What, she runs away?"

"Yep. Loud noises spook the heck out of her, for some reason. The front screen wasn't latched, but that's probably a good thing. If it had been she'd have gone right through it. When she gets like that she runs until she's exhausted, unless somebody heads her off and gentles her down. I figure something terrible happened to her when she was a pup, and it was connected to a loud noise."

Daphne picked up the soggy towel and sat back on her heels. "You startled me."

"Well, you told me not to bellow out your name when I came in the door."

Daphne rolled her eyes. "There has to be a happy medium between that and sneaking up on me."

"Like what?"

He really didn't know, she thought. He'd never lived in a house with another human being. You didn't have to call out greetings when you shared a camper shell with your father who was often drunk.

Her voice softened. "You could try calling 'Daphne, I'm home.'"

"Yeah, I guess I could." He picked up one of the flowers that used to be in the vase. "Do you want to save these?"

"Sure, if the stems aren't broken."

"I'll go get something to put them in." Gathering the fragile flowers carefully, he left the room.

Daphne used the damp towel to wipe up the floor

GET 2

HOW TO GET YOUR 2 FREE BOOKS AND FREE GIFT!

1. Peel off the MIRA sticker on the front cover. Place it in the space provided at right. This automatically entitles you to receive two free books and an exciting mystery gift.

2. Send back this card and you'll get 2 "The Best of the Best™" novels. These books have a combined cover price of $11.00 or more in the U.S. and $13.00 or more in Canada, but they are yours to keep absolutely FREE!

3. There's <u>no</u> catch. You're under <u>no</u> obligation to buy anything. We charge nothing – ZERO – for your first shipment. And you don't have to make any minimum number of purchases – not even one!

4. We call this line "The Best of the Best" because each month you'll receive the best books by some of today's hottest authors. These authors show up time and time again on all the major bestseller lists and their books sell out as soon as they hit the stores. You'll like the convenience of getting them delivered to your home at our special discount prices . . . and you'll love your *Heart to Heart* subscriber newsletter featuring author news, horoscopes, recipes, book reviews and much more!

5. We hope that after receiving your free books you'll want to remain a subscriber. But the choice is yours – to continue or cancel, anytime at all! So why not take us up on our invitation, with no risk of any kind. You'll be glad you did!

6. And remember...we'll send you a mystery gift ABSOLUTELY FREE just for giving "The Best of the Best" a try.

SPECIAL FREE GIFT!

We'll send you a fabulous surprise gift, absolutely FREE, simply for accepting our no-risk offer!

Visit us online at
www.mirabooks.com

before standing. She'd need to replace his vase, although she doubted he even realized there had been a collection of them in one of the top kitchen cupboards. She suspected even the dishes had been left by the previous owner. Stony had just moved in and started living, or what he considered living. Without beauty and grace around her, Daphne would consider it more like merely existing.

He came back with the flowers stuck into one of the ugliest drinking glasses Daphne had ever seen. It had some sort of action figures painted on the sides of it in garish greens and oranges, but she wasn't about to criticize his choice, not when he looked so earnest as he carefully balanced the arrangement and set it down on the lamp table. "How's that?" he asked.

"Terrific. Thank you."

"I'm sorry about your candlestick. It looked real pretty."

"I'm sorry about your vase."

"That was mine?" He looked up with a smile. "Didn't even know I had any vases. I wondered where you found something to put all those flowers in. The house looks nice, Daphne. Real nice. Especially this room. It was just a dust catcher before, and you've made it very..." He fell silent as the warmth in his eyes gradually turned to heat. "Very inviting," he finished, his voice husky. He cleared his throat and glanced away.

Her heart thundered in reaction to the stark desire she'd glimpsed in his eyes. There was no candlelight now, no full moon, no romantic setting. Yet the electricity between them was as strong as it had been last night.

"I, uh, noticed you fixed up the fireplace, just like you said you would." His chuckle sounded forced. "Now my reputation will be saved, right?"

"According to the principles of feng shui, it should help." *Unless you try to seduce your houseguest, in which case nothing will save your reputation, or your houseguest's heart.*

He glanced at her. "I need all the help I can get, I guess. Are you about ready to go to town?"

"I was." She glanced down at her skirt, which was split along the side seam at the hip, revealing a section of hot pink silk. "Give me a couple of minutes to change clothes."

His gaze had followed hers to the glimpse of underwear, and when she looked up at him, she could almost read the thought smoldering in his blue eyes. For one wild moment, she imagined him slipping two fingers into the ripped seam and tearing the garment away.

"I'll go check on the dog," he said, and left the room abruptly.

7

DAMN, Stony thought as he walked quickly down the hall. *Even in broad daylight I want that woman.* He couldn't remember the last time he'd felt this way. If he'd *ever* felt this way. He was used to nighttime passion, the kind ignited on the dance floor of a country-western bar and finished in a rented room. He'd had some good times, but when daybreak came, he'd always been back in control. Not with Daphne, apparently.

He walked into the kitchen and crouched down to stroke the dog's velvety head. "That lady's something else, Dog," he murmured. "Lord knows what I've let myself in for this time."

The retriever thumped her tail gently. She seemed over the worst of her scare, but she'd probably be content to sleep in the corner for the rest of the afternoon, judging from past episodes. Stony scratched gently behind her ears and tried not to think about pink underwear.

His first glimpse into Daphne's room had been enough to start his thoughts in the wrong direction. As she'd stretched up to reach that little curtain thing she'd made, her skirt rode up just enough to make the view interesting. The longer he'd stood watching her, the tighter his jeans had become, as he imagined slipping his hand up inside that little skirt.

Finally he'd decided he'd better say something instead of standing there gawking, and by speaking to her, he'd caused all the commotion. He hated for the dog to get so scared, but thanks to the dog he hadn't been able to join Daphne when she fell back onto the bed. Because he most probably would have flopped down on the mattress right after her, pushed her skirt up to her waist and satisfied the lust raging in him. In the middle of the day. Lord.

He heard her footsteps as she came into the kitchen, and he took a deep breath, hoping the worst of the madness inside him had faded.

"You think she'll be okay while we're gone?" she asked.

"I think so." Stony pushed himself to his feet. "Ready to go?"

"Yep." Daphne walked over and leaned down to stroke the retriever's head. "Take care of yourself, Chi." Then she straightened, picked up the purse she'd laid on the counter and started toward the front door.

Stony followed. This skirt had more of a flare and swing to it as she walked, which drew Stony's attention just as surely as the snugger one had. He had to face the fact his attention was tied to this lady as securely as if she'd thrown a heel loop on him.

"I think it's a good idea to get groceries and start using this kitchen," Daphne said as she opened the screen door. "The kitchen's in the wealth and prosperity sector of your house, so it needs more movement and energy if this ranch is going to be a booming success."

"Is that right?" Stony had no idea what she was talking about, but he enjoyed the sound of her voice just the same. He walked beside her down the stone path to his truck. "I keep waiting for the karate chops to start. Are you some sort of black belt in this?"

She glanced at him with a guilty look on her face. "I have a confession to make. Feng shui has nothing to do with self-defense."

He stopped in the middle of the walkway and stared at her. "You mean you just attack people straight out?"

She seemed to be working hard not to laugh. "Feng shui isn't about fighting, at all. The boys misunderstood, and I was angry so I let the misunderstanding go on. It's a philosophy. Part of it has to do with managing space, which is how I got interested. It fits right in with interior decorating."

"Well, I'll be damned. You don't smash boards with the edge of your hand or do those fancy kicks?"

She grinned. "Nope. I just decorate rooms."

He continued toward the truck and opened the passenger door for her. "The boys will be mighty disappointed. This morning Jasper told me they were hoping you'd feng shui the bunkhouse and break up some of that old furniture they're sick of."

"Do they really want to redecorate the bunkhouse?"

Stony forced himself to think about her question and not the glimpse of leg he got when she climbed into the truck. "Well, yes and no." He closed her door and walked around to get behind the wheel. "To tell the truth, they mostly want to meet you. Jasper and Ty are the only ones who've seen you, after all, and the rest of them—Ramon, Andy and Big Clyde—are dying of curiosity after all those weeks of writing to you." He started his trusty old pickup.

"Big Clyde?" She chuckled. "You really call him that?"

"That's what he told us to call him when he hired on. And he's big, all right. Steady as they come, too, with real horse sense. It says something about Jasper's salesmanship that he was able to convince Big Clyde to go along with the magazine trick." Stony closed his window and flipped on the air-conditioning, something he didn't always use but thought Daphne would appreciate, seeing as how she was all dressed up.

"Jasper is something of a salesman, isn't he?" Daphne said.

Stony glanced at her. "What's he been trying to sell you? Never mind, let me guess. He's trying to convince you that I'm a lonely, motherless cowboy who doesn't realize how much he needs a woman around. Am I right?"

"He cares about you, Stony. Maybe he's a little misguided, but—"

"He's a *lot* misguided."

"Maybe so."

Stony shifted uneasily in his seat. "Anyway, you're here now, and the other hands want to meet you, so I promised them I'd bring you down there this afternoon after we get back from town."

"I can walk over to the bunkhouse myself," she said. "I'm interfering with your schedule enough as it is."

"I have some business to discuss with Jasper, anyway." And between now and then he'd think of something that would qualify, he thought. He didn't want her spending time with his wranglers without him being around. Ramon fancied himself a lady's man and Ty had already indicated an interest, so Stony wanted to keep a close eye on the goings-on between the men and Daphne. That was all he needed, to have his wranglers start mooning around after this woman. It was bad enough that he was doing it.

DAPHNE NOTICED HIS possessive stance and decided not to comment on it. Still, it was interesting that he was willing to grocery shop rather than have them both eat down at the bunkhouse, and that he didn't want her wandering over to see the wranglers by herself. If he truly had no interest in continuing a relationship with her, he shouldn't care.

"Then you have a total of five men who work for you?" she asked.

"They're *supposed* to work for me. Half the time I think they work for Jasper and I'm just the one providing the paychecks every month." He sighed. "But I guess that's okay. Without Jasper I never would have made it through these first couple of years. He advised me on what cattle to buy, how much hay to plant, when to move the herd—nearly everything. His family owned a ranch when he was growing up. They lost it, so he took to rodeoing, but when I told him I wanted to buy a ranch, he volunteered to be my foreman. Whenever I had doubts about my plan, he kept me pumped up. Without Jasper, there would be no Roughstock Ranch."

"Now, *that* wasn't in the letters," Daphne said.

"If I'd been writing them, it would have been. I owe Jasper a lot, which is why I couldn't fire him, not even for this stunt."

"Then I'd like to help him and the hands redecorate their bunkhouse. Why don't you tell me something about the rest of them, so I'll have a better idea of where to start?"

"Now, don't go making too much of this project, Daphne. You need to concentrate on the people in town."

She almost laughed at his not-so-subtle attempt to limit her interaction with his men. "I promise not to get carried away. Just fill me in on everyone's personality."

Although she had to pull some of the information out of him as they continued down the road, she gradually formed a picture of Andy, only twenty and a red-headed prankster who often got himself and anyone around him in trouble. Ramon was apparently a sentimental type who was also a smooth talker, as opposed to Big Clyde, a man of few words.

"I think those men could all benefit from having a feng shui arrangement in the bunkhouse," she said at last.

Stony grinned. "You mean they have a reputation sector, too?"

"I can tell you don't believe a word of this."

"Not much. It doesn't make sense to say that if you fix up a part of the house, it's going to magically improve your life, unless you unplug a drain or something. Now, that makes sense."

"Then I suppose you wouldn't be interested in hearing about feng shui astrology, either."

"Astrology? Oh, boy." He shook his head. "I wouldn't be telling people about this, Daphne. We're not very New Age in Rio Verde."

She refused to let one bullheaded cowboy rain on her parade. "I have to tell them. It's the basis of my new business. Without feng shui I'm just another decorator."

He chuckled. "In Rio Verde you'll be the *only* decorator. In fact, I'm sort of surprised that Jasper got you two prospects. Most folks around here hang a set of horns over the fireplace and a picture of cowboys on horses over the couch and call it good."

"That's because nobody ever suggested something else. I think feng shui could be a big hit."

"You don't have to take my advice, but I'm warning you to go easy on it. I can't picture folks around here believing that a vase of flowers is going to protect their reputation or make them healthy, wealthy and wise."

"Don't they tack horseshoes over the barn for good luck?"

"I'm not saying we're not superstitious but we've got our own brand, and imported brands might not go down too well."

"We'll have to see about that, won't we?" She thought he was shortchanging the residents of the town and maybe even his men on the ranch. At least she hoped so.

"I'd just hate to see you disappointed."

She thought about that as they reached the outskirts of town, and she wondered if he'd also hate to see her business fail, which might make him continue to feel responsible for her.

She turned toward him. "Look, if I don't get a decorating job lined up in two weeks, I'll go back to San Antonio and look for work in a big department store or something. So don't worry that I'll hang around forever, trying to get people to buy into my feng shui ideas."

He looked startled by the announcement. "Two weeks? Well, I don't know. That doesn't seem like enough time, Daphne."

She'd thought he'd agree immediately and look relieved to have the matter settled. His hesitation surprised her. "I think it's important to set a timetable, so that you won't feel as if this is some sort of open-ended arrangement and begin to resent my being here."

He parked the truck in front of a small café and turned to study her. "The fact is, I don't resent your being here. And that surprises the hell out of me. Now, let's get a bite to eat before we go shopping."

LUNCH IN THE CAFÉ PROVED to be a repeat of dinner, as people came up to be introduced to Stony's "cousin" from Hawaii. Daphne caught a couple of them winking at Stony as they said the word *cousin.*

"I'm going to start fixing this situation," Daphne said. "The next person who comes over to be introduced is getting a pitch for my decorating business. Maybe that will make them realize that I'm here to open a business and that you and I aren't lovers."

"At least not currently," Stony said, nonchalantly picking up a french fry.

Warmth coursed through her. "I told you I've erased that from my memory. As far as I'm concerned, nothing ever happened between us."

He dipped his french fry in ketchup, popped it in his mouth and chewed as he gazed at her. Then he swallowed and leaned forward. "Then why do you get that pink flush on your cheeks and that sparkle in your eyes when you talk to me?"

"I don't." She could feel the blush rising to prove her lie.

"You do. These folks aren't blind, Daphne."

"You're the one who's giving them ideas. I've caught you looking at me with those big cow eyes."

He tugged his Stetson down and cleared his throat. "I was probably just staring into thin air, thinking about the price of beef, and your face happened to be in the way."

"So you don't think about that night, either?"

"No more'n you do, sweetheart."

"Then I can't imagine where people get the idea that there's something between us." She noticed a paunchy cowboy heading toward their table. "Okay, here comes someone. I'm going to see if he wants his house decorated."

The man clapped Stony on the shoulder. "Haven't seen you in here in a coon's age, boy."

Stony glanced up. "Been busy, Hiram. How's it going?"

"The drought's a pain in the behind, but other than that, okay. Are you going to introduce me to this lovely lady?"

"Sure thing. Hiram Connelly, meet my cousin from Hawaii, Daphne Proctor."

"Ma'am." Hiram touched the brim of his hat and smiled, revealing a bad-fitting set of dentures. "For your sake, Stony, I hope she's your kissin' cousin."

Daphne winced. This might not be easy. "Stony was kind enough to say I could stay at his place while I set up my business here in Rio Verde," she said.

Hiram hitched up his belt. "Jasper said something about that when I saw him in the feed store yesterday. Somethin' about you being able to order drapes and carpeting and such for folks here in town."

"I'm an interior decorator."

"That's it," Hiram said with another big smile. "I knew there was a fancy name for it."

"Maybe you'd be interested in my services yourself, Mr. Connelly?"

"Well, the wife was talking about ordering new drapes, but she usually just gets 'em out of the catalog. Are your prices gonna be about the same as the catalogs'? I'd like to help out, if it didn't cost too much more for the drapes."

Daphne was beginning to see the scope of the problem, but she pushed bravely on. "Actually, my job is to help you and your wife choose colors and fabrics to enhance your lifestyle. That fee is in addition to the cost of the items, but my clients consider my services well worth the money."

Hiram looked doubtful.

"Is your life as exciting as it could be, Mr. Connelly?"

Stony coughed.

Hiram's face grew pink. "I shoulda said first off, the drapes are for the living room. We put new ones in the bedroom last year. They block out everything."

Now it was Daphne's turn to blush. "That wasn't what I meant." She hurried to repair the damage. "When I decorate a house, I use the Oriental technique of feng shui to enhance your home and your lives."

"Fung whatzit?"

She barreled on. "For example, let's say your health hasn't been the best recently."

"My arthritis kicks up in the winter, is all."

"I would evaluate the health-and-family area of your house, make adjustments to allow the *chi* to flow more freely, and see if that didn't help your arthritis."

Hiram stared at her as if she'd just touched down from Mars. "Nothing's wrong with the plumbing. Our *chi*, or whatever you called it, flows just great. And I don't think you get arthritis from bad plumbing, anyhow."

Daphne was about to explain the meaning of *chi* when Stony put a hand on Hiram's arm, and she had the good sense to shut up.

"Take it from me," Stony said, "the woman can make your house real pretty. I'm finding out these decorators have all sorts of fancy names for things, names that simple men like us will never understand. Have Gloria give Daphne a call. By the time the kids and their families come home for the Thanksgiving holiday, you'll have a showplace."

"I dunno, Stony. I thought the drapes would be about all we'd need."

"Hiram, trust me. You have no idea what you need

until Daphne shows up and tells you. Besides, I'll bet Gloria would have fun talking to Daphne about all this stuff, and you'd be a hero 'cause you suggested it."

Hiram smiled at that. "You're probably right, but I have a feeling this is gonna cost me."

Looking pleased with his success, Stony tipped back his chair and winked at Hiram. "You can't put a price on having a happy woman around, right?"

Hiram's smile grew broader. "You tell me. Up until recently, you've claimed not to want any woman around, happy or otherwise. Seems like your 'cousin' here is domesticating you, son."

"Uh, well—" Stony's cocky grin faded.

Daphne rushed to his rescue. "His aunt Thelma, who's my mother, will be glad to hear you think so, Mr. Connelly."

"Then you mean you really are his cousin?"

"Why, Mr. Connelly, the family almost begged me to help Stony upgrade his living conditions when I came down here to open my business."

"Upgrade?" Stony protested.

"Gee, will you look at the time?" Daphne said, consulting her watch. "Agnes Farnsworth will be wondering why I haven't called."

"Agnes is gonna have you decorate her place?" Hiram asked.

"That's the plan," Daphne said. At least it was her plan. Soon she'd discover if Agnes agreed with her.

"Well, that settles it." Hiram tugged the brim of his hat down. "If Agnes got her house all fixed up with this fung shwazie stuff and Gloria didn't, I'd never hear the end of it. Gloria will be calling you, Daphne. Nice meetin' you."

"Same here, Mr. Connelly." After he left she glanced at Stony and lowered her voice. "Thank you for helping me get the job. I'm sorry about the 'upgrade' remark, but it seemed like the sort of thing a cousin would say, and I wanted to convince him that's all we were to each other. The way you were talking me up he was convinced I was your mistress."

Stony rubbed his chin. "Yeah, you're right. He was. And I guess you are fixing to upgrade my living conditions, at that. Your room is already up about ten notches from where it used to be."

"But that upgrade comment sounded superior and snooty, and that's not how I really feel about working on your house or anyone's. I just love making things look nice. If I can also improve people's lives through feng shui, so much the better."

His gaze grew speculative. "According to this philosophy of yours, what sector is your room in?"

She was hoping he wouldn't ask. "I don't know if I've done enough to substantially change anything for you in that area, so it probably doesn't matter."

"Come on, Daphne." He grinned at her, his expression teasing. "You took a depressing little hole in the wall and made it into a nice room. Don't you think I deserve to know how my life is going to change as a result? What part is it?"

She pushed back her plate. "We should get going. We have to shop, and I need to call Agnes Farnsworth before Gloria Connelly gets to her."

"You're stalling, Daphne. How am I going to know if

this stuff works unless you tell me what changes to expect?"

She looked him straight in the eye. "It was the only bedroom I thought I should pick under the circumstances, and I didn't locate myself there on purpose. I would prefer to have located myself somewhere else, to be honest."

"So you do believe your changes will make a difference in my life, or you wouldn't be so skittish about this question. What's that corner of the house supposed to affect in my life, Daphne?"

She swallowed nervously. "Love and marriage."

8

STONY WORRIED ABOUT that love-and-marriage sector for the rest of the afternoon.

He thought about it while they stopped at a pay phone so Daphne could call Agnes Farnsworth and her other contact from Jasper, Elmira Wermser. Daphne had success with both Agnes and Elmira after telling them that Gloria Connelly had agreed to have her house feng shuied. She made an appointment to meet with Agnes the following morning and Elmira in the afternoon.

Stony smiled and congratulated her, but the back of his mind was still occupied with that pesky love-and-marriage corner of his house.

He told himself it was just some silly superstition, but he'd lived around superstition all his life as a rodeo man. In his experience, if someone believed in something strong enough, superstition or not, it generally came true.

That meant Daphne expected his life to change in the areas of love and marriage. To top it off, she was living in the house, so wouldn't the same thing happen to her? Stony didn't like it, not one bit.

Maybe that was why he picked a fight with Daphne while they were shopping for groceries.

"We got meat, we got potatoes, we got bacon and

eggs, bread and beer," he said as she started toward the vegetable bins. "That's enough."

"What about stuff for salads?"

"I don't eat salads."

"That's not true. You ate one with dinner last night."

"It came with the meal. I don't like to pay for something and not eat it."

She folded her arms and gazed at him. "All right. I'll pay for the vegetables, then." She started toward the bins again.

"Don't buy any on my account," he called after her. He noticed her picking up a bundle of broccoli. "And don't be buying any of that. I hate the smell of that when it's cooking almost as much as I hate the taste when the darned stuff is cooked."

She put it in her basket, anyway. "I happen to love it, and it's very good for you. I'll cook it while you're gone if you're so fanatical about it."

"That's not fanatical. That's normal common sense. Broccoli is just plain plug ugly from the get-go. I don't want to even look at it in the refrigerator."

Her jaw tensed as she moved toward the display of lettuce. "I'll put it out of sight, okay?"

"I'll smell it, anyway! I can smell it from here!"

She whirled toward him, eyes blazing. "If you don't sound like some grumpy old bachelor set in his ways!"

"I suppose you feel obliged to *upgrade* my diet, too, don't you? Well, forget it, lady. That green smelly stuff is not my speed."

She held up the broccoli and shook it in his direction. "It's only a green plant, for heaven's sake. You act as if I'd suggested bringing home a live skunk."

"That's exactly what it smells like when you cook it! A damned polecat. And I don't know why you have to go stinking up my kitchen when you could have something else like...like corn!"

She dropped the broccoli into her cart and wheeled it toward him, her chin high, her eyes glittering. "And I'll have you know that corn's not a vegetable, Mr. Smarty Pants."

"Is so."

"Is not," she snapped. "It's a grain, dammit." She grabbed a chicken out of his cart and threw it into hers. "That's all I want from your basket. Go buy your food. I'll be out in a while with my food, which I will cook and eat when you're nowhere in sight." Then she wheeled her cart directly toward the broccoli and started loading up on it.

"Fine!" He was almost to the checkout counter before he came to his senses. The whole point of this shopping expedition had been to buy food they could cook together while she was here. If she planned to cook for herself and not include him, he wouldn't need the steaks and potatoes in his cart because he could eat down at the bunkhouse like he usually did. And that would leave her to eat alone every night. It didn't sit right.

He pulled his cart off to one side and waited for her to come along. Finally she did, and boy, did she have hers piled high with veggies. She could feed a corral full of rabbits for a week on that load.

She caught sight of him and immediately looked in the other direction. Nose in the air, she started to sail right past him.

"Okay, you don't have to cook it when I'm gone."

She paused, regal as all get out, and turned her head slowly in his direction. "Did you speak to me?"

"I guess I can stand to have a little broccoli in the kitchen now and then."

"Really?" She widened her eyes as if in total shock. "Oh, I wouldn't, if I were you. It's not manly. The smell will probably make you impotent."

He choked and glanced around to see if anybody might have heard her. Sure enough, Sarah Rankle, the woman who ran the beauty parlor, was staring at them with a knowing smile on her face. The incident would be all over town by tomorrow.

He sighed. "Let's just go home, Daphne."

"Are you quite sure you can ride in the same truck with a bagful of broccoli?"

"If it means we can get out of this store and on down the road, I would ride in the truck with a bagful of road apples. We're causing a scene."

"You started it."

He was having trouble getting that big chunk of pride down his gullet, but he finally managed. "You're right, I did. I apologize."

Her smile burst forth like the sun after a rain. "Apology accepted." She pushed her cart forward and he followed with his.

As they unloaded their baskets onto the conveyor belt at the checkout counter, she turned back to him. "I bought some cheese. I make a wonderful cheese sauce to go on the broccoli. I'll bet you've never had it like that."

"No."

"You'll love it."

"Look, I'm not planning to eat—" He caught her look of warning and closed his mouth. "I'm sure I will love it," he said, smiling sweetly at her. "Yum, yum."

Because he didn't shop for food, Stony didn't know the matronly checkout clerk whose name badge read Trudy, but she apparently knew who he was.

"A man should eat his greens, Stony," she said as she bagged the groceries. "Protects your prostate."

Daphne pretended great interest in the tabloids near the counter, but Stony could see the grin she was trying so hard to hide.

"Thanks for the advice, Trudy." Stony paid the bill. "I'll keep it in mind."

Daphne must have had some sympathy for him because she kept her laughter contained until they were in the truck. Then she broke up, laughing until the tears came.

"Just knock yourself out," Stony said. "Doesn't bother me to be the laughingstock of the whole town. No, ma'am."

She wiped her eyes and grinned at him. "You deserve it, making such a big deal out of my buying a little broccoli."

"A *little*? We could feed the town of Rio Verde on what you bought, if they'd even eat it, which I doubt. I'll bet the store owner was relieved to see you come along and clean him out before the stuff went bad."

She glanced at him, her eyes still filled with laughter. "Trudy was right, you know. Eating greens is good for you."

He liked it when she laughed, even if he was the butt

of the joke. He liked the flush on her face and the sparkle in her dark eyes. Fighting with her hadn't solved
any of his problems. He still wanted her.

"I'm glad to hear you're concerned about my prostate, too," he said casually. He checked her reaction to
that before returning his attention to the road. She
looked a little nervous. "From what I've heard, there
are other things that are good for a man's prostate besides eating his greens. If you're going to worry about
my health, shouldn't you be tending to all areas of it?"

Let her deal with that, he thought, smiling to himself. But she'd probably have some snappy comeback.
He'd sort of enjoyed the way she stood up to him on
the broccoli issue.

When she remained silent, he wondered if he'd been
too crude. "Hey, it was just a little joke." He turned his
head to look at her. "I—" Whatever he'd been about to
say vanished from his mind when he saw desire burning in the depths of her eyes. "Oh, sweetheart."

In seconds he'd pulled off the road and cut the engine. He flipped off his seat belt and turned toward
her.

"No," she said in a throaty whisper. "I bought ice
cream. It'll melt."

"Let it melt." He combed his fingers through her
hair and cupped the back of her head. "And don't tell
me you've wiped the other night out of your mind. It's
driving you crazy, too."

The answer was in her eyes. With a muttered oath he
reached around and unfastened her seat belt.

"Stony—"

"Don't worry. I couldn't make love to you in the

front seat of this truck if I wanted to. I'd kill myself on the gearshift. But I can damn sure kiss you, and that's what I intend to do." He smiled at her. "I won't compromise your virginity with a kiss, will I?"

She let out a long sigh that sounded like surrender. "It's a mistake."

"It won't be my first." Angling his head, he urged her toward him and tasted her rosy lips. Lord, but she was ready for that kiss. With a whimper she got right into it, scooting as close as the gearshift would allow and opening her mouth for his tongue.

It seemed years since he'd enjoyed the delights of her mouth, and he couldn't seem to get enough. His erection strained against the fly of his jeans as he delved deeper and she moaned softly against his mouth. Enough of his brain remained in working order to keep him from unbuttoning her blouse. After all, they were right near the road in the middle of the afternoon.

But no one could see when he reached beneath her skirt and pressed his fingers against her damp underwear. Pink. He remembered his glimpse of the color from earlier in the day when her skirt had torn. Thinking of that inviting pink silk barely covering her femininity only drove him crazier. He knew how she'd feel if he pushed the material aside and touched her there. He remembered how warm and moist she'd been when he'd slipped his hand between her thighs on the night they'd made love. He remembered the way she'd cried out when he brought her to orgasm.

She wanted that now.

From outside a horn honked.

"Go, Stony!" hollered a voice.

Dazed and disoriented, Stony lifted his mouth from Daphne's and gazed out the front window. A red pickup sped off down the road, arms waving wildly out of both windows. He recognized the truck—it belonged to Sam, who owned a neighboring ranch.

He looked back into Daphne's flushed face.

Her voice was no more than a breathless whisper. "We should go."

"Yes. This isn't the time or place."

"There...is no time or place."

"Are you so sure?" He pressed his fingers firmly against her.

She gasped. "Just because I want you doesn't mean I have to give in to that."

"No, I guess not, sweetheart." He eased away from her. Damn, but his jeans fit tight right now. "But if you decide being a virgin isn't all it's cracked up to be, come and see me." He refastened his seat belt. "I'll be just down the hall."

DAPHNE CHANGED INTO JEANS and a T-shirt while Stony put away the groceries. She changed her damp underwear, too. So much for pretending she had no lingering feelings, she thought. Not only were they lingering, they were raging out of control.

She and Stony hadn't made any conversation the rest of the way home. Everything had been said and her choice was clear. She could live in keeping with her principles and sleep alone, or she could spend her nights locked in primitive passion with Stony for the rest of the time she stayed under his roof. Damned if that second option didn't sound mighty good right now.

Daphne zipped up her jeans and sighed. She'd worked through this question before, and had come up with an answer—short-term gain wasn't worth sacrificing long-term satisfaction. Sure, she could gamble on love making its way into the equation with Stony somewhere along the line. She was half in love with him now, although she realized that could be a carryover from the letters, which he'd inspired but definitely didn't write. As for him, he was very much in lust, but Daphne didn't kid herself that he loved her.

When she returned to the kitchen, the groceries were all put away and Stony was giving Chi one of the doggy treats Daphne had thrown into the cart at the last minute. For reasons she couldn't explain, she drew great comfort from watching him with his dog.

She leaned against the counter. "I see you found my little extravagance."

"Yeah. She loves them. Big Clyde always does the shopping for the ranch, and I never thought to ask him about getting some of these."

"I thought it might be a way to retrain her so she won't get so scared about loud noises. You could make a little noise, like slapping the top of the table, and then when she starts to run you could get her back and give her a treat while you talk to her."

Stony straightened and brushed off his hands. "That's a good idea. I'm afraid someday she'll take off and get out on the main road where she might get hit by a car. When she gets scared like that, she doesn't show good sense. I've had to tell the boys they can't have target practice out behind the barn anymore, because she can't stand it.''

Daphne walked over and leaned down to give Chi a pat. ''She's lucky to have an owner like you.''

He looked startled. ''Oh, she's not really my dog. I'm just keeping her for the time being, because she had nowhere else to go. Somebody's bound to claim her sooner or later.''

''After all these months? I doubt it.'' She used both hands to give Chi a thorough scratch behind the ears. ''You're Stony's puppy, aren't you, Chi?''

The retriever whined softly and thumped her tail against the blanket.

''You're dead wrong,'' Stony said.

At the harsh note in his voice, Daphne glanced up in surprise.

''She just happens to be here, and with more training, she might even become a cattle dog. But she doesn't belong to me, in the sense that she's a pet. I don't have pets. Don't believe in them.''

Daphne started to argue that by giving the dog a home, food and affection he'd turned her into his pet, but she had a feeling logic didn't figure into Stony's pronouncement. He was kidding himself that he hadn't lost his heart to this dog, so he wouldn't have to face his vulnerability if something should happen to Chi. But Stony was vulnerable, Daphne thought. More than he knew.

He glanced up at an old kitchen clock on the wall. ''We'd better get on down to the bunkhouse before it gets any later. The boys are probably pacing the floor wondering where we are.''

"Wait. Let me get my feng shui book. That way I can show them there's not a single karate chop in the whole thing."

"Personally I'd advise you to let them go on thinking you could throw them over your head if you had a mind to."

She frowned. "You want them to be afraid of me?"

"The idea has a certain appeal."

"And why is that?"

"Think about it, Daphne. You're the only woman on a ranch with a bunch of cowboys. My men treat ladies with respect or I wouldn't have them working for me, but they can hardly be blamed for having certain thoughts. If they're afraid you could kick them into the middle of next week, they'll think twice before acting on those thoughts."

She folded her arms. "Then maybe I shouldn't have told you the truth, either."

He shook his head and smiled. "With me it makes no difference, because after the other night, I know what's at stake. And Daphne, I'd risk getting kicked black and blue just to have the chance to make love to you one more time."

The magnetism of his blue gaze nearly drew her across the kitchen and into his arms. Using willpower she didn't know she had, she started out of the kitchen. "Let's go, then."

"All right." Stony gave Chi a quiet command and the dog stayed behind.

Daphne wondered if Stony realized how the dog loved him, or if he chose not to think about such uncomfortable things. Probably the latter.

They had to pass the barn to get to the bunkhouse, and Daphne remembered how much she'd longed to get back on a horse again once she arrived. She'd pictured long sunset rambles with Stony as they toured the Roughstock property. That wouldn't happen, but maybe he'd loan her a mount for an hour or two.

"I realize it's a lot to ask," she said, "but I'd love to borrow one of your horses for a ride one of these days," she said. "That is, if you have one you could spare."

"I reckon I do." He glanced down at her. "I didn't know you could ride."

"I suppose that's one of the things that confuses me. I gave you my whole life history in those letters, but I keep forgetting that you didn't read them. Jasper and the men did. They know how much I love riding, but you don't."

"I guess there's a lot I don't know."

"Guess so." She wished he'd read her letters. Of course, she didn't even know if Jasper and the men had kept them. Maybe somewhere along the line she'd ask.

The bunkhouse was a low, rambling wooden structure in need of paint. She might suggest that for starters. There was movement at one of the windows, and she imagined the curious men peeking out and ducking back, not wanting to be caught sizing her up.

Stony gave a sharp rap on the door. It opened immediately.

"Come in, come in," Jasper said, his mustache twitching. "We're all here."

"I'll just bet." Stony stood aside so Daphne could go ahead of him into the bunkhouse.

A card game had obviously been in progress before she arrived. The men had stood up from the table so quickly that somebody had knocked over a chair. They all smelled of soap and shaving cream, and they whipped off their hats and stood shifting their weight uneasily.

"So here are the guys I've been writing to for weeks," Daphne said, gazing at them each in turn. She already knew Jasper and Ty, of course, and from Stony's description she picked out Big Clyde, a hulking man with a kind face. Stony had failed to tell her how attractive Ramon was, even with the split lip he'd earned in the bar fight. Stony's silence on Ramon's sex appeal made her smile to herself. And then there was Andy, his green eyes wide and a cowlick sticking up from his carrot-red hair.

"We're honored that you're here," Ramon said, flashing even white teeth.

"No joke!" Andy said. "It's like a visit from the queen of England or something! Except I don't think the queen knows any fighting moves, so this is even better."

"I'm warning you boys," Ty said. "You might not be so happy when she starts breaking up the furniture. Before y'all know it, you might not have a table to eat off of or chairs to park your butts in."

Andy looked excited. "Are you going to break the furniture? It's just that Ty's right about the table. It's the only one we got. So maybe you could start with something else. Ty's got an old nightstand that—"

"Hey!" Ty said. "What about that wobbly shelf of yours, Andy?"

Daphne smiled. "Don't worry. I'm not here to break anything."

"But she could," Stony added. "You should see this woman in action."

"Has she tried some of her moves on you, Stony?" Andy asked.

"A few. Impressive."

Daphne was sadly afraid she was blushing. Darn Stony, anyway. She knew he wasn't talking about self-defense. In his subtle way, he was reminding her about what they'd shared, just in case she happened to forget.

She cleared her throat. "I want to thank you, Jasper, for those two leads. I have appointments with both women for tomorrow."

"And Gloria Connelly should be calling," Stony added.

"Hot damn," Jasper said, a grin appearing on his weathered face. "That's great news."

"In the meantime," Daphne said, glancing around, "would y'all like me to suggest some decorating changes in your bunkhouse?"

"It's gonna cost us plenty, right?" Ty asked. "I mean, you'll have to start from scratch, because we ain't got a thing worth saving, to tell the truth, so—"

"Will you let the lady say somethin' before you go rainin' on the parade?" Jasper glared at Ty. "We'd love to have Daphne help us fix up the place, wouldn't we, boys?"

Everyone except Ty gave an enthusiastic response.

"I want her to teach me some feng shui moves," Andy said. "Might come in handy next time we go into town for a couple of beers."

"Next time we go into town, we're leaving you home, amigo," Ramon said, gingerly touching his injured lip.

"Okay." Daphne rubbed her hands together and assessed the room—bunks lined up military fashion and shelves and nightstands tucked in between them. She wished she could consult her book. She wasn't exactly sure what to do, but the pressure was on to do something, and fast. "First thing we need to do is get rid of these right angles. The table needs to be in the middle of the room, and the beds arranged in a circle out from there, like spokes on a wheel."

The men all stared at her.

"We're promoting the free movement of *chi*," she explained. "*Chi* is the Oriental word for the life force, and it likes curves better than straight lines."

Jasper recovered himself first. "Y'all heard the lady," he said, striding over to his bunk and tugging it toward the center of the room. "Start movin' furniture, boys! We're gonna get that *chi* circulatin', by doggies!"

9

Stony had never heard such nonsense in his life, but his men were acting as if they loved the idea of rearranging their furniture.

Daphne edged over to him. "I was going to suggest painting the outside, but that might take a lot of time and money, huh?"

"Yep." He watched in amazement as the circle of bunks took shape. Big Clyde produced a tape measure and proceeded to make sure each bunk was the same distance from the table and the other bunks.

"So how about if I just suggest painting the door?" Daphne said. "Would that be too wild?"

"Just the door? I guess not. Somebody could do that in one evening, without taking daylight for it."

"Good. And while I'm in town tomorrow, I'll look for some inexpensive material for curtains."

"*Curtains?*"

"Something jaunty."

"What's next?" Andy said, coming up with a huge smile on his face. "Are you gonna get up on the table and show us how you can stand on one foot, like they did in *The Karate Kid*?"

"She's not getting up on the table," Stony said. "Not now, and not in the future."

"Aw, come on, Stony," Andy said. "I've never seen a real expert."

"According to the expert," Stony said, "you boys are about to get some curtains."

"Curtains?" Andy's smile faded.

"Yeah, curtains!" Ramon said, coming up to clap Andy on the back. "You know, those things that civilized folks hang in their windows. Daphne is trying to give you a little class, señor Andy."

"Curtains just get dirty," Ty said. "And they never hang straight, and they usually don't match nothin'. I tried havin' curtains once, and they just hung there and got dirty."

"So you wash 'em," said Big Clyde.

"Exactly," Jasper said, glaring at Ty. "We'd love to have us some curtains, wouldn't we, boys?"

Each of the cowboys, with the exception of Ty, tried to outdo the other in his enthusiasm for curtains. Stony had never seen the like. His men had gone loco.

Big Clyde whipped out his tape measure again. "I'll measure them windows for you, ma'am."

Daphne smiled happily. "Thank you. That way I'll know how much material to buy. I also thought I'd pick up a small can of paint in town, so we can paint the front door. You can't expect good fortune to find your door if it doesn't stand out a little bit. What do you think of red?"

"Red?" Stony almost choked on the word. "You're gonna paint the bunkhouse door *red*? It'll look like a cathouse!"

Daphne gave him a withering look. "It will not. It will invite the *chi* inside."

"That ain't all it'll invite," Stony mumbled.

"Just watch. A red door will enhance everyone's career."

"You reckon Stony's gonna give us a raise?" Andy asked.

"Don't count on it, son," Stony said. "After buying curtain materials and red paint, I may be broke."

"Nonsense," Daphne said. "The ranch will start doing better economically as a result of the changes, so it all evens out."

"In order to do better, we need some rain," Big Clyde said. "There's not enough grass, and them cows ain't gettin' as fat as they should."

Daphne slapped her hand against her forehead. "I can't believe I haven't thought of this before. Y'all need a fountain."

Stony's brain began to whirl. The woman was a runaway train.

"Well, now, we mostly just drink out of the tap," Jasper said. "A fountain is fine for parks and such, but I don't think—"

"Maybe she means a fountain for the cows," Andy said, his eyes twinkling. "I mean, why didn't we think of that? We could just put one of them drinkin' fountains out in the middle of the pasture, and the cows could all line up, just like kids on a playground. And then—"

"We don't need no fountains with you running off at the mouth," Jasper said. "I'm sure Daphne wasn't talking about settin' up some fountain for the cows."

"No." Daphne grinned at Andy. "But what a picture. You have quite an imagination, Andy."

"See, that's the chief trouble with him," Ramon said.

"Actually, I wasn't talking about a drinking fountain, either for people or for cows," Daphne said. "I was talking about a water feature."

Everyone looked blank.

"For decoration," Daphne said. "You know, an attractive display of running water."

"Ah," Ramon said. "A water feature. *Si, señorita*. Like in the center of a village."

"Exactly. Only something elaborate like that would cost a lot of money. I'll bet we could build one for next to nothing in the ranch house yard. We could just dig up some—"

"Hold it." Stony was beginning to worry. "Curtains and paint are bad enough, but now you're talkin' excavation."

"Oh, not much," Daphne said. "And really, building a fountain is a marvelous way to coax the rain into coming. Leave it to me and the boys. In no time, you'll have a lovely water feature right outside your front door. If you leave your bedroom window open, you'll be able to go to sleep listening to the soothing sounds of water rippling over rocks."

He gazed at her. "I suppose I could use the distraction."

Daphne's cheeks grew pink and she looked away. "Is everybody agreed on the fountain?"

"I think it sounds real nice, Daphne," Jasper said. "Just tell us what you need us to do."

"One thing for sure, we won't have to split any of the rocks for it," Andy said. "Daphne can just whack those rocks with her bare hand. Wham!"

"It'll attract bugs," Ty said. "And the water will turn green and slimy before you know it. I vote we don't build it."

"Well, you're outvoted," Ramon said. "There was a fountain in the *plaza* of the village where I grew up in Chihuahua. I used to play there all the time. It's a good idea."

"I'll help dig," Big Clyde said.

"What about the water for it?" Stony asked, figuring he was the only man here with a working brain. "Is it smart to use water for a fountain when we're in the middle of a drought?"

"Maybe she's right, though," Ramon said. "Maybe a fountain will end the drought. You never know."

Stony sighed. Once again, control seemed to be neatly taken out of his hands. Oh, sure, he could refuse to cooperate. He was the owner of the Roughstock, and his men wouldn't cross him if he really put his foot down. But Stony believed in a more democratic working situation than that. If painting the bunkhouse door red and building a fountain in his front yard would make them all happy, he'd go along.

"Okay," he said. "I guess the Roughstock is about to get a water feature."

DAPHNE CHOSE NOT TO COOK broccoli for dinner that night. She recognized a man strained beyond the bounds of patience, so she suggested they pan-fry a couple of steaks. The evening was too warm to turn on the oven. While Stony tended the steaks, she made a salad and set the table with the chipped dishes from the cupboard.

She had to make do without either placemats or a tablecloth, and there was certainly no centerpiece unless she brought in one of the vases of flowers from the living room. Longing for some atmosphere, she considered setting a candle or two on the table, then decided against it. Creating a romantic setting was just asking for trouble.

"Steak's ready," Stony announced from his position in front of the stove.

"Salad's ready." She moved past him with the brimming salad bowl. She'd been careful to keep a reasonable distance between them, although it wasn't easy in the kitchen's close quarters.

"Then let's eat." Stony served the steak.

Daphne sat down quickly so he didn't have to decide whether or not to hold her chair. He'd done that at the restaurant the night before, and she'd been charmed with his manners, but perhaps it would be better if he didn't perform those little courtesies for her anymore. They could lead to interludes she wouldn't be able to control.

When Stony joined her at the table, he picked up his napkin and looked around at the table setting. "You know, I wouldn't have been able to tell you if I even had two plates that match."

"I can see why. The dishes are in the cupboard every which way. The whole setup needs to be revamped."

He shrugged. "It never mattered to me. I only use a coffee cup and a glass now and then. I don't sit at the table except to do paperwork. This is the first time I've actually eaten a meal here."

"According to what I know about feng shui, you

could be sabotaging the success of the ranch by not using this kitchen much."

He cut into his steak. "Should I leave the water running in the sink and pretend that's a fountain?"

"I realize you don't believe a word of this, but as for
the sink, you should keep the drain closed so wealth
doesn't flow away. Same thing goes for the bathroom,
which is in the creativity-and-children area of the
house."

His gaze snapped up to hers. "I'm a rancher. I don't
need to be creative. And as for children, I'll never have
any."

Her first thought was that he had a medical condition that would prevent him becoming a father. That
would explain a lot about his reluctance to marry. Men
were often skittish about such things. "I'm sorry to
hear that, Stony. But you know, lots of people adopt
these days, so I wouldn't rule out—"

"I didn't say I *couldn't* have children. I just said I will
not have them. I don't want a wife, and I don't want
kids. Simple as that."

His matter-of-fact announcement startled her. Men
often said they weren't ready for a commitment, but
they usually left the door open for marriage sometime
down the line. Stony had just quietly closed and locked
that door.

"Why?"

He continued eating his steak, but he wouldn't look
at her. "Just don't."

A dark lump of misery settled in her stomach. "Do
you dislike women and children so much?"

"Nope." He swallowed a bite and glanced up at her.

"Kids are okay, as long as they're somebody else's. And I happen to like women a whole lot, as you might have been able to tell the other night. I like dogs, too. That doesn't mean I want a pet or a wife."

"They are *not* in the same category!"

"I didn't say they were. I was just making a point. The salad's not bad, by the way. Why aren't you eating?"

"I...don't feel very hungry." She pushed back her chair. "Listen, why don't you give my steak to Chi? I think I'll go for a walk before it gets completely dark."

He regarded her quietly. "I know it sounds terrible that I don't want a family. Most guys do. But I know myself, and I'm just not the type. I'm sorry if that upsets you, but it's the truth. If you thought otherwise, you're probably thinking of the guy in those letters. That guy isn't me."

"That's obvious." She crumpled her napkin beside her plate and stood. "I'll be back to help with the dishes. I just need some air."

"Maybe I'd better go with you."

"I'd rather go alone." He was the last person she wanted with her at the moment.

"Then take the dog with you. There might be snakes out this time of the evening, and she'll let you know if they're around."

Daphne had forgotten about poisonous snakes. And dusk was a prime time for them. "Come on, Chi," she said. "Take a walk with me, okay, girl?"

The retriever hopped up from her bed in the corner and trotted over to Daphne's side. Daphne started out of the kitchen.

"Don't go too far," Stony called after her. "Please."

"I won't. I don't want to cause you any problems."

Once outside the front door, she fought tears. Her dream was finally and truly dead. Even though she'd told herself to abandon all hope that Stony could ever be the man she wanted, she hadn't done that until now. She'd allowed herself to continue to care for him, even to fall a bit in love with him.

She hadn't expected miracles. Stony would naturally be resistant to having a woman thrust on him, but deep in her heart, she'd believed Jasper knew what he was doing.

Wiping furiously at her eyes, she headed in the direction of the barn. Horses were good company at a time like this. Horses and dogs. She was glad Chi trotted along by her side, giving silent comfort.

The barn door stood open on this warm summer night, and once inside, Daphne took a deep sniff, enjoying the familiar scent of hay, old lumber, leather and horses. A cricket chirped nearby, and a horse blew air through its nostrils. She could hear the sound of munching. Dinnertime.

A pretty little horse with a white star on its forehead poked its nose out of the first stall and gave Daphne the once-over.

"Darn, I should have brought carrots," Daphne said, heading toward the friendly horse. The light was fading fast, but she could still make out that it was a chestnut, one of her favorite colors. "Or broccoli." The laughter seemed to stick in her throat. Her little scene with Stony at the grocery store seemed a million years ago. They'd had a domestic spat, and the very typical nature of it had fed her fantasy that there might be a happily-ever-after to this story. She'd been a fool.

"What's your name, pretty baby?" she asked the chestnut as she peeked into the stall and discovered the horse was a mare, as she'd suspected from the delicate bone structure. She stroked the mare's soft muzzle and looked into her brown eyes. "I'm surprised they keep you around," she murmured.

The mare's ears flicked forward.

"I hate to break it to you, sweetie, but this ranch is strictly for manly men." Daphne scratched along the base of the mare's burnt orange mane. "The owner doesn't want pesky females in his life. It's a wonder he keeps any heifers, except he is in the business of raising cattle. He must hate that."

"Daphne, is that you in there?"

She sighed. She wasn't in the mood to deal with Jasper. "It's me."

"I wager you and Stony had a fight."

Daphne continued to stroke the mare's neck. "Not really."

"Sure sounded like it to me. He came down to the bunkhouse lookin' ornery and wanting to scare up a card game. Brought his bottle of J.D. When I asked him where you were, he said he didn't know, but the dog was with you, so you were probably okay."

"He doesn't really care if I'm okay or not, Jasper."

"Oh, I believe he does." Jasper came over to her and leaned against the stall door while he fished in his back pocket for his can of chewing tobacco. "He made it sound real casual, but he pretty much asked if I'd mosey around the place and see if I could find you. Said you wouldn't want him to look for you, but somebody better, seein' as how you didn't know your way around yet and it was gettin' dark."

Daphne turned toward him. "Jasper, give it up. Stony might feel responsible for me the way he'd feel responsible for any living creature on this ranch, but he'd rather not have me around if he could avoid it. I've let you talk me into believing otherwise, but it isn't true. It's cruel to lead me to believe Stony could ever care for me."

Jasper stuck a plug of tobacco under his lower lip and closed the can carefully. "I've played fast and loose with you, ma'am, and I admit that."

"That's putting it mildly. You've had me on a roller coaster, Jasper, and I don't appreciate it."

"I don't blame you none. I done it all for that boy, you know. It just about killed me when he said he'd never get married. If his daddy only realized..."

Daphne knew it wasn't wise to hear yet another story that might soften her heart, but Stony was a puzzle she couldn't resist trying to solve, in spite of everything. "What do you mean?"

Jasper settled his tobacco beneath his lip and leaned against the stall. "I wish you coulda knowed his mama. Jolene was quite a woman—educated, strong-minded. While they traveled around to all the rodeos, she home-schooled Stevie, which is why he talks better'n most of us and even knows some poetry she made him learn by heart."

"Wait a minute. Did you just call him Stevie?"

Jasper looked startled. "Did I? Must've been thinkin' about the old days that did that. Stony's given name is

Steven, but after Jolene died he turned into such a little poker face that everybody took to calling him Stony. I don't suppose anybody but me remembers his real name. 'Course I would, bein' his godfather and all.''

"His godfather. I didn't realize." That certainly helped explain Jasper's meddling ways, Daphne thought. He obviously took his role seriously.

"Not many know that, either, and I'd appreciate it if you wouldn't mention that I told you either of them things, his real name or me bein' his godfather. The other hands don't know, and I think Stony wants it that way."

"I understand."

"Now, Jolene, she was the strong one in that marriage, and she passed that on to her son. Stony's daddy is basically weak, and when Jolene died, he started on the bottle and hasn't stopped since."

Daphne could feel her anger toward Stony slipping away, and with it the protection anger could give her against a broken heart.

"Kids have funny logic sometimes," Jasper continued. "Stony made up his mind that he shouldn't get married, because if somethin' happened to his wife, he'd turn into a drunk like his daddy. He could barely stand losin' his mama, and so he thinks lovin' someone is too dangerous. Riding bulls, that don't faze him. But love, that scares the spit out of him, even though he's got a lot of love just achin' to get out."

"He loves you," Daphne guessed.

"I believe he does. And the dog and that bay gelding of his. And even his sorry excuse for a daddy. From the signs, I think he could come to love you."

"Oh, Jasper." Daphne sighed and rested her head against the chestnut's warm neck. "You do ask a lot of a girl."

"I found me one who's up to the job."

"I'm not so sure. Did you see the look on his face when I suggested a fountain? He hates change."

"You're gonna get your fountain, ma'am. Whatcha need me to do?"

Daphne lifted her head and glanced at him. "A truckload of big, smooth stones would be a start. I'm thinking of making a waterfall."

Jasper nodded. "I'll see to it."

"The waterfall will be a piece of cake, Jasper, but I have my doubts about turning Stony around."

"Just so's you don't give up. Come on, I'll walk you back to the house. Everythin' will look brighter in the mornin'. Always does."

After Daphne bid Jasper good-night, she went into the kitchen and found it clean. There was a note from Stony saying her dinner was in the refrigerator. She found it there, neatly wrapped. She shared some of the steak with Chi and used the rest to make herself a sandwich.

From the sound of things, Stony wouldn't be back very soon, so she decided to occupy herself by rearranging the kitchen cupboards. While she was at it, she even moved the table to a different spot and took a vase of flowers from the living room to put in the middle.

Finally she felt tired enough to go to sleep, so she turned out the lights and went into her room. Too bad she didn't have a granny gown to wear to bed, she thought as she put on another of her filmy, short night-gowns. But she'd chosen nightwear with a different scenario in mind.

Jasper's revelations had helped her understand Stony better, she thought as she drifted off to sleep. But now that she knew what she was up against, she wondered if Jasper wasn't foolishly hoping for a miracle.

10

A LOUD CRASH brought Daphne wide awake and sent Chi tearing out of the bedroom, her toenails skidding on the wooden floor. As Daphne leaped out of bed, heart pounding, she heard a string of colorful curses in a voice she recognized. With a sense of relief, she headed down the hall. At least the intruder was a known quantity.

The kitchen light flashed on just before she reached the doorway, and the cursing had changed to muttering. She walked just inside the room and surveyed the damage. In a repeat of her bedroom accident, the table had been tipped over and the vase of flowers lay broken and mangled on the floor. Chi cowered in her bed in the corner, and Stony was on his hands and knees, his hat shoved to the back of his head while he talked to the dog.

"Ish all her fault, Dog," he said, weaving a little. "Ever'time I turn around, somethin's been moved. I jish wanted a glash a'water. Ish that too mush to ashk?"

"I moved the table," Daphne said. "I didn't know you'd try to find your way around in the dark."

Stony continued to address Chi. "Ish her. Devil woman."

"Oh, that's me, all right." Daphne walked over and

picked up the small plastic trash can. "All my attempts to make the place look nicer are really an evil plot to cast a spell on you and make you my slave."

"I wish she'd be my shlave," he muttered to the dog. "I'd kish her all over."

Even though Daphne knew how drunk he was, that remark had an effect on her. Her hand trembled slightly as she crouched down to pick up the pieces of broken vase and the flowers. He must have stepped on them, because they were mangled beyond hope.

"I think you'd better go to bed, Stony," she said, carefully kneeling in the carnage. "Chi seems okay, and I'll clean this up."

Still on all fours, he scooted around so he was facing her. "Come with me," he said, a goofy grin on his face.

"I don't think so."

"Why not?" He sounded like a whiny little kid. "I wash good to you."

Too good. She continued picking up the shards of glass. "It's against my principles. Did you win at cards?"

"Didn't play long. Jashper and me took a bottle t'the barn. Got a little shmashed."

"I noticed."

"Le's go t'bed, you'n' me."

"No. Besides, you're too drunk to accomplish anything, anyway."

"Am not." He started crawling toward her.

"Wait! There's glass—"

He yelped and picked up his hand. The heel of it was bleeding. "Somethin' bit me!"

"Oh, for heaven's sake. Don't move." Taking care

not to step on any remaining bits of glass herself, Daphne got up and went to the counter, where she ripped a paper towel off the roll and dampened it at the sink. Grabbing a whisk broom, she brushed the area in front of him quickly before kneeling down and taking his hand in hers.

She pressed the damp paper towel against the cut, then took it away again to assess the injury. Fortunately it was small. A few moments with the pressure of the damp paper towel should stop the bleeding long enough to get a bandage on it.

"I can shee down the front a your nightie."

She glanced up at him. "Don't look."

"I like to. Beaut'ful. Let me kish you there."

"No." She checked his wound again, all the while trying to convince herself his drunken suggestions weren't arousing her. But they were.

"It'll feel s-o-o-o good."

"Enough of that talk, Stony. I'll help you up and we'll go into the bathroom for a bandage. Then you can get right into bed." Moving under his armpit, she draped his arm around her shoulders and tried to get him up off his knees.

He didn't budge. "Come t'bed with me. Wanna be inside you."

"No. Now, come on and help me here."

"Okay." He heaved himself upward with obvious effort. "Mebbe I'm drunk."

"It's possible." She did her best to keep him steady as they wobbled across the kitchen and down the hall to the bathroom. Along the way his hat fell off.

"Need m'hat."

"I'll get it later." Once inside the bathroom, she leaned him against the wall while she turned on the light and searched for a bandage.

"You're pretty as a piglet," he mumbled. "Wanna kish you all over."

"So you said." She found the bandage and put it over the cut, smoothing the adhesive strip gently in place. "Okay, now to bed."

"I need help."

She looked into his eyes and saw a gleam there, as if through his whiskey-induced fog he'd figured out how to coax her to bed with him. "I'll get you as far as the bed, but I'm not joining you in it. I'm holding out for a man who truly loves me. Let's go." She hooked her shoulder under his armpit and they made their clumsy way back down the hall.

"I truly love going t'bed with you, Daph."

"That's not the same thing as loving me."

"Close."

"Not even close." She got him through the door and over to the bed. "I guess you can sleep in your clothes." Releasing her hold, she allowed him to topple sideways onto the mattress. As he did, he pulled her down on top of him.

She struggled, but he had a pretty good grip for a drunken man. Something crinkled under his shirt as she tried to get away. "What's inside your shirt?"

"Letters."

"My letters?"

"Yup."

"Did you read them?"

"Yup. Pretty nightie." He rolled over, pinning her beneath him.

She didn't know if the letter-reading had been Jasper's idea or Stony's, but apparently that's what had kept Stony so late, having drinks with Jasper and reading her letters. But now wasn't the time to discuss them, if he even remembered what he'd read.

"Let me up, Stony."

"In jus' a minute." He cradled his head against her breasts. "Nice." With a sigh of contentment, he went to sleep.

Gradually his hold on her relaxed, and she knew that soon she'd be able to wriggle out from under him and leave him to sleep off his overindulgence. But she didn't need to rush. Closing her eyes, she reached up and gently ran her fingers through his hair.

STONY AWOKE LATER THAN usual, and the chirping birds outside his window gave him no pleasure whatsoever. He threw a pillow at the open window and the movement scared the birds away. Sinking back onto the bed, he massaged his aching head.

He'd been plowed the night before, but not so plowed that he didn't remember knocking over the table and Daphne taking care of things after that. He'd pulled her down on the bed with him, rolled on top of her, and...if he'd made love to her, he sure didn't remember. And if he *had* made love to her and couldn't even relive the pleasure now, that would really tick him off.

Chances were he hadn't been successful with her, considering he was still wearing all his clothes, even his boots. He doubted she would have dressed him afterward.

Then he remembered the packet of letters and patted his shirt. Still there. Unsnapping his shirt, he pulled out the envelopes, a little crinkled for having slept on them all night. Reading about Daphne's hopes and dreams in those pages had been a painful experience, dulled a little by good old Jack Daniel's.

One thing was certain from the letters—Daphne was determined to choose the right husband the first time and not end up like her mother, who was on her fourth marriage. Daphne had thought he was her answer, her knight in shining armor. He must be a hell of a big disappointment to her.

He smelled bacon. She must be up and cooking already. With a groan he heaved himself out of bed and staggered down to the bathroom. It was filled with her scent and he groaned again. Thanks to her, he was hungover, feeling guilty and also extremely horny. Damn poor combination.

A shower and shave improved things some. Wearing only a towel, he returned to the bedroom. He almost wished she'd come back to check on him and find him half naked. Then nature could sort of take its course, and at least one of his problems would be handled.

Cagey woman that she was, of course, she didn't show up while he dressed. She could catch him off guard by parading around in little bits of satin and lace—last night they'd been yellow, as he recalled—but she apparently sensed when he might be wearing nothing but a smile and stayed away.

And to be fair, it was really his own damned fault he was in this condition. If he hadn't already made love to her, he wouldn't be going crazy wanting seconds. He understood now why they gave out free samples at the ice cream shop.

Although his stomach felt a little queasy this morning, the aroma of cooking bacon tickled a sweet memory of his mother making breakfast around a campfire when they'd spent a few days in the mountains of New Mexico. He wasn't prepared for the fierce ache in his heart as that memory took hold.

He walked over to the window, fighting unexpected emotions as he gazed out on the ranch. His mother would have loved this place. She'd talked about owning a ranch some day, and it hit him this morning that he'd probably bought it with her in the back of his mind. And that was pretty stupid, considering she would never see it, unless he wanted to believe all that religious stuff about people looking down from heaven.

He glanced skyward, feeling ridiculous for even doing it. A hawk circled in the clear sky. Yeah, sure. His mother had come back as a hawk and was scouting out the ranch her son had bought. What a bunch of bull.

Still, he kept watching the hawk, an uncomfortable lump in his throat, until it wheeled out of sight over the granite bluffs on the far horizon.

"Stony?"

He turned and saw Daphne standing in the doorway wearing a sky blue summer dress. He tried to say something, but his throat wasn't working quite right, so he just stood there like an idiot, staring at her. All the loving words she'd written in the letters came back to haunt him. She looked so sweet, so beautiful, that he would have given all his rodeo buckles just to be allowed to hold her for a few minutes.

"Are you okay?" she asked.

He nodded and cleared his throat. "Rough night."

"I know."

He was afraid she did know—the terror that had made him drink too much last night as he was reading her letters, the fierce needs she inspired in him, the bottomless well of sadness he never wanted to tap. The expression in her dark eyes told him that she saw more than he'd ever revealed to another human being. With her, his famous stone face didn't seem to stay put.

"I...have some bacon ready." She made a small gesture toward the kitchen. "I wasn't sure if you'd want any, or how you like your eggs."

"Thanks. I think I will eat a little something." He managed a crooked smile. "I didn't smell broccoli, so I guess I'm safe."

Her answering smile took his breath away. He realized if he walked over to her now and took her in his arms, he might never have the strength to let go.

He swallowed. "Go ahead. I'll be right there."

Uncertainty flashed in her eyes and was gone. "Okay." She turned away and started back toward the kitchen. "Sunny-side up or over easy?" she called over her shoulder.

"Sunny-side up. Cheerful-looking." His mother had always said it like that. He'd eaten his eggs that way all his life, but he'd never repeated the phrase until this minute. He rubbed a hand over his face. He almost felt as if he'd been thrown from a bull and things were breaking up inside him. He needed something, or someone, to hang on to. But Daphne was not a safe choice.

As Daphne drove into town that morning, she wondered for the hundredth time if she'd made a mistake in not going over and putting her arms around Stony when she'd come into his room and seen the stricken look on his face. To comfort him had been her first instinct, but she'd been too afraid of rejection to act on it.

She had no real idea what he'd been thinking about while he stared out the window. Maybe it had to do with the letters he'd read the night before, or maybe drinking last night with Jasper had stirred up memories of his unhappy past. He'd probably been able to shove those painful thoughts away as long as nobody disturbed his careful personal routine. But Jasper was determined to shake him up, and so far she'd been helping Jasper do exactly that.

Whatever had caused that haunted look in his eyes, he'd wiped it away by the time he came to the kitchen for breakfast. They had discussed plans for the day, both hers and his, and even what to cook for dinner. Through it all Stony had been polite but detached, as if she didn't affect him one way or the other.

He was behaving that way out of a sense of self-preservation, she knew. If he began to feel threatened enough, he might even send her away. She felt as if she were sitting on a smoldering volcano with no way of knowing when the thing might blow. If she wanted to avoid being hurt, she'd be wise to clear out soon. Unfortunately, her heart was now in a position to overrule her head.

Using the map Stony had drawn, she found Agnes Farnsworth's house, a white clapboard similar to several others along a tree-shaded street only two blocks from Rio Verde's business district. Lawn sprinklers whirled in front of several homes, and with school out for the summer, children had gathered in one large yard to play tag.

It looked like a very conservative neighborhood, Daphne thought with a sinking heart. Stony had told her people wouldn't take to feng shui in a small town like Rio Verde, and maybe he was right. Thanks to Jasper and some fast talking on her part, she had two appointments, but that didn't mean the women would go along with her ideas after she explained them.

But Rio Verde would be a good place to raise a family, Daphne thought. She'd visited the little town a couple of times when she'd lived on her stepfather's ranch about thirty miles away. When she was a teenager eager for excitement, Rio Verde had offered her little. Now as a grown woman desperate to put down roots, she thought it offered just about everything she could want, if only some of the residents could be open to her decorating concepts.

Her business success wasn't the only consideration, though. And whether or not she could remain happily in Rio Verde if Stony rejected her was a question she didn't have the courage to answer.

Her feng shui book tucked into her small briefcase, she rang the Farnsworths' doorbell and took a deep breath. This was her first potential client, and she was nervous as a cat. She'd expected people to be excited and intrigued by her new concepts, but so far the reaction had been confusion and disbelief. Sure, the wranglers were going along with her ideas, but Jasper had probably threatened them with bodily harm if they didn't. She knew there was a good chance Agnes would listen politely and send Daphne on her way.

A slight, dark-haired woman of about fifty answered the door with a smile. "I've been so anxious for y'all to come, Daphne, honey, I almost couldn't stand it! Now, get yourself in here and explain to me about this Chinese thing. I love Chinese food, especially the fortune cookies, so why shouldn't I love this, too?"

Daphne wanted to hug her.

LATE THAT AFTERNOON, Stony and Big Clyde were supposed to be gentling a green horse in the corral, but Stony had a hard time keeping his mind on the job. He kept watching the dirt road, looking for the rooster tail of dust telling him Daphne was coming home.

"If you keep looking down that road and don't pay more attention than you been doin', this horse is gonna throw you for sure," Big Clyde said as he held the horse's bridle while Stony eased his foot into the stirrup.

"I just hope my truck didn't break down on her," Stony said. "I've been meaning to replace the water pump, and I'm just afraid—"

"You know the folks around here," Big Clyde said with his typical logic. "Nobody's gonna leave a woman stranded beside the road in this county. A lot of them have those cell phones now, too. We'd have a call by now if she was broke down somewhere."

"I guess you're right. Easy, Sunshine," he crooned to the buckskin as the horse pranced sideways. "We're gonna be fine." Mounting gradually took more strength than swinging into the saddle, but Stony thought it was worth it not to startle a green horse. He moved almost in slow motion as he put weight on the stirrup and gradually hoisted himself up, bringing his right leg over the saddle. He started out by standing in the stirrups and then gradually settled down on the leather. The horse trembled.

"Turn him loose," Stony said in a low voice to Big Clyde.

Big Clyde slowly released his hold on the buckskin's head.

The buckskin stood a moment without moving. In the lull Stony made the mistake of glancing toward the road again, and this time he saw the truck coming. He wondered how her day had gone, and if she'd landed the two decorating jobs she'd gone after. He wondered if she'd want to go riding when she got home, which had been his latest brainstorm, or if she'd be too tired. He—

With one spectacular buck, Sunshine threw him sky high. He came down hard on his butt in the dirt and sat there cursing himself for being one mush-brained cowboy.

Big Clyde, of course, was laughing his head off. "I warned you, boss. You can't be breakin' horses and thinkin' about women at the same time."

Stony grimaced and stood, brushing off the seat of his pants as he went to retrieve his hat.

About that time the truck pulled up next to the corral and Daphne hopped out. "Are you okay? I saw you on the horse, and next thing I knew you were sailing through the air."

Even worse than having Big Clyde witness his indignity was having Daphne see it. "I'm fine," he said, although he thought he might have turned his ankle some in the process. He tried not to limp as he walked over to the edge of the corral where she stood. "How did things go in town?"

"Spectacular."

He leaned on the top rail and gazed at her. "You look like they did. You're grinning all over." He couldn't help smiling himself, seeing the triumph shining in her eyes. "Agnes and Elmira went for the feng shui, then?"

"They can hardly wait for me to transform their lives. They're telling their friends, too." Her voice quivered with excitement. "I'm a hit, Stony."

It was a good thing they had the corral fence between them, he thought, or he'd probably have picked her up in a bear hug and swung her around. He'd been worried sick that on top of all she'd been through at the Roughstock, she'd also face rejection in town. "That's great," he said. "Really great. Say, I was wondering, after I finish up here, if you'd like to take a little ride, see some of the ranch."

If it was possible for her to glow even brighter, she did. "I would love that," she said. "Just let me change out of my skirt. I'll be ready in a jiffy." She started back toward the truck.

He stayed where he was for a minute, pleased as hell with the success of his suggestion.

She turned back before climbing in the truck. "Thanks for asking," she said, and her smile was as big as Texas. Then she got into the truck and drove over to the house.

Stony felt a little dazed by her happiness, some of which had to do with him. He didn't have much experience making women happy, unless he counted making them happy in bed. He'd thought that was all he was capable of. Apparently not. Who knew?

11

STONY DISCOVERED he'd made Daphne even happier by saddling Morning Star for her to ride. It seemed Daphne and the little mare had struck up a friendship the night before. Morning Star looked almost like a pony next to his big gelding, Jolly Boy, but she was the perfect size for Daphne.

Judging from the sun, Stony figured they had about an hour of good daylight left, so he decided to take Daphne up to Lookout Hill, then down to Wayward Creek and back home, which should take up most of the hour. The edge was gone from the heat that had battered the countryside for most of the day. It was one of Stony's favorite times. He whistled to the dog and they started off.

"The range isn't as green as it normally is this time of the year." He automatically handed her his reins when he dismounted to open a gate leading into a meadow. "We keep moving the herd around to get the most of what grass there is. So far we're not desperate. But like Big Clyde said, the cattle aren't fattening up like they did last summer."

"I have a feeling your luck is about to change," Daphne said. Without being told, she led his horse through the opening. She'd obviously been on ranch-land before and knew how two riders got through a gate. "I picked up some premixed cement, a submersible motor and some PVC pipe while I was in town," she said.

"For the fountain," Stony said, as he remounted and they started off side by side with the dog romping a few yards away.

"Actually, it'll be more like a waterfall. Jasper said he'd get me a truckload of rocks."

A waterfall in his front yard. Just what he didn't need. "Daphne, I really don't think—"

"Don't worry. I paid for the supplies with my own money. And the rocks are free."

"You shouldn't be spending your money, either. We both know that a waterfall isn't going to make it rain, so you're wasting a lot of time and effort."

She smiled serenely at him. "*You* may know a waterfall in the front yard won't work, but I don't. You can't discourage me today, Stony. I have two new clients and the prospect of several more. You may say that has nothing to do with my rearranging and cleaning the living room, which is in the career sector, or cleaning out the kitchen cupboards, which are in the wealth-and-prosperity sector, but I say it has everything to do with it."

"Well, however it happened, I'm glad you got those two jobs. To be honest, I didn't think anybody would be interested in your feng shui."

"Jasper obviously picked the right person when he talked to Agnes Farnsworth. She loves new ideas."

Which put him in his place as a person who didn't, thought Stony. And maybe that was the right assessment. Besides, believing in the feng shui stuff could be dangerous to his carefully guarded bachelor status.

"Stop." She held up a hand. "Do you see the deer?"

"Where?"

"Uh-oh. Chi's going to scare them away. There they go, through the trees."

He squinted in the direction she was pointing and finally made out the pair of white-tails disappearing over a ridge. The buck had a pretty nice set of antlers on him. "Hey, Dog! Get back here!"

The retriever reluctantly returned, her tongue hanging out from the run.

"Do you hunt?" Daphne asked as they continued riding.

"Never took the time."

"I'm not much of a fan of it, myself, especially killing something as beautiful as deer. I guess once I saw *Bambi*, that did it for me."

He remembered the movie, although he hadn't thought about it in years. He remembered his mother taking him to see it one winter afternoon, and how he'd been ashamed of crying when Bambi's mother was killed. His mother had said it was okay to cry when something was really, really sad, but he'd been around rodeo cowboys all his life, and he hadn't believed her. He still didn't. A man just wasn't supposed to cry. But he'd never taken up hunting, either.

"I'm...I'm sorry," Daphne said.

He glanced at her and started to speak, but he had to clear his throat first. He wondered if he was coming down with a cold. "About what?"

"That was thoughtless of me, to bring up *Bambi*."

"You mean because of the mother?"

"Of course because of the mother."

"That was a long time ago, Daphne. I hardly think of it anymore." At least he hadn't until the past three days. And he didn't want to start thinking about it now, either. "Come on. We have a lot yet to see." He pushed Jolly Boy into an easy canter across the meadow, checking to make sure Daphne stayed with him.

She did, sitting the little mare like a pro. He felt sorry he'd waited until now to offer her the chance to ride. She obviously loved it.

Their pace slowed as Stony led them up through an oak grove toward Lookout Hill. Even the trees looked a little stressed by lack of water, he thought, and the wildflowers were few and far between. Yet his worries about the drought couldn't ruin the sense of peace and satisfaction that came over him when he rode out here in the evening after a hard day's work.

As they topped the hill, his cares slipped away as they always did when he gazed out on his land. Well, his and the bank's, to be perfectly accurate, but as long as he could make the payments, he considered the Roughstock his.

"Oh, Stony." Daphne's voice was hushed, almost in awe.

She couldn't have responded any better, as far as he was concerned. If she'd just said the view was pretty, or started asking him where his property ended, or something like that, he'd know she didn't understand how special this spot was. But somehow she did understand, which is why she stayed silent and just looked, the way he always did.

Only this time, he found himself looking at her. The sun hovering just above the horizon gave off an orange glow, and Daphne seemed to be surrounded by it. It ignited flashes of fire in her hair and tinged her cheeks the color of nectarines. She just might be the most beautiful woman he'd ever seen, he thought. Logically that didn't make any sense. He'd dated a rodeo queen once, and a professional model another time. But in his mind they didn't hold a candle to the picture Daphne made wrapped in the light from the setting sun.

Then it occurred to him that in looking at Daphne, he was seeing more than a pretty woman, more than just surface beauty. After reading her letters he knew more about her than he had about any of the others he'd dated. Her letters had revealed her grit, her wacky creative side, her generous and trusting heart—too trusting, sometimes.

She turned to him, her eyes alight with wonder. "Thank you for bringing me up here."

He merely nodded, unable to form a reply to save his soul. The reply he was thinking of—climbing off his horse and hauling her down into his arms—would have serious consequences. Yet making love to her here, on top of this hill, seemed like the right thing to do. More and more, making love to her seemed like the right thing to do under any circumstances. He was afraid he was becoming obsessed with the idea.

"You must enjoy showing this to people," she said. "It's so beautiful."

"I...never have."

She stared at him.

"Not like you mean, anyway, showing it to a ranch visitor. The boys and I ride up here when we're scouting for missing critters, sometimes, but as a pure pleasure ride, I always come by myself. And bring the dog, of course. She loves it up here, too."

"You didn't even show this to your father?"

"I did ask him if he wanted to take a ride and see the place, but it was pretty cold and he...said he'd rather not."

Her expression became grim. "His loss."

Stony shrugged. "He never wanted to own property, so I guess seeing my ranch didn't mean all that much to him."

"Or it meant more than he was willing to admit."

"Who knows?" The conversation had taken an uncomfortable turn. The subject of his father always made him uneasy. He'd been so sure that once he bought the ranch, he'd be able to convince his father to come and live there. It hadn't worked out that way.

He tugged his Stetson down over his eyes. "Well, if I'm going to show you Wayward Creek before dark, we need to get a move on."

IT WAS NEARLY DARK by the time they finished putting up the horses and walked toward the ranch house, Chi following at their heels. But even in the dim light Daphne could see the pickup-load of rocks in Stony's front yard.

"They did it!" Daphne couldn't believe so much bounty in one day. Two people had hired her to decorate their homes, and Stony had taken her on a sunset ride to a special hill where he'd never taken anyone else. She considered that significant. And now she had rocks for the waterfall.

"I suppose you'll be wanting to borrow some of my men to help you put the thing together tomorrow."

"I was afraid to ask, but yes, I will need a little help."

"Who do you want?"

You. But she knew better than to ask him to help her build a waterfall he didn't want in the first place. The result would have to be a wonderful surprise. So she picked the man she thought could get the most done in the least amount of time. "Big Clyde."

"Okay."

Excitement pumped her full of energy. "Tonight I'll sew up the curtains for the bunkhouse, and tomorrow I'll—"

"Sew them up on what?"

"I rented a sewing machine while I was in town."

"Did you buy the red paint for the door, too?"

"Sure did. And I—"

"So you plan to hang curtains, paint the door and build a waterfall, all in the same day?"

She decided not to tell him about her additional beautification plans. "Sure. We'll start early."

"Tell you what. I'll give you the whole crew, for one day, so we can get this out of the way once and for all. You can direct them to do anything you want. But at the end of the day, they're mine again. How's that?"

She beamed at him. "That would be terrific. Uh, does that include you?"

"No." He held the door open for her and Chi. "I'll run some errands in town tomorrow. I have a feeling it would hurt me too much to watch my men feng shuiing the day away."

That remark put a little dent in her happiness. She flipped on a lamp as she walked through the living room. "You may not think that what I'm doing matters in the grand scheme of things, but it does. People behave differently when you place them in environments with different colors and textures and sounds." She turned on the kitchen light and went to a cupboard to get Chi some kibble.

"That's what I'm afraid of." He hung his hat on a peg. "I like the way my men behave just fine."

"That could be because you don't know what their potential is. And everything around them affects that." She poured kibble into Chi's dish and walked back to the cupboard. "Even something like your hat hanging on the wall affects the mood of this room," she said. "It's a macho sort of symbol."

"Yeah?"

She shoved the dog food into the cupboard. "You're affected by interior and exterior decoration whether you know it or not."

"I know one thing. I'm affected by you."

She closed the cupboard door and turned. He was right there, pinning her against the counter.

He cupped her chin. "The way you move, the way you talk, the way you smile. You're driving me crazy." He released her chin and wrapped her in his arms. "And don't pretend you don't like this, because I know different." He brought his mouth down on hers.

In that moment she knew it was love that made the temptation of his lips so hard to resist. She'd loved him long before she'd met him, and although she'd tried to kill that emotion, he'd rekindled it when he'd looked at her so hauntingly this morning. He'd fanned it into a full blaze during their sunset ride, and now she longed to show him the depth of her feeling.

When his tongue sought entrance, she gave it, needing that firm thrust, needing the taste of him, needing the warmth and passion coming off him in waves. He unbuttoned her blouse, and she didn't stop him. The front clasp of her bra gave way beneath his fingers and he caressed her, his calloused hands bringing her the same joy they had the first night she'd felt his touch.

His kiss became deeper, more suggestive, and her knees grew weak. His erection pressed firmly against her, bringing a rush of moisture between her thighs. She moaned softly, wanting all he had to offer.

He lifted his mouth a fraction from hers. "I want you so much," he murmured. "Please, Daphne."

Want. It wasn't the word she was looking for. Her heart quivered. "I want you, too."

"Then, please, sweetheart." He cupped her breast and stroked his thumb back and forth across her taut nipple. "Please..."

"First I need to know..." She tried to catch her breath. "I need to know if we'd be making love...or having sex."

He went still in her arms. "Are you asking me...to say I love you?"

His question was enough answer. "No," she said, pain knifing through her as she pushed him away. He was caught so unaware that he almost stumbled.

"Daphne—"

"I would never ask that."

He gazed at her, confusion in his blue eyes. "Then why won't you just go to bed with me? I know you want to."

"Yes, I want to." She fastened her bra with trembling fingers. "But not if it's only about sex."

"Daphne, if you're holding out for those three little words, you have the wrong man. I've never said them to a woman and I never intend to. Is it so terrible to enjoy good sex without all the mushy stuff? I would never cheat on you like that other guy."

She buttoned her blouse. "I believe that about you, Stony." She looked him in the eye. "But I deserve a man who can tell me he loves me. When I'm giving the gift of my body, I deserve to be told that I'm loved, not just that I'm wanted."

"I don't see the big difference!"

Heartsick and disappointed, she gazed at him. "Then why not say it?"

"I'm just not the type." He met her gaze for a moment longer before turning and going over to retrieve his hat. "I'll be down at the bunkhouse."

Chi followed him out the door.

EVEN THOUGH STONY HAD organized a special trip to the store to buy food, they had yet to eat a dinner in this kitchen together, Daphne thought as she washed up the dishes from her chicken-and-broccoli casserole. They would have eaten together, although much later, if she'd just been willing to go into his bedroom with him first. He would have been so mellow she probably would have been able to convince him to eat broccoli.

She set up the sewing machine. Using the measurements Big Clyde had given her, she cut and stitched the red bandanna material she'd bought into café curtains for the bunkhouse. Sewing was the sort of mindless job that gave her lots of time to think. And she had much to think about.

She'd been foolish to expect a declaration of love from Stony tonight. Just because he'd looked at her with such wistfulness this morning, and just because he'd taken her on a ride to his special place this evening, that didn't mean he was ready to say that he loved her. But she couldn't help wondering if he was beginning to.

The trouble was, he probably thought the only thing wrong with him was sexual frustration. She thought he was driven to make love to her for deeper reasons than that. Of course, one way to prove it was to give in and go to bed with him. But if she was wrong and he wasn't any closer to commitment after they made love than he was before, she'd be in worse shape than ever. No, she had to hold fast to her convictions.

TO DAPHNE'S SURPRISE, Big Clyde volunteered to hang curtain rods for her. She'd have expected Ramon or even Jasper to do it, but Jasper told her confidentially that Big Clyde was a genius at measurements. Daphne sent Andy, the most creative one, to scour the area for wildflowers and interesting grasses to use in arrangements inside the bunkhouse. Jasper corralled Ramon and Ty and herded them off to dig the shallow pit Daphne had marked out for the waterfall.

While Big Clyde worked on the curtain rods,

Daphne painted the door, which dried quickly in the summer heat. In between coats, she threaded the café curtains onto the wrought-iron rods. Big Clyde wasn't much of a talker, so Daphne held up the conversation by explaining the various feng shui sectors and how they applied to the bunkhouse. The hefty cowboy listened, not saying much, but he looked interested.

Finally, when the curtain rods were all in place, he pointed to the building's far right corner with his screwdriver. "So your book says that there's the spot for love and marriage?"

"That's it. The head of your bunk is just inside it."

Big Clyde blushed. "Thought so."

Daphne gazed at him. "Is there someone special in your life?"

"Kinda. The lady what runs the library. She don't know it, though."

Daphne bet not. Being a man of few words, Big Clyde probably hadn't told her. "Would you like to give a little feng shui help to the situation?"

He looked nervous but hopeful. "Could we?"

"You bet."

"I don't want the boys to know what we're doin'. I'd never hear the end of it. You won't say nothin', will you?"

"Of course not. But making it inconspicuous is a bit of a challenge." She thumbed through her book and found the section on posing objects to encourage couple interaction. Big Clyde needed something decorating the iron rails of his headboard that would signify a pair, but it couldn't be anything that would alert the other hands as to what he was trying to accomplish.

She glanced around the bunkhouse, searching for an answer.

Then it hit her. "Do you have some spurs you don't use every day?"

"You mean my fancy ones, with the silver on them?"

"That would be perfect. And a little piece of rawhide, if you have it."

Big Clyde went back to the big closet all the hands shared and soon emerged with his spurs and a length of rawhide. "You gonna do a trick?"

"Sort of." She worked as she talked. "We'll link these spurs together and tie them to the top rail of your headboard, so it'll look like a cowboy-style decoration. But it really stands for two people linked together." Daphne wasn't sure if this was completely accurate feng shui, but her intention was good, so that should count for something. "I'd also recommend you start talking to the lady," she said for good measure.

Big Clyde surveyed the linked spurs and gave her a gap-toothed smile. "I'll surely try, ma'am. And I thank you."

"I got a whole bunch a purty weeds!" Andy sang out from the doorway. "Where you want 'em?"

"Let me take a look," Daphne said, stepping into the sunshine to evaluate the two buckets of wildflowers and different types of grass. The array of colors would look properly rustic, and she'd already decided to talk somebody out of an old pair of boots, which she could transform into vases by inserting water glasses down the shaft. "This is wonderful, Andy," she said. "I especially like the—"

"Don't touch that!" shouted Big Clyde, jerking her

back from the bucket. "Somethin' moved in there!" He released her and stepped forward to peer into one of the buckets. Then in a surprisingly quick move for such a big man, he reached down and pulled out a foot-long snake, grasping it just behind its head.

Daphne stepped back, heart pounding. But after looking more closely she could see it was a small, completely harmless bull snake.

Big Clyde didn't look particularly harmless as he advanced on Andy. "You did this on purpose!" he thundered.

Andy got red and backed away. "Just for a joke. To see if she'd scream. The snake wouldn't hurt her."

"I should make you swallow this here snake," Big Clyde said, dangling it in Andy's face. "But that'd be cruel to the snake." He jerked a thumb back at Daphne and his voice dropped to a low growl. "This here's a lady, and if you pull any more of your tricks on her, you'll answer to me. Now, say you're sorry."

Andy peeked around Big Clyde, his face beet red. "Sorry, ma'am. Didn't mean no harm."

Her heart went out to the poor kid, whose active imagination obviously wasn't challenged enough by the work he did. "Apology accepted," she said, taking a deep breath. "Now, who's ready to help me make a wildflower wreath for the door?"

"Andy'll make it, and I'll hang it," Big Clyde said.

"A wildflower wreath on the door." Andy looked a little worried. "Won't everybody make fun of us?"

"Not while I'm around," said Big Clyde.

12

DAPHNE HAD picked up a booklet on building waterfalls and fountains when she was town, along with a good-size motor and plenty of flexible PVC pipe. When she, Big Clyde and Andy walked over to check the progress in the front yard, they found a sizable hole being dug by Ty and Ramon while Jasper studied Daphne's booklet. Chi watched the proceedings from under the only tree in the yard, a large oak.

Jasper glanced up as Daphne approached. "How many of these contraptions have you put together?" he asked.

She smiled at him. "None. But how hard can it be? The pump sucks the water in and the pipe squirts it out. The rest is just details."

Jasper squinted at her. "You ain't put any together before?"

"I told you she didn't know what she was doin'," Ty said, leaning on the handle of his shovel. "It's gonna be a swampland out here in no time."

"You just don't appreciate the music of falling water," Ramon said. "On a moonlit night, this will be a beautiful spot."

"A lawn sprinkler woulda done the trick," Ty said.

"Stony ain't got no lawn," Big Clyde pointed out. "Just the one tree and lotsa dirt."

"You know what?" Andy said. "After we finish the waterfall, we should dig up some bushes and plant them around the edges of the pond. It'll look like a park."

"It'll look like a pig wallow," Ty predicted darkly.

"Don't mind him," Ramon said. "Is this deep enough for what you had in mind, *señorita?*"

"Looks like a swimming hole," Andy said with a grin. "Which gives me an idea."

"We don't want nobody skinny-dippin' in this here waterfall," Jasper said, glaring at each cowboy in turn. "Save your shenanigans for the stock tank."

Daphne evaluated the hole the men had dug. Actually, it was a little deeper than Daphne had planned on, but she wasn't about to say so after all that hard work. "It's perfect. Let's start putting in the rocks and building up the falls part."

"We've just been waitin' for Big Clyde before we started moving rocks," Ty said. "Better get the liniment. I'm expecting some ol' boy will throw his back out liftin' them things."

Jasper gazed at him. "That settles it. Everything that cowboy complains about always turns out great." He handed the booklet to Daphne. "You're the straw boss on the project, ma'am. Come on, boys, let's get 'er done."

THE MERCILESS SUN BEAT down as the men positioned rocks and cemented them into place. In the heat the cement set almost instantly. Daphne made sure drinking water was always available, even for Chi. The construction was a noisy process, but the racket was steady, not abrupt, so Chi didn't seem to mind. Jokes and laughter mingled with the clatter of rocks as the men all predicted how they'd spend the money the waterfall would bring them. Daphne felt a little like Snow White supervising the five dwarfs.

By early afternoon they had all the rocks in place for the waterfall that would cascade down into the pool. A PVC pipe hidden inside the stair-stepping rocks would draw water from the submersible pump in the bottom of the pool to the top of the waterfall. Daphne's excitement grew as her concept began to take shape.

She also realized as the men toiled through the hot afternoon how much she'd come to care for these rowdy yet tenderhearted cowboys. They were the ones who'd landed her in such a mess with Stony, but she'd never find it in her heart to blame them for it.

"Let's break for lunch and let this-here concrete set," Jasper called to the men.

"I'll fix lunch in the house," Daphne offered.

"We'll use the hose and clean ourselves up some," Big Clyde said.

"Lunch'll be ready in ten minutes." Daphne hurried inside. She'd never thrown sandwiches together so fast in her life. She laid them out with plates and napkins on the kitchen table and set out some cans of pop and beer.

In exactly ten minutes Jasper knocked on the front door.

"Y'all come in," Daphne called.

The men scraped their boots on the mat before filing quietly inside. They glanced around with interest at the living room.

"Looks nice, *señorita*," Ramon said. "Much better."

The other men murmured their agreement.

"'Course Stony probably didn't like it," Ty commented. "He never was one for changing things around."

"He didn't like it at first," Daphne admitted, "but now he does. Just take a plate and whatever you want to drink and then sit wherever you like. We couldn't all fit around the kitchen table, so I thought we'd just eat buffet-style."

"It's sorta like a party," Andy said as they all got situated in the living room. "Like them potlucks they sometimes have at Rio Verde Baptist."

"Some of the ranchers have 'em, too," Big Clyde said. "Like on the Fourth of July."

"Yeah, the ones where there's a married couple running the place," Andy said, with a significant glance at Daphne.

"That makes things real nice when a couple's running things," Ramon agreed.

"Well, unless they get divorced," Ty said.

Jasper grabbed a newspaper and whacked Ty on top of the head.

Daphne swallowed a bite of sandwich. "Listen, guys, I get the hint. But your boss is not the least bit interested in a wife."

"He sure was worried about you gettin' back from town safe, yesterday, ma'am," Big Clyde said. "He was so busy lookin' for you, he got hisself bucked off."

Daphne was impressed with such a long speech from Big Clyde, not to mention the interesting information about Stony.

"And the night before that, when we was playin' cards, he kept bringin' up your name," Andy said. "Couldn't keep his mind on the game. I won about ten bucks off him 'cause he was so woolly-headed."

"I keep tellin' Daphne to give this some time," Jasper said. "He'll come around."

Big Clyde gazed thoughtfully around the living room. "Did you feng shui the whole house?"

"I've worked on most of it," Daphne said. "This room, the kitchen, my room. Not Stony's room, though."

"Well, there you go." Big Clyde put down his plate. "Time to move some furniture. Come on, boys."

Daphne leaped up in alarm. "Wait a minute. I don't know if we should just go in there and—"

"We won't hurt nothin'," Andy said, already halfway down the hall. "Just get the *chi* movin', like you did in the bunkhouse. Come on, Ty."

"The boss ain't gonna like this," Ty said, but he was already on his feet.

"This time I agree with you, Ty," Daphne said.

"He can always put it back, *señorita*," Ramon said over his shoulder as he headed after the others.

Jasper glanced at her and grinned. "You'd better get in there and tell 'em what to do. They're liable to get that *chi* movin' in the wrong direction."

"Guess I might as well be hung for a sheep as a lamb," Daphne muttered, as she put down her plate and started toward Stony's bedroom.

Half an hour later, Stony's four-poster was angled against one corner of the room and his dresser angled against another. Daphne watched in amusement as Ramon and Andy made up the bed and fluffed the pillows. She had to admit the room looked better already.

"He needs flowers," Big Clyde said. He left the room and soon returned with a bouquet from the living room. He positioned it carefully on the top of the dresser and stood back, arms crossed, to judge the effect. "Good."

Ramon walked to the doorway and surveyed the room from that vantage point. "It still needs something else, like the curtains you made for us. You got anything like that?"

She did. Not knowing if she'd ever have the chance to use it, she'd bought an extra-large lace tablecloth on sale, thinking how beautiful it would look draped over the tall posters of the bed. Yet she felt a little shy about trundling the lace out in front of everyone.

Big Clyde edged over beside her. "You need somethin' like my spurs, too," he said in an undertone.

She remembered how he'd allowed himself to be vulnerable in front of her and decided she might as well trust these guys with her tender feelings. "All right, I do have something. Wait here and I'll get it. I'll need some help hanging it, anyway."

Moments later she came back with the lace. "I want to hang this from the bedposts to make a canopy."

"That's real pretty, ma'am," Andy said. "But I have to tell you, seein' as how you can kick a guy clear into next week, I thought you'd go in for silk things with dragons on 'em."

"Sometimes that's nice, too," Daphne said with a smile. One of these days she would explain everything to these cowboys, but now didn't seem like the time.

"Now, if four of you will each take a corner and lift it up over the bedposts, I think it will just hang there."

Even if she'd had a camera, she wouldn't have embarrassed the cowboys by taking their picture. But she would have loved to capture the moment when Big Clyde, Andy, Ramon and Ty lifted the lacy material and gracefully draped it over the tall bedposts. It was a tableau she wouldn't soon forget.

From her pocket, she withdrew two lavender sachets tied with ribbons that she'd been keeping in her suitcase to freshen her clothes. Fastening the ribbons together, she hung the twin sachets over a central finial on the headboard. Then she glanced at Big Clyde, who nodded his approval.

Andy grinned as he looked around the room. "If that don't get his *chi* movin', I don't know what will."

"And now we'd better get our butts movin' if we expect to finish that fountain," Jasper said. "Everybody rinse your plate and then come on outside."

"Thanks for rearranging the room, guys," Daphne said, giving them all a smile.

Ramon winked at her. "Maybe we'll have potlucks around here yet."

With one last look at the bedroom, Daphne followed the men down the hall. With a vision of the canopied four-poster lodged in her mind, she wasn't dreaming of potluck dinners.

An hour later Jasper came to stand beside her while Big Clyde lifted the motor down into the pool and connected it to the pipe going up inside the falls. "Is that motor big enough for the job?" Jasper asked.

"I got the biggest one they had. I thought nothing

would be worse than having some wimpy little trickle of water coming down the rocks."

Jasper nodded. "Yep. Don't want no puny-lookin' waterfall, that's for sure."

"By the way, I appreciate you telling the men to go along with the feng shui stuff. You probably don't believe in it."

"Oh, I wouldn't say that. Went over to that part of the world when I was in the navy. I'm not one to say my way is right and another is wrong." He gazed at her. "As for the boys, they would do about anything you asked 'em to do. They feel plumb responsible for you, after what we done." His eyes twinkled. "Besides, you was the cream of the crop, so a'course we was all bound to like you. We picked you out of a big stack."

"Lots of women wrote to Stony?" She'd always wondered.

Jasper chuckled. "So many that I'm never tellin' him. He'd get hisself a swelled head."

"A hundred?"

"More like three hundred. We spent hours down at the bunkhouse goin' through 'em, and nearly killed ourselves slippin' everything outa sight when Stony would show up."

"My goodness." The news that she'd been chosen out of a large field made Daphne feel better, even if Stony hadn't been the one doing the choosing.

"Now, back to this-here waterfall motor, we gotta plug it in somewheres."

Fortunately Daphne had thought of that. "For now, we'll just use a heavy-duty extension cord and run it inside the house. Maybe later it can be wired up in a fancier way, but I want to make sure the water's running by the time Stony gets home.''

Jasper glanced up at the sun. ''Then we'd better get that cord and start fillin' this hole with the hose. That boy usually gets bored with town after a few hours and hankers to be back home at the Roughstock.''

''He really does love it here, doesn't he?''

The old cowboy nodded. ''He sure appears to.''

''And from what he's told me, he owes you a big debt for making his dream come true. He said he couldn't have done it without you.''

Jasper flushed with pleasure. ''It ain't true, but it's nice to hear. Stony can do anything, once he puts his mind to it. I mighta made things a little easier for him, but he'd have this ranch with or without me. Once he latches on to an idea, you can't shake him loose.'' He grinned. ''That's what earned him all the prize money on them bulls. He had an idea he was gonna ride 'em to the buzzer, and that was that. Them bulls was outgunned.''

Daphne smiled at that, but she couldn't help thinking that Stony's stubbornness might be a liability as well as an asset. After all, he'd held on to his ideas about love and marriage for a very long time.

''If you'll get the hose, I'll get the cord,'' Jasper said. ''I can hardly wait to see ol' Stony's face when he gets home.''

CURIOSITY BROUGHT STONY home a little sooner than he'd anticipated. He'd thought about staying in town until well past bedtime, just so he wouldn't be tempted to grab Daphne again and try to seduce her. She wanted more than he was capable of giving, so there was no point in getting himself worked up for nothing. He'd been a fool to try anything the night before, and he was determined not to make that mistake again. The best defense was to stay away from her.

That didn't explain the little pot of African violets he'd bought, but he'd seen the damned things and remembered from her letters that she loved violets. He'd thought of the two flower arrangements he'd been a part of destroying, and how nice this little pot would look in her room.

In fact, the whole time he was in town, whether he was prowling the aisles of the hardware store or arranging for a delivery from the feed store, his mind was either on Daphne or on the ranch and what sort of craziness was happening there today. He should have put a stop to the whole feng shui thing a long time ago, but he hadn't had the heart. Besides, with the loyalty Jasper and the men seemed to feel for Daphne, he might not be wise to lay down an ultimatum that would force them to choose between the boss and the lady.

His concern about the ranch made him hurry through the list he'd brought, and by midafternoon he'd run out of errands. He'd even spent some time under a shady tree installing the new water pump on his truck. Unless he wanted to stop in at the bar or just park the truck and take a snooze, he had nothing to do except go home. Home was where he wanted to be, anyway, so he pointed the truck toward the Roughstock and stepped on the gas.

Deciding to make a detour by the bunkhouse before

he faced whatever was going on in his front yard, he pulled up in front of the structure and groaned. Not only was the door bright red, but it had some sort of weed and flower *wreath* on it, and Christmas was months away. It looked like a dormitory for sweet young maidens, or not so sweet, considering the red door. It definitely didn't look like a bunkhouse where five Texas cowhands lived.

Almost afraid of what he'd find, he climbed down from the truck and opened the red door. Sure enough, red bandanna curtains hung café-style at the windows, and more red bandannas were draped over the night-stands and chests of drawers scattered around the bunkhouse. He couldn't figure out why Big Clyde's fancy spurs were tied onto his headboard like that, but if he sat up real quick he'd find himself scalped.

Additional weed-and-flower bouquets tacked on the walls and tucked inside somebody's old pair of boots just made him shake his head. Couldn't even have a card game on the table without moving the center-piece. What was his ranch coming to? Next thing he knew Daphne would probably want to color-coordinate the saddle blankets and paint flowers on the shovels they used to muck out the barn.

Through the open windows came the sounds of the ruckus going on over at his house while they put to-gether Daphne's waterfall. With a sigh, he left the bunkhouse, closing the red door behind him. That red was going to be a hard color to cover up, once Daphne left the ranch. He couldn't believe the boys would want to leave their bunkhouse looking like that once they

weren't trying to impress Daphne with their love of interior decorating.

A shout of "Here he comes" greeted him as he
pulled up in front of what used to be his front yard.
Piles of dirt were everywhere, and the pond was much
bigger than he'd anticipated. Of course he'd been careful not to think about this too much. But whenever
thoughts of the project snuck up on him, he'd pictured
the pond as being about the size of a bathtub. The reality was considerably bigger. The rocks for the waterfall rose on the far side of the pond, but no water was
cascading down at the moment. The people were sure
rushing around, though.

Ty pulled a hose out of the pond and shut off the
nozzle while Andy and Ramon patted dirt around a
couple of bedraggled bushes they must have dug up
somewhere on the property, because Stony had never
seen anything like that in the nursery in town. Jasper
and Big Clyde were gesturing and talking in loud
voices about something. Daphne was nowhere in sight,
but the front door was open and an orange cord trailed
from the edge of the pond, up the steps and across the
porch to disappear inside.

Stony got out of the truck and walked toward the
pond. The dog trotted over to greet him and he patted
her absently, but his focus was on the structure in front
of him. He nudged his hat back with his thumb and
peered down to the bottom. "There's a hell of a lot of
water in there," he called across to Jasper.

"It took a hair more'n we thought it would," Jasper
called back. "But Daphne bought a good strong motor.
Should move that water just fine."

Daphne came to the door and waved to Stony. "You're gonna love this!" She popped back inside, and the motor at the bottom of the pond began to hum.

Thumbs through his belt loops, Stony faced the opening where the water was supposed to come out. "I don't think it's—"

The water gushed out, shooting completely over the pond and hitting Stony in the face with enough force to knock off his hat. Sputtering and yelling, he backed up and tripped over the dog, who was also trying to scurry away from the water. He landed on his butt in the mud being quickly formed by the shooting water.

The cascade of water ceased and he just sat there, soaking wet, and stared at the waterfall while his men killed themselves laughing. As a final insult, his dog shook herself right in front of him. Any place the waterfall had missed, the dog took care of.

Daphne hurried toward him, her face red as a beet. "I'm sorry. I had no idea it would do that. The motor must be too powerful."

Stony gazed up at her. "Good guess."

"You're covered with mud."

"No kidding."

"Can I...can I help you with anything?" She looked like she was trying not to laugh.

"Why, no, I can't think of a thing."

"Then I think I'll...go over and talk to the boys."

"You do that."

He sat there and watched her go into a huddle with his men, who as they talked with her kept glancing back at him with grins on their faces. He had the feeling that during the few hours that he'd been in town, she'd taken over more than his front yard and the decoration of the bunkhouse. She had those cowboys in the palm of her hand, and there was no telling what mischief they'd been up to.

Jasper's mustache twitched as he kept waving a piece of paper that looked like it could be instructions for the pump. Finally Andy took off his boots and socks, handed his hat off to Ramon and stripped off his T-shirt. Then he waded carefully into the pond, letting out a whoop of reaction as the cold water hit his heated body.

The water came up to his waist at the deepest part. "Here goes!" he called. Holding his nose, he sank out of sight. After what seemed like a very long time, he burst to the surface again. "I did it!"

"Did what?" Stony asked. He might as well get in on this little party.

"Adjusted the valve so it comes out slower. Go ahead, ma'am. Fire her up again."

Daphne started toward the house.

"Hold it!" Stony scrambled to his feet. "How do you know which way you adjusted it? You may have it set to hit my truck!"

Big Clyde glanced at the truck. "Could use a wash, boss." Then he favored Stony with his big gap-toothed grin.

"Oh, what the hell," Stony said as he retrieved his hat. "Let 'er gush." He walked over to his men. "So how do you boys like your boudoir? Shall I order up a pot of tea for y'all this afternoon? Maybe a few little finger sandwiches?"

He glanced around at the men, who all looked like

they were about to bust a gut keeping their laughter inside. Dammit, they were holding out on him about something. "Okay," he said slowly. "I'm guessing the froufrou bunkhouse and the gushing fountain aren't the only surprises in store for me. What else have you boys been up to?"

He didn't know if he ever would have gotten an answer out of them, because at that moment the waterfall roared to life, spewing out of the rocks and leaping ten feet across the pond to rain directly on his truck. With a sigh he remembered he'd left the windows down.

"Well, boss," Andy said from his position in the middle of the pond, "there's good news and bad news. The bad news is I musta turned that valve the wrong way, after all."

"Yeah, and what's the good news?"

"We just feng shuied your truck!"

13

"DAMMIT, JASPER, but we shouldn't be wasting water like this." Stony watched as the geyser was shut off again and Andy submerged to adjust the valve once more.

"That's a fact," Jasper agreed. "We didn't count on no waste, though, and if we drain the pool now we'll waste what we already put in there. And we need to get that pump workin' right or we'll have a slimy swamp, just like Ty said."

Stony had to concede Jasper's point. The project had gone too far to stop it now.

Big Clyde came over to Stony and cleared his throat. "Uh, boss?"

"Yeah."

"I know you think this is foolishness."

"Yes, I do."

Big Clyde took a deep breath. "I don't."

Stony glanced up sharply into the big man's face. "You don't? You're the soul of logic around here! This feng shui is the most illogical bunch of nonsense I've ever come across!"

Big Clyde shuffled his size sixteen boots. "Daphne, she explained it to me, boss. It's about—" He paused and gazed off into space, obviously struggling to express himself. "It's about movin' things around. You can't leave things the same. They get...what's that word, Ramon?"

"Stagnant." Ramon gestured toward the pool. "Like that, with no water flowing."

"Yeah." Big Clyde's face brightened. "Stagnant."

Andy popped up from the bottom of the pool again. "I think I got it this time!"

Jasper made a megaphone of his hands and turned toward the house. "Plug it in again, ma'am!"

Stony braced himself for another gusher. Instead, water bubbled merrily out of the opening at the top of the rocks and spilled over the various levels to splash into the pool below.

A cheer went up from the men. Andy threw up handfuls of water in celebration, and even Stony had to admit the effect was kind of nice.

Big Clyde put a hand on Stony's shoulder. "She means well."

"I know." Stony sighed. "Everybody around here means well. I just feel as if I landed in the middle of a carnival."

Big Clyde grinned at him. "Stuff's movin'."

INDEED. STONY STOOD in the doorway of his bedroom and stared at the transformation. Before coming in the house he'd taken off his shirt and muddy boots and brushed off his jeans as best he could. Then he'd made a quick trip down the hall to put Daphne's violets in her room. He'd wondered as he passed by his room if there was something different about it.

There sure as hell was, he discovered as he returned from Daphne's room and took a better look at his own.

He didn't dare step in there without a shower. Maybe even a manicure.

He tried to work up some righteous anger, but instead he was floored by how inviting the room looked. Although he would never have imagined such an arrangement, it seemed like the only way the furniture should be set up. He wanted to hate it, because then he could reestablish his authority by demanding that Daphne put everything back the way it had been before. Unfortunately for his authority, he liked what she'd done.

"The boys helped me."

He turned to find Daphne standing in the hallway, her expression anxious.

She twisted her hands together nervously. "I thought it was a bit of an invasion of your privacy, so I'd understand if you're upset. If you are, I'll get a couple of the hands to come in and we'll put it back the way you had it."

"I don't want to put it back. Much as I hate to admit it, this looks good, better than the way it was."

Relief showed in her dark eyes and she smiled.

"But I would be interested in why you did it."

"Uh..." She glanced away. "The boys thought as long as we'd feng shuied everything else, we might as well do your room."

He crossed his arms over his bare chest, wishing he could hold her close while they had this fascinating discussion. He had an idea where such talk could lead. "And which one of them brought over the lace tablecloth to hang from the bedposts?" He snapped his fingers. "I know. Big Clyde had one in his hope chest. I should have figured on that."

She blushed. "I bought the tablecloth when I was in town yesterday. It was on sale."

"We don't have a table that big." He heard himself say *we* and winced. The word had come to his lips so easily. Too easily.

She crossed her arms in imitation of him. He wondered if she had as big an urge to hold him as he had to hold her.

"I might as well tell you that when I woke up in that bed the first morning I was here, I looked up at the bedposts and imagined how pretty a lace canopy would look draped over them," she said. "Then I found your note and...well, I stopped dreaming about lace canopies."

He studied the expression on her face, trying to read what was going on in that mind of hers. "You must have started dreaming about them again at some point, if you bought that tablecloth."

"I'm a designer. I saw the lace tablecloth on sale and naturally thought of your bed."

"I like the way your mind works. You should go shopping more often."

She glanced away. "I thought of your bed purely in a decorative way."

"Uh-huh. You're the one who lectured me about how colors and textures affect people. What did you suppose would happen while I'm lying in bed looking up at that filmy material you chose to hang there? You don't think I'll dream of you and the bits of lace trimming on your nightie, the one you're wearing as you lie not twenty feet away from me? You don't think this lace roof over my bed will drive me absolutely, completely around the bend with wanting you?"

She looked back at him, and the conflict going on in her mind was obvious. "You're right. It's not fair. We should take it down." She started to move past him.

He caught her arm. "Oh, no, you don't. That's staying up there." He pulled her close but resisted the urge to kiss those full lips. "And you have an open invitation to sashay down the hall any night and enjoy it with me," he murmured, watching her eyes darken. "I'll even let you lie on your back, so you can appreciate the pretty pattern of the lace while I'm deep inside you."

She wrenched from his grip and fled. He heard the front door bang after her. With a long sigh he started toward the bathroom for a cold shower. At least he had the satisfaction of knowing that the canopied bed would prey on her mind as well as on his. And she had no one to blame for that but herself.

A BRISK WALK FINALLY reduced Daphne's tension to the point where she could face Stony again. She returned to her room to comb her hair before starting on dinner and found the pot of African violets. Although there was no note or card, she knew they had to be from Stony. Her heart quickened with hope.

Yet when she tried to thank him for the violets as they sat down to dinner, he shrugged off the gesture as if buying them for her had been almost an afterthought. Frustrated with his refusal to acknowledge even the slightest bit of sentimental feeling for her, she remained silent through the meal and avoided him for the rest of the evening. But in the days that followed, she took very good care of the little pot of violets.

With the waterfall in place, she also checked the sky every morning, hoping to glimpse rain clouds on the horizon, but the sky remained relentlessly blue and the land grew thirstier every day. Several times she caught Stony eyeing the waterfall and she knew he was begrudging the water it took, but the birds and small animals loved it. The yard became a colorful gathering place for wildlife.

Daphne had little time to watch the activity, though. Her carton of catalogs and samples arrived, and her growing business kept her on the move with constant trips to town. Although sexual tension remained high between her and Stony, she managed to keep her yearnings in check during the brief times she was with him. Unfortunately, she thought about his canopied bed more than was good for her during the restless nights, and consequently wasn't as alert as she would have liked to be for her third meeting with Agnes Farnsworth.

As they sat on Agnes's sunporch surrounded by catalogs, Daphne gulped from her glass of iced tea and hoped the caffeine would keep her awake. During the first appointment Daphne had learned that Agnes was the mother of two daughters, both married. One lived in Rio Verde, and this morning Agnes mentioned hiring Daphne to feng shui her daughter's house as a Christmas present.

"I'd love to," Daphne said, glancing up from the color wheel she'd been consulting. By agreeing to a job so far in advance, she was also committing herself to stick around. With luck, that wasn't a foolish thing to do. "It couldn't be a surprise for your daughter, though. You'd need to make sure she and her husband want it done. Not everyone goes for the concept."

Agnes gazed at her. "For instance, like your cousin Stony?"

Daphne could feel the warmth stealing into her cheeks. "Right."

Agnes put down her glass of iced tea and leaned across the wicker cocktail table. "Daphne, I'm a plain-spoken woman, so you'll have to forgive me for being blunt, but you're no more Stony's cousin than I am."

By now Daphne's cheeks felt like a couple of stove burners. "What makes you say that?"

"Remember last time you were here I asked you a little about your family and Stony's? You managed to change the subject, not once, but twice. Most folks, especially Texas folks, love to explain all about their kin."

Daphne squirmed. "Well, I—"

"And just now, at the mention of his name, you lit up like a stoplight. I'm not a gossip and I won't give away your secrets to the whole town, but if I'm going to have you redoing my house and then Suzanne's house come Christmas, I want to know who I'm dealing with. You're not in trouble with the law or anything, are you?"

"Goodness, no!" Daphne put a hand on her pounding heart and sank back against the cushions of the wicker love seat.

"Then, what brings you to Rio Verde? I have a hard

time believing you traveled all the way from Hawaii to this little Texas town just because you had a burning urge to start a business here. It's a nice-enough place to live, but our chamber of commerce usually has to bribe folks to transfer a business to Rio Verde."

Daphne quickly thought through her options. If she insisted on sticking to her story, Agnes might decide against the redecorating job. If Agnes backed out, that could affect her other clients, because Agnes was apparently the ringleader among the women in town. Besides, Daphne liked Agnes, and lying to her had never felt like the right thing to do.

She started to pick up her glass of tea and realized her hand was shaking too much to take a drink without spilling it everywhere. She put the glass down.

"Oh, my stars, you are upset." Agnes hurried around and moved the catalogs so she could sit next to Daphne and put a comforting arm around her. "What is wrong, darlin'?"

Too much caffeine, too little sleep and too much stress had Daphne fumbling in her purse as tears gathered in her eyes. "It's just...it's just *everything!*" she burst out. Embarrassing herself in the process, she started to sob.

With a mother's instinct, Agnes had soon dragged the whole story out of her.

Daphne dabbed at her eyes and blew her nose. "This is so unprofessional. You're free to cancel our agreement, Agnes."

"Cancel it?" Agnes patted her hand. "I'll do no such thing. In fact, I'll help you rummage up some more clients."

"Well, thanks, but I—"

"You deserve it. Thanks to Jasper and his gang, you were plopped down in the middle of nowhere and expected to build up a business from scratch. That isn't easy to do, but I'm sure you can do it, because you have spunk and wonderful new ideas. I'd consider it a privilege to help you."

Daphne choked back a fresh flood of tears. "Thank you."

"But like any mother on the face of the earth, my help comes with some advice. You're free to take it or not. I'll make the same rule with you as I do with my two girls. If you don't take my advice, don't come complainin' to me about poor results."

"You probably think I should move away from the Roughstock Ranch, and you're probably right. It's just that I—"

"Why would you want to move away? Aren't you in love with him?"

Daphne glanced at her and slowly nodded.

"Have you told him that?"

Daphne shook her head.

"Then tell him. Don't wait for him to say the words. These men are slow. The good ones are, at any rate. The Romeos of the world say it every five minutes, just to get what they want, but Stony isn't like that. My advice is to make him a good dinner, give him a good time in bed, and then tell him how you feel."

"Agnes!"

Agnes regarded her gravely. "Told you I was plain-spoken. Have the courage to put your cards out on the

table, is what I say. Now, about the living room walls,
what do you think of purple?''

MAYBE IT WASN'T FAIR, but Stony partly blamed
Daphne and the lace canopy for Jolly Boy stepping in a
gopher hole. If Stony hadn't been short on sleep from
lying in bed thinking about the interesting shadows
that lace would make on Daphne's naked body, he
might not have been running his horse so fast that he
hadn't seen the gopher hole until it was too late. He
could have steered around it. Then again he might not
have, but he felt better laying the blame on Daphne,
her sexual appeal and her decorating schemes.

Thank God Jolly Boy's right front leg was only
sprained. Stony was in no emotional shape to handle
anything worse. Rio Verde's only vet was headed out
to do an emergency cesarean on a neighboring
rancher's mare and wouldn't be available, but he as-
sured Stony that ice treatments throughout the night
would probably be adequate for Jolly Boy's sprain.

Stony realized that if he wanted to find a silver lining
in the cloud, it would be that he'd spend the night in
the barn putting ice on Jolly Boy's leg and wouldn't
have to face the sweet agony of lying in that canopy
bed tonight, just down the hall from Daphne. He was
damn near close to breaking on that score.

Jasper had offered to spell him during the night, but
Stony didn't want to trust the job to anyone else, not
even Jasper. He'd owned Jolly Boy for ten years, and
although he'd tried to tell himself that any mount
would do and he shouldn't get attached to just one, he
always chose the big bay when it came time to saddle

up. For the next little while he'd have to ride another horse to give Jolly Boy a chance to heal, but he didn't want that to become a permanent situation.

"I'll see that you get somethin' to eat, then," Jasper told him as he left the barn. "And I'll tell Daphne what happened."

Stony looked up from his job of wrapping Jolly Boy's foreleg prior to immersing it in a bucket of ice. "I'd appreciate that. Tell her she can switch off the waterfall. I won't be there to hear it tonight." He hated to admit how much he'd enjoyed the sound of the water each night. It had been like camping next to a rocky stream. True, it had probably heightened his sexual frustration, because the splashing water had a sensual tone to it. Hell, these days everything had a sensual tone to it.

Stony had expected one of the boys to bring him a plate of food from the bunkhouse, but instead Daphne showed up with fried chicken, potato salad and an ice-cold beer, all packed into a little basket. The food smelled wonderful, but he nearly forgot his hunger when he emerged from the stall and took a good look at her. Red Riding Hood meets the wolf, he thought grimly.

She'd changed out of her town clothes into the cutoff jeans he liked so much. But the part of her outfit that had his mouth watering was her blouse. None of the buttons down the front seemed to be fastened. Instead, she'd tied the thing together just below her breasts. Unless he was a poor judge of such things, and he usually wasn't, she wore no bra underneath.

If she'd decided to drive him completely insane, this was the outfit to do it with. But damned if he'd make a move on her, because if he did, she'd probably set up all her conditions again. He didn't want to deal with conditions.

"I was sure sorry to hear about Jolly Boy." She handed him the basket. "Is it all right if I go in to see him?"

"Sure. Just talk easy to him so he doesn't try to move suddenly and pull his foot out of the bucket." He stood watching as she unlatched the stall and slipped inside. Definitely no bra. That couldn't be an accident. A woman like Daphne didn't just *forget* to put on underwear.

"Go ahead and eat," she said over her shoulder. "You must be starving."

"Yeah." *Oh, yeah.* "Thanks." He sat down on a bale of straw and started in on the meal while he listened to her croon softly to his horse. Another sensual sound to add to the list. Damned if he wasn't getting aroused just thinking about that tempting blouse of hers. One little tug and the whole thing...but he needed to put that thought clean out of his mind and concentrate on the meal she'd brought.

He'd eaten most of his dinner when she came back out of the stall and latched it behind her. "This is really good," he said. He took a sip of beer and swallowed. Perfect temperature on the beer. "Did you make the potato salad?"

"With my own two hands. In my experience, most guys like fried chicken and potato salad."

That caused him to lift his eyebrows. "You mean you made this because you thought I'd like it?"

"As a matter of fact."

Oh, he sensed a trap coming. Feed a guy good, tantalize him with the promise of sex, and then refuse to go to bed with him unless he proposes. He was a little tired of the game. He gazed deliberately at her breasts. "Nice outfit."

"Mmm." She smiled.

He took a shaky breath. She could play this better than he could, apparently. "Look, Daphne, I appreciate the food, but you'd better take the basket and go back up to the house before I forget myself. I know you wouldn't want that without me having a wedding ring in my pocket, and I can guarantee I don't have one of those."

She just smiled that tantalizing smile that made his fingers itch to rip off her clothes and back her up against the stall door. "Jasper said I should turn off the waterfall," she said. "But I had an idea that might help Jolly Boy."

"Please don't try to tell me that Jolly Boy will heal faster listening to splashing water."

"That's possible, but I was thinking he might heal faster with his leg in the water, especially with the pump on and the water moving."

He stared at her. "Daphne, that is a damn fine idea."

"Thank you. I'll help."

"You can help by taking this basket and getting your cute little fanny out of here. I have a horse to doctor." He held out the basket.

"What if I told you I've changed my mind about staying a virgin?"

The basket clattered to the floor of the barn as he stood there absorbing her words, his heart hammering.

"I'd say—" He had to stop and clear his throat. "I'd say you have damned poor timing." He gestured back to the horse. "Jolly Boy— Hellfire, woman, why *now*?"

"Because I can't stand it."

God, he wanted her. His erection strained at his jeans. But his horse needed treatment.

"Let me help you with Jolly Boy tonight," she said. "And then...we'll see."

"I can't imagine what sort of torture that will be. Maybe you should just go on back to the house and I'll..." He swallowed. "I'll see you in the morning."

"I want to be with you tonight."

He groaned.

She leaned down and picked up the basket, in the process giving him an eyeful. "I'll take this back to the house and meet you at the waterfall. Jolly Boy might be a little spooked by the whole thing, and I'll help you keep him calm."

"While you turn me into a wild man."

She smiled again, and he had to clench his fists at his sides to control himself. Then she turned and headed out of the barn.

"Better put on some coffee," he called after her. "It's gonna be a long night."

She glanced over her shoulder, an invitation obvious in her dark eyes. "Oh, it's going to be a very long night."

14

THE EVENING wasn't working out the way Daphne had planned, she thought as she started the coffee perking and rinsed Stony's dishes. The pretty table she'd set with candles and store-bought flowers would go to waste. But if Stony couldn't go to her, she'd go to him.

After making her decision in town today, she wasn't about to let circumstances defeat her. Luckily she'd thought to tell Jasper that she'd be keeping Stony company in the barn tonight and he and the other hands wouldn't have to worry about a thing. Jasper took the hint, she was sure. He'd even taken Chi down to the bunkhouse for the night. She and Stony would have complete privacy.

Gathering supplies for a night in the barn, she thought about the look on Stony's face when she'd told him of her intentions. A man who wanted a woman that much had to have some love wrapped in with his lust. As Daphne had packed up to leave Agnes's house that morning, Agnes had reminded her that if Stony only wanted sex, he could have satisfied his cravings with another woman by now. Such options were available to a man as attractive as Stony, even in a small town like Río Verde, Agnes had said.

Daphne had put all the evidence together and decided that Agnes was right. Stony loved her, but with his background he certainly wouldn't be the first one to say so. She'd demonstrate her love tonight and then tell him about it afterward. She doubted that he'd be unable to say those words back to her after the night she had planned for him.

She piled her supplies on the front porch and got down to the waterfall just as Stony arrived, inching along so that he wouldn't put too much strain on Jolly Boy's leg. The horse flicked his ears forward and snorted when he saw the waterfall.

"I'll hold him while you take off your boots," Daphne offered, walking around to the horse's head.

Stony turned over the lead rope to her. "You don't have to go in the water with him, too," he said.

"I want to." As she stood holding Jolly Boy, she nudged her shoes off. "I think with one of us on each side of his bridle as we walk slowly into the water, he'll have less chance of spooking."

"You're probably right. Okay, my boots are off."

"If I were you, I'd leave the hat and shirt behind, too. The closer we get him to the waterfall, the better, and you're going to get wet."

He gazed across the horse's neck at her. "So are you."

"Yes, but women aren't as free to take off their shirts."

"You're barely wearing it, anyway."

"I'll keep it on," she said, meeting his gaze. "For now."

"Tarnation, woman. I hope you know what you're doing to me, teasing me like this. Did you really change your mind?"

"Yes, I really did. Now, let's take this horse into the fountain. That should ease his condition...and yours."

Stony muttered something she couldn't quite hear, but his frustration came through loud and clear. Daphne smiled to herself and stroked Jolly Boy's nose.

As they eased the big bay into the water, Jolly Boy jerked his head up and trembled slightly.

"Whoa, son," Stony murmured. "This will be a good thing for that leg of yours. Just ease on down there. That's right. Got him, Daphne?"

"I've got him." The water was cold, but she waded in without hesitation so that the horse would absorb her confidence and follow along. The water crept up to her thighs and finally lapped above her waist. "Make sure he doesn't step on the motor."

"I'm trying to steer us around that. Okay, this seems like as good a spot as any. The water's churning up pretty good right here. Easy, Jolly Boy. Just stand still."

"I think this is perfect," Daphne said. Water splashed down on her until her hair dripped and her blouse was soaked, but she was in the shadow of the falls and no one would be able to see her in this light, anyway. She could barely make out the outline of Stony's head and shoulders as he stood on the other side of Jolly Boy. "It should really take the swelling down."

Stony chuckled. "On both my horse and me."

"That's probably a good thing," Daphne said. "Trying to fool around while we're holding this horse in the pool wouldn't be too bright."

"I had no intention of that," Stony said. "Fortunately

I can't see you worth a darn, anyway. I'm sure by now that blouse is..."

The moon peeked up over the roofline of the house, bathing Daphne in silver light.

Stony gasped. "Good Lord, woman," he said, his voice husky. "I can see right through that material. Can't you...do something?"

She glanced down at the transparent cloth. Sure enough, she might as well have been standing there naked. She shrugged. "I can't very well turn off the moon."

"You could turn around."

"You could look away."

Neither of them did either as the tension grew thick between them.

He spoke in a whisper. "Every blessed night I lie down in my bed, I can remember what you looked like stretched out on those sheets. I loved looking at your breasts. I love looking at them now, even if it's killing me."

"I remember the touch of your hand on them," she murmured as her nipples tightened in response. "The way you stroked me. The way you knew just how to—"

He groaned. "The cold water isn't working anymore, Daph."

"I think Jolly Boy's had enough of the water treatment for now, don't you? We can bring him back again later on tonight."

"And what will you be wearing then?" Stony asked in a choked voice.

"That depends."

"God." He took a deep breath. "Okay, let's turn him around and get him back out. I want to walk him to the barn just as slow as I brought him over here, so we don't wreck what we just accomplished."

"I'll take the coffee and...other things over to the barn and wait for you."

"What other things?"

"Supplies." She wasn't about to reveal all her secrets. She wanted him to be thoroughly curious and thoroughly aroused. From the look of him as they led Jolly Boy out of the water, she had a good start. Good thing he didn't want to walk fast. It would have been painful for him.

As Stony started leading Jolly Boy back to the barn, Daphne put on her shoes and retrieved her pile of goodies. She beat him to the barn by quite a while. He'd left his battery-operated lantern on in Jolly Boy's stall, probably so he wouldn't have to use the harsh overhead lights and disturb the other horses when he returned.

Quickly borrowing the light so she'd be able to see, she scattered a deep bed of straw in the empty stall just opposite Jolly Boy's. She wouldn't keep Stony from checking frequently on his horse, but he needed a break now and then, and she intended to give it to him. She spread a large blanket on top of the straw. Then she experimentally draped a red bandanna over the lantern. Perfect. She pulled the bandanna off again and tossed it where she'd be able to reach it easily.

Her luck must be running, she thought, because the stall happened to be in the love-and-marriage sector of the barn. She set the vase of pink roses in a corner of the stall, scattered some stray petals over the blanket, picked up the lantern and walked out, latching the door behind her.

She was waiting in Jolly Boy's stall by the time Stony led the big bay in. He'd put on his hat and shirt, but he hadn't bothered with the buttons. One look at him and desire seeped heavily into her body, making her ache with a ferocity that almost scared her.

"His leg looks much better," she said, somehow managing to sound as if she weren't ready to throw herself into Stony's arms.

"I think so, too. That was a real brilliant idea of yours." He gave her a brief glance. "But seein' as how your blouse isn't dry yet, I'd appreciate it if you'd step outside the stall until I get his leg wrapped up and back in the ice bucket."

"Then would you like a coffee break?" Her heartbeat quickened as she thought of what she had in mind.

He crouched down to wrap Jolly Boy's leg. "A coffee break?"

"I'll have a cup poured and waiting when you're finished."

He knelt beside the horse and glanced up at her. "I like it hot."

She quivered with the need to hold him. "It'll be hot. Bring your lantern with you."

A fire of unholy intensity burned in his blue eyes. "Damn if you aren't the most provocative woman I've ever known. Now get. Please."

She crossed the aisle of the barn and entered the stall on the other side. The interior was fairly dark, but fortunately she didn't have to see well to accomplish the next part of her plan. She started working at the damp knot keeping the front ends of her blouse together.

AS STONY THOUGHT ABOUT what Daphne was planning, he had trouble keeping his hands steady as he wrapped Jolly Boy's leg. No doubt about it, the tumbling water had helped. He'd make sure to get in at least one more session before daybreak. God knew what else might happen that night, judging from the signals he was getting from Daphne.

He had no idea what was going on with this woman who had caused such confusion in his life. But for some unknown reason, she'd given up her virgin plan and was coming on to him in no uncertain terms. He probably should be more cautious, but damn, she had him so worked up he couldn't think straight.

After he'd repositioned Jolly Boy's leg in the bucket of ice, he stood and rubbed the gelding's nose up under his forelock where the bay liked being scratched. "Take it easy, son, okay?" he said. "Stand quiet, like I know you can. I'll be back to check on you in a little bit. Right now I need to see what's going on with that feng shui lady."

With a final pat on the bay's silky neck, Stony picked up the lantern, went out of the stall and latched it. He glanced around, wondering where Daphne had disappeared to. He called her name softly.

"In here," she replied, her voice pitched low and sexy.

A shiver went up his spine. He noticed the door to the stall across from Jolly Boy's was open a crack. With his heartbeat pounding relentlessly in his ears, he stepped forward and slowly pulled the door open. As the glow from the lantern lit the interior of the stall, he caught his breath.

She lay on a blanket, propped up on one elbow. The delicate scent of roses, the earthy tang of fresh straw and the punchy aroma of coffee swirled around him as he stared at her. She was absolutely, gloriously naked.

With the blood roaring in his ears, Stony ceased to hear the night sounds of horses moving in their stalls, the crickets in the hayloft, an owl in the woods. In a daze, he stepped inside the stall.

She lifted a steaming mug toward him. "Coffee?"

He was so completely mesmerized by the gentle movement of her breasts as she lifted the mug that he couldn't organize his brain to give her an answer.

"I warned Jasper to keep everyone away tonight," she said. "But maybe you should latch the stall door, anyway."

Without taking his gaze from her, he closed the door with a soft click that seemed to echo through the barn. Then he walked forward, knelt on the blanket and set down the lantern. Slowly, so as not to spill hot coffee on her delicate skin, he took the mug she held out.

Keeping eye contact with her, he took a sip. "Good coffee." He could have been drinking motor oil for all he knew.

"Can I have a little?" she asked.

Silently he passed her the mug. She turned it around so that her mouth touched the spot where his had been before she took a drink. Her gaze never left his.

She lowered the mug and ran her tongue over her lips. "I wonder if you'd like to try an experiment?"

His voice sounded rusty. "What?"

"I've heard that it's a nice sensation for a man if a woman takes a little warm coffee in her mouth and then..." She glanced significantly at the fly of his jeans.

"Is that right?" His erection pushed painfully against the wet denim.

"You look uncomfortable." She set the coffee mug down and eased herself to a sitting position. As she draped a piece of material over the lantern, the stall took on a rosy glow.

He couldn't believe it. She'd turned a stall in his old barn into the sexiest place he'd ever seen.

"Those jeans seem way too tight," she murmured. Gazing at him, she got to her knees and started unbuttoning his fly.

He'd love to abandon himself to this, red light, roses and all, but he had to know just how complete her preparations had been before he lost his ability to reason. He caught her wrist. "What sort of...supplies did you bring?"

"Everything we'll need." Her voice was like velvet. "But you aren't going to require any *supplies* just yet."

"Oh." With the wild excitement surrender brings, he released her wrist. As she resumed her careful unbuttoning, he closed his eyes and battled for control. "Daphne, just the slightest... I'm...not going to be able to...hold out for very..."

"I'm not asking you to, cowboy. It's been a long, dry spell."

Her hands against his skin were like a match to a fuse. When her fingers encircled his erection, a low cry came boiling up from deep in his chest.

"Time for your coffee break," she murmured.

He opened his eyes and discovered that she'd put the mug to her lips once again. "You're really going to—" Then he lost the power of speech, because she really did.

The warm liquid of the coffee and the sensuous movement of her tongue were like nothing he'd ever experienced in his life. His control was going, and fast. He tried to pull away but she held him tight, and he didn't have the willpower to resist. It felt too damn good. Soon there was no stopping, and she loved him right to the end.

He cried out and might have lost his balance if she hadn't wrapped both arms around him and gradually eased herself up along his heated body, kissing and nibbling as she went. Gasping for breath, he filled his arms full of her. Her nipples slid tantalizingly against his bare chest, and he promised himself he'd explore the delights of her full breasts before long. Removing his hat and tossing it in a corner, he sought out the tender mouth that had so recently taken him to paradise.

She tasted of passion, and he grew hard again just remembering how she'd used that mouth on him. She might have played the innocent the first night they'd made love, but tonight she was all wanton sexuality. And he wanted her again.

She reached between them and wrapped him in her clever fingers once more.

He groaned softly against her mouth as she caressed him. She was going to kill him with pleasure. He needed to even the odds, but he was still all tangled up in his wet jeans and boots.

He lifted his mouth from hers. "Let me get rid of—"

"They're not really in the way." She ran her tongue over his lower lip. "And you'll just have to pull them back on when you go check on Jolly Boy."

Jolly Boy. With the way she was stroking him and planting little kisses all over his face, it took a couple of seconds before he remembered why he was spending the night in the barn in the first place. "I can just put my jeans back on. But I'm all tied up here. I can't move."

"Then I'll move you, big boy."

He wasn't sure exactly how it happened, but she shifted her body and he temporarily lost his balance. The damp jeans clinging to his thighs made him nearly helpless to maneuver, and before he knew it, she'd toppled him to his back on the blanket. He was definitely not in charge.

When she brought out a condom and rolled it over his throbbing erection, he ceased to care who was in charge. She kissed him thoroughly on the mouth before easing herself over him. He gazed up into her beautiful face as she lowered herself slowly, taking him inside her body with an expression of pure happiness. He felt the same way. At last they were together again.

He cupped her face. "Come here and kiss me," he whispered, guiding her down. As her lips met his, he wrapped his arms around her. He held her there, buried deep inside her warm body, chest to chest, mouth to mouth, and knew a sense of completeness he'd never felt in his life. Gratitude for being able to hold her like this surged through him. If he died this instant, he'd have no regrets.

Gradually she began to move, but the sense of oneness didn't leave him as she rocked her hips, increasing the pleasure for both of them. He loved the friction of her body against his, the catch in her breathing as she grew more excited. Soon it seemed as if their two bodies were no longer separate, as if they rode the same wild mount. He imagined his breath became hers, his heartbeat hers, going faster, faster, faster. Straining for the prize...reaching...needing...

Mouth seeking mouth, they poured their groans of pleasure into each other as the climax rushed upon them at the same moment. Then she lifted her head, gasping for breath in the same rhythm as he did. She leaned her damp forehead against his and he held her tight, tighter than he'd ever held anyone in his life. He didn't want to lose this miracle, this feeling of being totally *with* a woman.

Her lips brushed his and then she nestled her head against his shoulder. One arm wrapped around her, he cupped the back of her head and held her there as their hearts thudded in unison. He closed his eyes. He never wanted this to end, never.

But, as he'd learned so well, it would. He needed to prepare for that. But not now. Not just now.

EVEN THOUGH STONY TOOK the lantern to go check on Jolly Boy, Daphne could see well enough to straighten the blanket. She couldn't help smiling as she smoothed out the wrinkles and then lay back on the makeshift bed. Stony loved her. She'd felt it. If she hadn't been so bullheaded about keeping her virgin status, she might have found out sooner.

Then again, maybe he'd fallen in love with her over the days they'd spent together when they hadn't been intimate. Maybe she had done the right thing in waiting until now. It didn't matter, so long as she could look into his eyes and see the devotion shining there.

He'd held her as if he cherished the chance to do so. No man had ever held her quite like that, as if he never wanted to let go. Before he'd left the stall, he'd kissed her and stroked her cheek with such tenderness that she had no doubt about his feelings for her. He was, after all, the man she'd dreamed of when she'd been writing those letters. It had just taken a little while for him to realize that they were perfect for each other, just as Jasper had predicted.

The lantern light bobbed in the aisle of the barn as she heard Stony's footsteps approach. He smiled at her as he slipped inside the stall and set the lantern on the floor. "I don't care what you say." He leaned against the side of the stall and pulled off one boot. "I'm taking my jeans and boots off this time."

Her pulse quickened. "You mean you're not tired? You could sleep a little bit if you like. I'll keep watch and wake you in a little while."

He chuckled as he took off the other boot. "Sleep? When I'm having the night of my dreams?"

"So am I."

He peeled off his jeans and briefs, revealing that he was once more becoming aroused. "See what you do to me? I haven't been this quick to recover since I was seventeen."

"I just don't want to wear you out. You have obligations tomorrow, I'm sure."

"And I'm sure you do, too." He lay down on the blanket and pulled her into his arms, combing her hair back from her face with his fingers. "Do you want to sleep? If you do, I'll find the strength to leave you alone, somehow."

Her heart filled with joy as she twined her leg around his. "I can't imagine sleeping when we could do this."

"Good. Just a second." Releasing her, he rolled back toward the lantern, picked up the bandanna and tossed it over the light. Then he turned back to her and gathered her close. "Party time."

15

ABOUT AN HOUR before dawn, Daphne dressed and carried everything back to the house while Stony checked Jolly Boy one last time. They'd taken the gelding to the waterfall twice more during the night, and Stony had kept the horse's leg iced the rest of the time. Jolly Boy was going to be fine.

They were all going to be fine, Daphne thought as she deposited her bundle on the couch and went into the bathroom for a quick shower. Stony had asked her to wait for him in his bed. He'd promised to leave a note for Jasper that he and Daphne would be sleeping in.

"And we'll sleep?" Daphne had said, smiling.

"Maybe." He'd given her a wicked grin before going into Jolly Boy's stall.

The first glow of dawn lightened the sky outside Stony's bedroom window as Daphne crawled between the cool sheets and glanced up at the canopy. It was only shadowy fabric now, but soon she'd be able to make out the patterns in the lace. Stony had said once that he'd let her lie on her back so that she could see those patterns when he was deep inside her. She had no business getting aroused again after all the wonderful lovemaking she'd shared with Stony the past few hours, but desire stirred in her, anyway, just lying in his bed gazing up at the canopy.

The open window let in the cool breeze of early morning and the murmur of the water going over the falls. The sound relaxed Daphne, yet heightened her senses, as if she could feel the water slipping over her body in a liquid massage.

"I ought to be all played out," Stony said from the doorway as he leaned there and pulled off his boots. Then he sauntered over to the bed and braced a hand on each side of her head. "But damned if I don't want you again, seeing you lying here under that lacy thing, just like I pictured you."

She reached up and drew his head down. "I want you, too."

He resisted her. "I should shave first. And shower."

"No," she whispered as the water lapped at the rocks outside the window.

"Did you know your waterfall sounds like lovemaking?" he murmured.

"Yes."

The stubble on his chin pricked as he took her mouth in a fully suggestive kiss. She liked him this way, unshaved, musky and thoroughly male. He grabbed a fistful of the sheet covering her and pulled it completely off the bed. Then he swept his hand over her, seeming to mimic the sound of the water as he stroked his palm over her skin and left fever in the wake of his touch.

With no hesitation he slid his hand surely between her thighs. He slipped his fingers inside with the smooth certainty of what he would find, what he did find, that she was already drenched with arousal. She arched into his caress, moaning with the pleasure of it.

With a sharp intake of breath he eased away from her and fumbled with the buttons of his jeans. She watched his impatient movements as he tugged the jeans off, and wondered if she and Stony would ever lose the urgency that seemed to drive them toward this glorious joining of two bodies...two souls.

"The way I want you, you'd think I'd been away from you a week instead of thirty minutes." He moved over her.

Her body flushed with desire as she wrapped her legs around his, urging him closer. "I know what you mean."

"It's as if...I want to drown in you...."

She lifted her hips in invitation. "And I want you...to fill me. Please, Stony."

"Wait. We need—" He leaned toward the night table, opened the drawer and searched it. His breathing was ragged as he pulled the drawer out and it clattered to the floor. "Damn, where are they?"

She panted with need as the melody of the waterfall promised exquisite pleasure. "I forgot to put them back. They're in the living room. Oh, Stony...Stony, please!"

He looked into her eyes and she pleaded silently for what only he could give her.

He groaned. "The sound of the water is so..."

"Fill me," she whispered.

Clenching his jaw, he pushed in deep.

"Ohhh..." She'd had no idea lovemaking could feel like this, so liquid and supple. So absolutely, completely right. She opened to him in a way she never had to a man, arching upward with each thrust, her head thrashing from side to side as she cried out for more, more, more.

And he gave her all she asked, creating the perfect rhythm that sent her soaring upward until her body grew taut and quivering. He paused, and with one powerful thrust sent them both over the edge.

As her body erupted in a fiery, wondrous explosion, she could no longer hold back the words that had trembled on her lips all night. "I love you," she cried softly. "I love you, Stony."

He closed his eyes and gulped in air.

With growing dread she waited for him to speak. Finally she couldn't stand it any longer. Her voice trembled. "Say something."

He opened his eyes and gazed down at her, his eyes reflecting his inner torture. He took a breath, and then another. Finally he eased away from her and rolled to his back.

"Stony?"

"No matter what I say, it won't be what you want to hear."

She felt suddenly cold. "Why not? Stony, we've been as close as two people can be tonight, and I know you were feeling something pretty special."

He was silent for a long time, and when he spoke, the words came out like bullets. "I don't love you."

The words went deep, wounding her in a way that might never heal. She tried to blunt the impact. "I don't believe you."

"You think you know who I am, but you don't. You

know the guy Jasper made up in those letters, and that's not me. I don't have whatever's inside people that makes them fall in love, get married, have a family. I know that's the kind of guy you want, so you'd better stop wasting your time with me and go find him."

A robin chirped outside the window, and then another as the waterfall bubbled happily and the birds gathered there for a drink. The cheerful beginning of a new day mocked the desolation in Daphne's heart. She thought about arguing with him. She could point to all the evidence that proved him wrong—his devotion to Jasper, his father, even his horse and his dog.

But it didn't matter if she could see the truth. If he refused to even look, then he might as well be just as coldhearted as he pretended to be. It amounted to the same thing in the end. Maybe eventually he would become the sort of unloving man he pictured himself, if he told himself those lies long enough.

She slipped out of bed and left the room, her cheeks wet with silent tears. She wiped them away angrily. She didn't have time to cry. She had a lot of packing to do.

STONY LAY THERE a long time, listening to the sounds from Daphne's room. From all the banging around in there, he figured she was probably packing. By tonight she'd be gone. And that was a good thing. He needed her to leave now, before things got any messier. And she needed to go, for her own good.

He wondered where she'd end up. San Antonio, maybe. That way she could keep up with the clients she'd picked up while she was here. He thought of her looking for a place to live in San Antonio. She didn't know anybody there. Some parts of town weren't as safe as he'd like them to be. Damn, but he wished the tight feeling in his chest would go away.

Finally he faced the part he didn't want to think about. They'd just had sex without protection. What if he'd just made her pregnant? His gut twisted. She'd never tell him, not after that speech he'd delivered a few minutes ago. He couldn't figure out why he'd let himself get carried away like that. He could have left the bed and located the box of condoms. Instead he'd allowed himself to sink right into her softness.

The effect had been incredible, but he couldn't think about that now. He'd never had sex without protection before, and he never would again. Why he'd acted so irresponsibly with this woman remained a mystery. But he had to deal with it.

Sighing, he climbed out of bed and pulled on his briefs and jeans. The walk down the hall toward her bedroom felt like a condemned man's last journey. He'd rather ride the meanest bull on the circuit than talk to Daphne now about this subject.

He stood in the doorway of her little room. She'd put on a white bathrobe and she had her back to him as she grabbed things and threw them into the suitcase lying open on her bed. When he spoke her name, she whirled around. She'd been crying.

He should have expected it, but the sight of her tear-streaked face sliced him to ribbons. But what was worse was the glimmer of hope in her dark eyes, hope he was about to dash.

He cleared his throat. "What if you're pregnant?"

The hope died and she turned back to the suitcase. "I was the one who pushed you to make love without protection. I don't hold you responsible, just myself."

"I could have refused."

Her laughter held no joy in it. "I had you bewitched with the feng shui waterfall. Nope, it's my problem to deal with. If it turns out that I'm pregnant, which I'm probably not, I'll handle it."

"How?" He couldn't believe she'd get rid of the baby. That wasn't like her.

"None of your business."

"It is my business."

She spun around, and fury had replaced the hopeless look on her face. "You just told me you don't have what it takes to be a family man. So you've given up your rights, in my opinion."

"I'm not talking about rights. I'm talking about financial obligation. I would...pay support, for you and the...baby." He had a hard time getting the last word out. It seemed to lodge in his throat, and his heart was hammering like a son of a gun.

Her chin lifted. "All right, if it would bother your conscience, I'll take money. It's pitiful that's the best you have to offer in such a situation, but I suppose it wouldn't be fair to the baby if I didn't take at least that."

"So you'll let me know?"

"I'll let you know." Her expression grew bleak.

He fought the urge to take her into his arms. But unless he planned to lie and tell her how much he loved her, unless he decided to marry her, he shouldn't touch her ever again. "That's settled, then. Guess I'll go on down to the barn."

"I need a way to get to San Antonio today."

"I'll ask Jasper to drive you."

"Thank you."

He stood looking at her and thought this might be the last time they'd ever see each other. A great black void seemed to open inside him at the thought. He experienced a moment of panic that scared him so bad he knew he had to either leave the room or beg her to stay, as if he stood on the edge of a soft shale ledge, not sure if it would give way at any minute under his feet.

Her expressive eyes lost their hard glitter and grew soft. She opened her mouth, as if to say something.

He struggled for breath. "I gotta go," he said, and bolted.

"YOU DAMNED COWARD!" Jasper's mustache twitched furiously as he paced back and forth in front of the bunkhouse. Periodically he glanced at the bright red door with its decorative wreath, as if to remind Stony of Daphne's many talents.

Stony had decided he might as well notify Jasper now that Daphne would need a ride to San Antonio, before Jasper settled into his work for the day. Stony had figured on Jasper being unhappy that Daphne was leaving, but he hadn't judged correctly on how upset his foreman would be, or how many details of the breakup he'd pull out of Stony. The other wranglers were still inside and would probably stay there until Jasper's fit blew over.

"She has the guts to say she loves you, and you turn tail and run!"

"I can't give her what she wants," Stony said, his jaw tight.

"The hell you can't!" Jasper jammed his Stetson down hard over his ears. "You're plumb crazy about that woman, and you know it!"

"I got used to her, is all. Once she's been gone awhile, I'll forget all about her."

Jasper glared at him. "The sickening thing is, that's what I'm most afraid of. That woman woke you up, son, and if you let her go, there's little hope for you. Oh, you'll walk around and eat and sleep and play cards, but you won't be a whole man, not by a long shot."

The black void that had opened up inside Stony as he stood looking at Daphne for the last time seemed to grow larger. He crossed his arms over his chest, as if he could squeeze the void back down to size. "You're talking pure nonsense, Jasper." He hoped Jasper couldn't hear the slight tremble in his voice. "Some men are cut out for a wife and some aren't. I'm not, and you just won't accept that. And you're ticked off because your little plan didn't work."

Jasper's eyes narrowed. "Oh, it worked. It worked too good. You're in love for the first time in your life, and you're just too scared to admit it."

"I don't love her!" His sense of panic grew.

Jasper got very quiet. "Just because your mama died don't mean Daphne's gonna die and leave you, too, Stevie."

He stared at Jasper as the blackness inside threatened to swallow him. His protest came out in a hoarse croak from his suddenly dry mouth. "That's not my name."

"Used to be, back when you still had a heart."

He had to get out of there, and fast. "Have somebody check on Jolly Boy, and make sure Daphne gets to San Antonio before the day's over."

"Is that an order...boss?"

From the time they'd started working the ranch together, Stony had never given Jasper a direct order. He'd asked him to do a few things, and on the big jobs they'd discussed options, argued a few times and compromised on the final decision.

"Yes," Stony said. "That's an order." Then he headed for the barn to saddle Sunshine, the half-broken horse he'd been training. The challenge was just what he needed right now.

JASPER STOOD IN THE living room waiting as Daphne fed Chi doggy treats in the kitchen and struggled to tell the dog goodbye. Stony had left the house while Daphne was still in shock, and adrenaline had carried her through the packing, but somehow saying goodbye to the retriever seemed like an impossible task.

Finally she got to her knees and put her arms around the dog. "I wish I could take you with me," she said, her voice choked with tears. "But I'll be living in an apartment in the city and you'd hate that."

Chi whined and licked Daphne's face.

"And besides, I guess...Stony needs you more than I do." She buried her face in the dog's fur and cried softly. "Take care of him, Chi. He won't let me do it."

The dog's sigh sounded almost human as she rested her muzzle on Daphne's quivering shoulder.

Finally Daphne released the dog and got shakily to her feet. "Goodbye, Chi." She reached down to stroke the silky head once more before starting out of the kitchen.

Chi followed her.

"No, sweetheart." Daphne motioned her back. "You have to stay here."

The dog flopped down and put her head on her paws as she gazed soulfully up at Daphne.

Daphne's heart broke as she turned away from the dog and marched into the living room. "Let's go, Jasper."

He nodded and picked up her suitcase. Then he glanced at her. "This ain't as heavy as when you first came."

"I threw away my book and materials on feng shui."

"Now, why'd you go and do a thing like that?"

"Because it doesn't work!" As if to emphasize the point, she reached down and yanked the plug on the extension cord powering the waterfall. Ignoring Jasper's frown, she walked through the front doorway as he held the screen open for her.

"You didn't give it time."

"I don't have any more time! My love life is a wreck, my career in Rio Verde is probably over, and I couldn't even end the stupid drought!"

Jasper put her suitcase in the back of the pickup next to her box of decorating materials. "So you ain't gonna redecorate Agnes's house and the others?"

Daphne climbed into the cab of the truck. "I called

all three of them this morning and explained that I'd be working out of San Antonio now, and that I had serious doubts about the value of feng shui. Agnes wants to keep me on, but the other two sounded as if they'd probably back out."

Jasper didn't say anything more until they were headed down the ranch road toward the highway. That was probably just as well, because as they drove away, Daphne caught a glimpse of Big Clyde standing by the corral. He lifted his hat in a silent farewell that Daphne found so touching she had to swallow several times and blink back tears.

"I think you should call those ladies again and tell 'em feng shui works just fine," Jasper said.

"How can I do that? I have absolutely no proof that it does."

"Look out the window."

And that was the first time Daphne peeked out from behind her personal misery long enough to notice the dark clouds boiling up over the hills. They were coming in fast and hard, and they looked heavy and swollen with water.

"How soon?" she asked.

"The way they're movin', could be here in another hour. We're going toward it, so we'll hit it in less time than that."

"It could be coincidence, you know."

Jasper nodded. "Or your waterfall. And it seems to me you ended your own career by tellin' those ladies you don't believe in feng shui no more."

"That still leaves my love life, which is a total disaster."

Jasper sighed. "I knowed he was scared, but I didn't know how scared. I'm plumb sorry about how that worked out, Daphne. All along I've been promisin' you that things would get better, but now...well, I'm just not sure anymore."

His words ended any lingering hope she might have had regarding Stony. If even Jasper was giving up on him, then Stony must be really and truly lost to her. There was nothing more to say.

She watched the glowering clouds and thought how perfectly they matched her mood. A streak of lightning connected two dark thunderheads, creating an ominously deep rumble. As they traveled toward the storm, the next lightning flash brought an even louder crack of thunder. Jasper stopped the truck long enough to secure a tarp over her belongings. Soon afterward, the first big drops hit the windshield, and the thunder became deafening as lightning struck all around them.

"It's a noisy one," Jasper said. "Too bad you didn't ask for a quiet rain, but we'll take whatever we can get."

"It is noisy," Daphne agreed. "I—oh, my God, Jasper. We left Chi alone in the house! Did you close the front door?"

"Didn't think of it. Didn't see the clouds until we got outside, and then I was mostly thinkin' about you, not the dog."

"Turn around, Jasper. We have to go back."

"Stony'll probably ride in and take care of her."

Daphne shook her head. "I'm not counting on him. Besides, we're the only ones who know she's in there and can just push through the screen door if she gets scared. And she will get scared. I haven't had time to retrain her like I'd hoped. Turn around, Jasper."

"Okay, but Stony ain't gonna like it if I don't get you to San Antonio by dark."

"Too bad."

"You see, Stony, he gave me a direct order." Jasper pulled over to the shoulder and waited for traffic to clear before making a sharp U-turn. The tires skidded on the slick pavement, but Jasper straightened the truck out and stepped on the gas.

"Well, you can blame it all on me."

Jasper looked at her and grinned. "Nope. Not gonna do that. That boy oughta know better than to give me an order in the first place. I used t'change his danged diapers."

16

ON THE TOP OF Lookout Hill, Stony sat on a rock and wrestled with his demons. For the first time in his life, he couldn't see a way out. Whether he blamed it on Daphne, feng shui, Jasper or his own damn stupidity, he was in love with the woman. Desperately in love with her.

And that was after only a few days of contact. How bad would it be after five years, ten years? By that time she'd make the sun rise and the moon glow. He couldn't imagine becoming that dependent on a living thing. Living things died.

So he was better off to let her go and try to forget all about her. Eventually he wouldn't remember the way her eyes crinkled up when she laughed, or the pattern of freckles across her cute little nose, or the shape of her mouth, or the joyful way she cried out when he made love to her.

The hell he wouldn't.

Cursing under his breath, he stood and paced back and forth, wearing a path in the dry grass. Having Daphne by his side would mean facing every day with the knowledge she could be taken away from him. He wouldn't be able to stand that. Yet not having her meant facing every day alone, haunted by her smile, her voice, the memory of her touch. And that would be hell.

He wanted to blame all this on Jasper and the men, but he couldn't. A grown man had the power to make his own decisions, no matter what others threw in his path. He could have refused Daphne that first night, but he'd needed her so. He could have ignored Jasper and sent her away the next day. Somehow he could have scraped together enough money that it wouldn't have seemed a completely heartless thing to do. He'd told himself that he'd asked her to stay out of guilt, but that wasn't true. He'd asked because he'd needed her, even more than he'd needed her the night before.

Loving her that first night had put a hole in the dam, a hole that had widened with every hour, every day they'd spent together. Now his emotions were in full flood. Despair closed over him. He had no idea what to do to save himself from complete destruction. It seemed to him that either path led to ruin.

Sometime during his endless pacing he paused long enough to notice the clouds on the horizon. He stared at them in disbelief. Surely her waterfall hadn't ended the drought. Feng shui was just a stupid superstition. And yet...just yesterday he'd noticed that beef prices were rebounding. He'd put it down to coincidence. This morning he'd finally faced the fact that he was in love with a woman, an event he'd never expected to happen in his life.

A chill traveled up his spine.

Then he saw the rooster tail of dust from Jasper's truck as the foreman drove Daphne away from the ranch. Feng shui or no feng shui, she was gone. If this stuff was supposed to be so powerful, something would have kept her from leaving, but there she went, down the highway and out of his life.

He stared at the truck until he couldn't see it anymore. The wind picked up, making his damp cheeks sting. There was something he should remember, he thought, but he didn't seem to have the power to move, much less think of what he should do next. He just stood there staring at the spot where the truck had gone over the rise and disappeared.

Lightning zigzagged between the dark storm clouds, and when he closed his eyes the imprint of the jagged flash remained. That was how his memories of Daphne would be, he thought. All he'd have to do was close his eyes and he'd see her. His cry of frustration mingled with the rumble of thunder, and in that moment he knew what he should remember. The dog. Thunder would scare the dog.

Sunshine wasn't trained well enough to ground-tie, so he'd looped the reins around a low branch of a nearby tree. Hurrying back to the horse, he quickly untied the reins and started to vault into the saddle. In the middle of his vault he wondered if he'd just made a really dumb move considering how green this horse was. As he landed on his rear in the dirt and Sunshine galloped away, he knew for sure.

Sunshine would run back to the pasture gate they'd come through on their way up here, so Stony wasn't afraid of losing him, but now he was on foot, and it was a long walk. He wasn't sure he could beat the storm home, and if the dog wasn't locked up, she'd spook at the first crack of thunder. He glanced over at the advancing clouds and headed out.

DAPHNE GRIPPED THE DOOR handle as Jasper pushed the truck as fast as he dared on the slippery road. She prayed that they could outrun the storm and get back to the ranch before the thunder became loud enough to frighten Chi. Her prayers went unanswered. By the time they turned down the dirt road, the storm was crashing all around them and rain fell in sheets that quickly turned the road to mud.

"Stony's most likely at the house with her," Jasper said.

"I hope so." Daphne had no desire to see Stony again, but if it meant Chi had someone to comfort her, Daphne would suffer through another encounter.

"You're gonna hafta stay another night, y'know. It makes no sense to turn right around and head back for San Antonio in this gully-washer."

Daphne had figured that out, too, but she couldn't imagine sleeping another night under the same roof as Stony. "Maybe you can have him sleep down at the bunkhouse with y'all," she said.

"Might not be safe. I reckon the boys are ready to strangle him."

"Well, he's not safe with me, either."

He glanced at her, a gleam in his eye. "Gonna use some of your feng shui moves on him? The boys was hopin' you would. Said it would serve him right."

"Jasper, I have a confession to make. I don't know any moves. There's nothing about feng shui that involves self-defense. I let you and the boys keep thinking that because everybody seemed to enjoy the idea. I'm just a decorator."

"Now, that's where you're barkin' up the wrong tree. You ain't *just* anythin'. You're the finest lady I've had the privilege to know since...well, since Stony's mama was alive."

Daphne's throat tightened with grief. She'd miss Jasper. She'd miss them all, when it came to that, except for Stony. She couldn't describe the loss of Stony with such a simple word. "Thanks, Jasper. That's a wonderful compli—" She forgot whatever it was she'd meant to say as they drove around to the front of the ranch house. "Oh, no."

The wind whistled across the front porch, catching the screen door and slamming it back on its hinges. Inside, the house was still and dark. Stony wasn't home.

STONY CURSED HIS BOOTS as he ran. They weren't made for cross-country running, and that was a fact. He was soaked through from the driving rain, and a bolt of lightning had split a tree not thirty feet from him. The impact had thrown him to the ground and raised every hair on his body to full alert, but he was okay.

He hoped to God that Jasper was driving carefully and would get Daphne to San Antonio without skidding into a ditch or worse. He topped a hill where he could look down on the ranch house. Sure enough, there was Sunshine standing at the pasture gate, waiting for someone to show up and take him to the barn. Stony quickly scanned the area to see if the dog was anywhere around. But dammit to hell, the screen door was flapping in the wind.

The dog was gone. Stony knew it as certainly as he knew Daphne was gone. The house stood empty and dead, all the life sucked right out of it. Once the ranch had been all he wanted—land was solid and dependable, land would never fail him. But it couldn't love him.

With a groan of despair, he started down the hill. She'd named the dog Chi. It was a word meaning the life force, she'd said. He had to find the dog. If he lost Chi, how could he ever hope to keep Daphne?

Then he heard a truck on the road. It sounded like Jasper's truck, but that couldn't be right, unless.... He didn't even form the thought, as if thinking such a thing would jinx it.

The truck stopped in front of the house. Stony was concentrating so hard on the passenger door that when it opened he stumbled on the uneven ground and almost fell. *She'd come back to him!* He wanted to call out to her, but she'd never hear him over the storm.

He reached Sunshine, and the gelding was so soaked and miserable he didn't even shy when Stony grabbed the reins and opened the gate. He led the horse through and closed the gate, forcing himself to do all that needed to be done, despite the fact that all he wanted was to grab Daphne and never let go. She'd come back to him.

She and Jasper hurried into the house. As he approached the house, leading Sunshine, they came out again.

Daphne spied him and started to run, with Jasper fast on her heels. "Where's Chi?" she called.

So she hadn't come back because of him, he thought grimly. She'd come back because she was worried about the dog. Well, so was he. And they'd find her. And then...he'd find the courage to say what had to be said, no matter how much it terrified him to lay his heart on the line.

"I don't know where she is," he said as he drew nearer. "I started back to check on her and Sunshine threw me."

"Are you okay?" Seeming to ignore the rain pelting down on her, she glanced over him as if checking for injuries.

His throat tightened. And he'd tried to throw away her love, her caring, her life-giving presence, out of fear. His voice was husky with regret. "I'm better now that you're here."

"Well, I'll be danged," Jasper said. "Maybe this-here horse knocked some sense into you."

Daphne met his gaze, confusion in her dark eyes. "Stony, I—"

"Let's find Chi."

"I'll take Sunshine to the barn and get the boys to help look for the dog," Jasper said, sounding almost cheerful despite the stream of water cascading from the crease in his hat brim.

"Thanks." Stony handed him the reins. "I'll cover the east pasture and over to the creek. You divide up the rest among yourselves according to who has four-wheel drive. We'll meet back here in thirty minutes. Then if necessary we'll head out again."

"I take it you don't want to use horses," Jasper said.

"Not with the lightning. But we'll find her." He glanced at Daphne. "I'd like you to come with me."

She still looked very confused. "Okay."

RAIN DRUMMED ON THE ROOF of the cab. Daphne held on to the dashboard as Stony drove through mud holes and along paths that could barely be called roads. Every so often, he'd stop and they'd both get out, slipping in the mud, and call for Chi. As the minutes wore on, Daphne's fears increased. The ranch was huge, and they had no idea which way Chi had run when the thunder started. She'd had a long head start.

"Don't worry. We'll find her," Stony said after their third try brought no results.

"Right."

He fought the shimmying wheel and put the truck in a lower gear. "You don't sound very sure about that."

"I want to be sure, but there's so many places she could go, and so many things that could happen."

"But having her around is good feng shui, right?"

"Don't make fun of me now, Stony," she begged. "I've made a terrible mess of things with my belief in that system, and I admit it. I've thrown away all the books and I—"

"You did *what*?"

She winced. "I suppose that irritates you, after the way I insisted on the waterfall and painted the bunkhouse door, and—"

"About that waterfall, have you noticed what's happening outside?"

"Well, sure, it might be raining, but—"

"You rearranged the kitchen, and I noticed yesterday that beef prices are up."

"That's probably coincidence."

"I thought so, too. But then you came back to me."

She stared at him, openmouthed.

"I know you came back because of the dog, but it doesn't matter. You're here." He veered around a puddle that looked more like a lake.

Her chest grew tight, restricting her breathing. "You...really want that?"

"Yes." He gripped the wheel hard as the truck bounced over a deep rut and the wheels spun in the mud.

His reply whirled in her brain, making her dizzy. "But—"

"Your feng shui works great, Daphne. And that's why we're going to find Chi."

She tried to get her bearings. Stony was saying that he believed in feng shui, and that he wanted her here with him, but they would come to nothing if he couldn't admit to his love. And love was the only thing that would carry them through.

"There, through the trees! I think I saw her!" He slammed on the brakes and leaped from the truck. "Chi! Come here, Chi!"

Daphne jumped from the cab and ran after Stony. Twice she nearly fell in the mud. "Chi!" she called, trying to see through the rain pelting her in the face.

A bark echoed through the woods.

Stony made a megaphone of his hands. "Chi! Come here, dog!"

The retriever burst from the cover of the trees and headed straight for them.

"Oh, Chi," Daphne whispered as tears mingled with the rain. "Thank God." She reached Stony just as Chi did, and the three of them got very muddy in the ensuing welcoming party.

"Come on," he said, laughing. "Let's take this mutt home."

Home. Her heart ached with longing. But all he'd said was that he wanted her there. That wasn't enough to build a dream on. She'd like to ask him some questions about that statement of his, but she wanted to look into his eyes when she asked them. Right now there was a very wet and happy dog between them, and Stony had to concentrate on his driving or they'd end up in a ditch.

There was much rejoicing among the wranglers when Daphne and Stony returned to the bunkhouse with Chi in tow.

"Now everythin' can git back to normal," Big Clyde said.

"You know what we should have?" Andy said. "One of them potluck suppers. Daphne can make something, and a couple of us will make something, and we'll all git together and eat it. What y'all say to that?"

"People get food poisoning at them things," Ty said. "Food's left out, and it spoils, and blamo, everybody's throwing up."

"You talk too much, amigo," Ramon said, laughing.

Stony glanced up from where he'd been rubbing Chi with a towel. "I think it's a great idea, but let's do it tomorrow night."

Daphne knew she'd have to stay tonight because of the weather, but if Stony only wanted a mistress, she'd have to leave again tomorrow, whether he wanted her around or not. She had to protect her heart. "I might not be here tomorrow night," she said.

Stony looked at her. "Sure you will."

"We need to talk," Daphne said.

Stony smiled. "That, too." He handed the towel to Ramon. "Would you mind taking over here for a while?"

"Sure thing, Señor Stony."

Stony stood and walked over to Daphne. "If you boys will excuse us, we have to go up to the house and discuss the menu for the potluck tomorrow night."

"Can I invite somebody?" Big Clyde asked.

"He means the *librarian*," Andy teased.

Daphne glanced at Big Clyde and could tell from his blush that matters were progressing with his love life. Maybe feng shui worked for some people, but she wasn't counting on it for herself.

"Invite anybody you want," Stony said. "See y'all later." He took Daphne's arm and propelled her out the door and into the rain.

"I'm not going to bed with you, Stony Arnett," Daphne said, once they were far enough away from the bunkhouse that no one could hear.

He kept steering her toward the ranch house with a firm grip. "Why not? Did you become a virgin again this morning?"

"As a matter of fact, I did."

"It's not often a guy can deflower a virgin three times in the space of a week."

"You won't be setting that record, either. I'm through letting this chemistry between us divert me from what I truly want, which is a home and a husband who loves me."

Stony paused in front of the main house and swept out an arm. "How's that?"

"What do you mean?"

"For the home part of what you want. I realize it's not paid for, but I'm working on that. It needs a touch more fixing up, but I know a good decorator. So taking into consideration the mortgage and the condition of the place, will it do?"

Heart pounding, she turned to him. The look in his eyes made her forget the rain.

"And the second part of the question is, will I do?" he murmured, drawing her close. "I'm a little worn around the edges, haven't taken much care of my heart, but I know somebody who can help me fix that, too."

"Oh, Stony." He hadn't said the important things, but she was melting, just the same.

He tilted her face up to his. "I've never said this before, so it may not come out so smooth. But it seems that I love you and—"

"*Seems?*"

He sighed. "I knew I wouldn't get it right."

Her pulse was racing, but she fought to keep her head at this critical moment. "You either do or you don't. There's no *seems* about it."

"Then I do. I definitely do."

"Do what?"

"Tarnation, woman! Love you! I—love—you! Is that good enough?"

"Oh, Stony!" Wild with joy, she threw her arms around his neck and peppered his face with kisses.

"Hold it! That's not the end of the speech."

"It's enough for me. Kiss me."

"Not till I say what I need to say." His hand trembled as he touched her cheek, and his gaze was anxious. "I've been practicing in my head ever since we found Chi, and I'm gonna ride this baby to the buzzer."

Her heart squeezed at the determination and love in his voice. "All right, cowboy," she murmured.

He took a deep breath. "I love you and I want you to be my wife." He let out the breath in a long sigh. "There. It's done."

Her throat tightened. He'd faced the scariest monster in his universe...for her. "I love that speech."

"Now it's your turn to say something."

Dreamily she traced the line of his dear mouth, the mouth she'd come to love before they'd ever met. "But I already did, this morning."

"It could stand repeating, under the circumstances."

She looked deep into his eyes. "I love you, Stony." She watched the passion ignite with her words. "And I want you to be my husband. Will you kiss me now?"

"It's raining."

She smiled. "So what's your point?"

"I have no idea." And he proceeded to kiss her until their wet bodies were plastered together and they were on the verge of indecent behavior. Lifting his mouth from hers, he drew in a ragged breath as he rubbed his thumb across her lower lip. "I understand you're a virgin, Miss Proctor."

"That's right."

"Are you planning to save yourself until your wedding night?"

Desire raged within her, yet she managed to keep her tone prim. "I don't think that will be necessary."

He swept her up in his arms. "Glad to hear it."

"Maybe before our wedding night I'll become one again, just on general principles."

He chuckled. "Sweetheart, as often as I plan to make love to you between now and then, I don't think you'll be able to claim virginity with a straight face, even on general principles."

She gazed up at him as he carried her over the threshold and into their new life. "Then I'll just have to do it with a smile."

_____ Epilogue _____

"WE SHOULDN'T BE havin' this-here potluck reception outside," Ty said. "It'll rain for sure. Or the wind'll come up and blow these flower doodads off the tables."

"So where should we hold it, amigo?" Ramon asked as he readjusted the tilt of a centerpiece of wildflowers and white paper wedding bells. "In the barn?"

"Don't pay no attention to him," Jasper said. "I'm just hopin' Big Clyde remembered to pick up the beer kegs on his way home from the church. Ever since he started courtin' that librarian, seems like his brain's been stuffed with horsehair."

"Do you think Daphne's gonna like how we done the centerpieces?" Andy asked. "Did we get enough pink and red in there for the feng shui to work good?"

"You're a fine one to be worried about flowers," Ramon said. "Sprinkling red pepper in Stony's sheets like you did. Good thing I caught you doin' it."

"Good thing I put you in charge of Andy," Jasper said.

"Aw, I didn't mean no harm," Andy said.

"I know." Jasper tugged the brim of Andy's hat over his eyes. "You just can't help yourself." The foreman stood back and surveyed the ranch yard. "Well, if Daphne don't like the flowers, she ain't gonna quarrel with the way we got them tables arranged, stickin' out from the center table like spokes in a wheel. The *chi's* gonna be whippin' around this place like nobody's business."

"Hey!" Andy shouted. "Here comes Big Clyde, and there's kegs in the truck. We're gonna have us a party!"

"I'm tellin' you, potlucks are risky," Ty said. "Sure as the world, every blessed person will bring bean dip. We won't have no potato salad, or fried chicken, or—"

"Quit your jawin' and help unload them kegs," Jasper said. "Folks'll be here any minute now."

Big Clyde hopped down from the cab. "You boys done a nice job with them tables and flowers. Looks real good."

"Where's your *señorita?*" Ramon asked.

Big Clyde blushed, as he always did when the librarian was mentioned. "I asked if she'd bring Stony's dad and Daphne's mom back from the church, seein' as how I had to detour and pick up the beer."

"Good thinkin'," Jasper said. "Now, let's get them kegs up on the porch."

Big Clyde opened the tailgate. "That ceremony was real nice and all, with Stony's dad as best man and Daphne's mom as matron of honor, but I think you shoulda been best man, Jasper."

"Nope." Jasper pulled a keg toward him. "It was the way it was supposed to be."

"But you made everything happen," Andy said. "Big Clyde's right. You shoulda been up there."

"I think so, too, *señor*," Ramon said. "You've been more of a papa than that other *hombre*. Being best man would have been like a reward for all you've done."

"Will you look at that," Ty said. "Here comes

Stony's truck, and sure enough we don't have the beer unloaded. I just knew we'd be scramblin' around at the last minute. We gotta hurry up and—"

"Hold on to your britches, cowboy," Jasper said, grabbing Ty's arm. "Ramon said somethin' about a reward. We all deserve a reward, if it comes to that." He stood with his hands on his hips and gazed over at the parking area while Stony stopped the truck, climbed down and walked around to the passenger side.

As Stony helped Daphne down, being careful to keep her white dress out of the dust, she glanced up at him and smiled. He paused, took off his Stetson and gave her a long kiss.

Jasper stood watching, and then turned to his men. He blinked and cleared his throat softly. "There's your reward, boys."

FREE Bath Spa Experience
With two proofs of purchase from
specially marked Harlequin novels.

FREE
Bath Spa
OFFER
Proof of Purchase

Special Limited-Time Offer

IN U.S., mail to:
Harlequin Quiet Moments Bath Spa Offer
3010 Walden Ave.
P.O. Box 9023
Buffalo, NY 14269-9023

IN CANADA, mail to:
Harlequin Quiet Moments Bath Spa Offer
P.O. Box 609
Fort Erie, Ontario
L2A 5X3

YES! Please send me my FREE Introductory Bath Spa Experience Kit so I can savor
Quiet Moments without cost or obligation, except for shipping and handling.
Enclosed are two proofs of purchase from specially marked Harlequin novels and
$3.50 shipping and handling fee.

_____

Name (PLEASE PRINT)

_____

Address   Apt. #

_____

City   State/Prov.   Zip/Postal Code

FREE SPA KIT OFFER TERMS

To receive your free Bath Spa Experience Kit, complete the above order form. Mail it to us with two
proofs of purchase, one of which can be found in the upper right-hand corner of this page. Requests
must be received no later than August 31, 2001. Your Quiet Moments Bath Spa Experience costs you
only $3.50 for shipping and handling. The free Bath Spa Experience Kit has a retail value of $16.99
U.S./$24.99 CAN. All orders subject to approval. Products in kit illustrated on the back cover of this
book are for illustrative purposes only and items may vary (retail value of items always as previously
indicated). Terms and prices subject to change without notice. Sales tax applicable in N.Y. **Please
allow 6-8 weeks for receipt of order. Offer good in Canada and the U.S. only.**

Offer good while quantities last. Offer limited to one per household.

425 UDN DAL9   © 2001 Harlequin Enterprises Limited
                                                                    HNCPBS1

QUIET MOMENTS™

Introducing a guilt-free way to pamper yourself and restore the healthy positive balance in your life.

Indulge yourself by mailing the Free Bath Spa Experience order form. We'll send your beautiful gift box overflowing with an array of delights. It's your guilt-free reward for always being there for others.

Let Quiet Moments pamper you from head to toe. Literally!

Mail in the order form, along with two proofs of purchase from specially marked Harlequin novels (and your shipping and handling fee), and we'll send you your introductory Free Bath Spa Experience Kit.

See offer terms on previous page.

HNCPBS2